THE SECRET PATIENT

Vaughan W. Smith

Fair Folio

Sydney, Australia

Fair Folio
www.fairfolio.com.au

The Secret Patient/ Vaughan W. Smith. -- 1st ed.
ISBN 978-0-9874694-4-1

For Dad

CHAPTER ONE

BEGINNINGS

Elizabeth stepped back from the curb as a bus hurtled past way too close. She felt the gust of wind and almost lost her balance. She was in too much of a hurry, and the place she was in needed caution.

"But I can't be late," she thought to herself, trying to justify the recklessness. She had an informant to meet, and she really needed to make it. So after a short pause, Elizabeth scanned the traffic and made a dash across the road.

She was heading into an old run-down part of town. It was a strange mix of established family homes and organised crime, which was maybe not so strange when you thought about it. That led her to believe that her tip was about a crime boss, or some sort of drug operation.

She desperately wanted to check a map, to verify where she was and make sure she was on the right track. But opening a map would be suicide here, it would mark her as an outsider, or worse a tourist waiting to get fleeced. She didn't have time for that kind of attention, or the ability to get out if it escalated.

Elizabeth kept up a fast walk, trying to look like she was hurrying somewhere and knew what she was doing. She spotted a man with a sun visor and bum bag pulling out a big paper map.

"A plant or a soon to be victim," Elizabeth thought, unwilling to engage with either. This was not the place to stick your neck out, because you could lose it in a heartbeat. She avoided eye contact and kept walking.

"Excuse me," the man said, but she pretended she didn't hear and kept walking.

"Excuuuse me," the man said again, this time placing a hand on her shoulder. Elizabeth almost jumped, and spun around swiftly. Something seemed wrong. Out of the corner of her eye she saw a street sign, and realised that she had walked past the meeting point. She focused on the man in front of her, keeping an annoyed look on her face while she tried to study him. He had sunglasses and bleached, short cut hair. She sensed that this was the guy, the contact.

"Sorry, I'm running late," she said, testing him.

"This won't take but a minute. I just need your help confirming my location. I'm trying to find the Golden Arms," he said. Elizabeth choked back a gasp as he spoke the code words. That had been the phrase she had arranged with her contact. Nobody else would have known to say it.

"I'll take a look for you," she said and moved closer to examine his map in detail. She hoped that whatever was happening would happen quickly, she didn't want a third party stumbling in and taking advantage of the situation.

"So I think we're around here," the man said out loud, pointing out a corner of the map where he was also holding a slip of paper. Elizabeth held out her hand to point at the same spot, slipping the folded paper into her hand expertly.

"No I think that's the wrong spot. Let me see," she said, pretending to study the map to give him a moment to add anything.

"What's...?" Elizabeth started to whisper, but she was cut off when she noticed the pressure on her arm. He was squeezing it with considerable force.

"No questions. The lead to the biggest story you will ever find is there," he whispered forcefully. Elizabeth took the hint and remained quiet.

"Yep I think I'm on the right track. Thanks for the help," the man said in a normal voice, and then walked off. Elizabeth's first reaction was to return back the way she came, but that seemed wrong. It would tip off anyone who saw her that she had been there to meet the man. That was a sure fire way to get them both into trouble. So she hurried on, wondering what her destination could be. She remembered a quirky bar a bit further ahead, that was popular enough to be a safer area.

Elizabeth walked with speed and purpose. But it wasn't potential danger or the chance of missing her meeting that spurred her on now, it was curiosity. She had to see what the tip was. But she didn't dare open it until she was seated in a quiet spot at the bar. So all she could do was speculate.

The man had a pretty big claim about the importance of the tip when he gave her the paper, but he didn't have the air of someone trying to show off. He was more trying to explain his urgency and get her attention. He was certainly desperate, posing as a tourist in the Black Jungle was a recipe for disaster. The area hadn't garnered the name by having special black fauna, but instead from the grimy interconnected mess of alliances and backstreets and beastly people that prowled them. Perhaps there was a reason he chose that location, because others wouldn't dare go there. She had been quite foolish turning up there alone, but she had sensed the importance of this tip. And she needed a new assignment.

Her thought pattern had distracted her enough that when she arrived at the Third Crow she almost walked past it. She had been there a few times, but she was still startled by the bar staff and their feathered outfits. The hats especially, were creepy when pulled down to cover their faces. She ordered a gin and tonic and then settled down into a cane chair in the corner lavished with tasselled cushions. After a half a glass she pulled out the note and unfolded it.

"What the hell," she whispered, confused by the contents.

Royal Monterey Hospital - CM

She flipped the note over, looking for more information. There was nothing else, the other side was blank. She folded the note and slipped it into her purse. As far as leads went, it was pretty flimsy. The informant had gone to a lot of effort to pass it on. He had seemed anxious and in a hurry, which could have been explained by the location. But he had convinced her of the importance of the information, and had also believed it himself. That was cause for investigation.

She didn't know where to begin. The note may as well have been blank for all the good it did her. But she needed something new to unearth, and she'd been given a lead. The least she could do was follow the trail, and see if anything came up. She smiled as she raised her glass to her lips. The tip was probably nothing, but hinted at being spectacular. And she would enjoy closing it down, even though the real excitement would be finding something there.

The next morning Elizabeth walked through the doors of the Stately Herald, the buzz of activity sounding pleasant to her ears. Her heart always skipped a beat when she walked past the framed front page article that had catapulted her to fame - 'MAYOR BURNT BY

INCRIMINATING DOCUMENTS'. It had been the biggest scoop in recent history, and nothing she had worked on since had measured up. She noticed a tall gaunt man with close cropped black hair and thick glasses standing over her desk. As always his pot belly seemed like it was intruding incredibly rudely. He was waiting for her, and she could see his anger simmering.

"Your editor would like to know why you ran out yesterday without filing your story," he said, the volume of his voice slowly building.

"My editor would know that it was just a fluff piece on the local hospital, and that it could wait. I had a tip George."

"Well, what was it?" George said, his anger a little deflected by curiosity.

"Too vague to bother mentioning, but the guy seemed spooked so there could be something to it."

"I don't want you wasting time on these spotlight seekers. You can work the normal stuff while you wait for the next big break. Have you even looked at the so-called fluff piece?"

"No."

"It's not that bad. It won't get you hospitalised and on the front page, but most people would see that as a good thing," George said, his anger subsiding.

"Yeah, I know."

"My rising star reporter isn't worth much if she isn't doing her job," George said, without venom but with honesty.

"Fair enough. Where is this fluff piece?" she asked.

"Royal Monterey Hospital. Brief is on your desk, where it's been all week. Today, Elizabeth," George said and walked away. But she didn't hear his last words. As soon as he had said 'Royal Monterey Hospital' her mind started ticking over with the possibilities. She was glad that she hadn't mentioned the tip to George. He would have reassigned the story to keep her away from the distraction. She sat down and picked up the manila folder that she had been avoiding. It now had additional interest, as well as being a way to keep her job.

As she scanned the folder for the notes on the story she realised that it was pretty much a fluff piece. A nurse was being recognised for twenty years' service and would be retiring soon. It was a nice opportunity to recognise the woman's dedication and service to others, but it was hardly hard-hitting journalism. But it would serve its purpose as an excuse for her to go digging at the hospital.

The notes also had when the nurse, a Robin Mellows, would be available for interview. Each day had a one to two hour window listed, up to today.

"Here we go," Elizabeth said to herself and picked up the phone. A few minutes later she had apologised for her late follow-up and organised an interview. The woman on the phone had said two-thirty in the afternoon but Elizabeth wrote down two in her diary.

"Can't hurt to be early," she thought to herself. It would give her some more time to look around under the guise of being bored.

"You doing the hospital piece?" a man's voice said. It was Peter, the other general reporter. Elizabeth looked over and noticed that his crazy tie for the day was a bright purple.

"Yeah, couldn't avoid it forever."

"It'll be a nice change, so much negativity comes through here," Peter said.

"That's what sells papers."

"I know. Still, learn to enjoy the happy ones. They'll be the ones that keep you in the game," Peter said, a big smile on his face.

"Yeah I guess," she said. She watched him turn back to his desk and continue his work. With the small tuft of hair on his otherwise bald head and his generally round shape Elizabeth couldn't shake the impression of him being an over-boiled egg. But he was a nice guy, and had been a reporter for almost twenty years.

"Maybe I'll be doing a fluff piece about him reaching twenty years soon," Elizabeth thought before turning back to her diary. She had nothing else pencilled in for the day. So she pulled out the slip of paper and examined it once more. The 'CM' had to be the key piece of information, but she wasn't sure what it meant. Her best bet was that it was the initials of a key person at the hospital who knew more. So she decided to keep an eye out for any people she met with those initials.

Elizabeth filled the morning with some prep and busywork. After a light lunch she drove out to the hospital and headed for the South Wing. It looked like an older hospital, with tired decor and dated trimmings. She walked up to the nurse station and waited to get their attention.

"Hello, may I help you?" the nurse said.

"Yes, I'm looking for Robin Mellows. I'm doing an interview for the Stately Herald," Elizabeth said.

"Oh yes, I'm afraid you're a little early, but she should be available soon. Would you mind taking a seat," the nurse said, gesturing at the old leather chairs in the corner. Elizabeth looked over the room and saw nothing of interest.

"Sure, but can you direct me to the bathroom first?" she said.

"Around this corner, second door. That's the visitor bathroom. If they're busy you can use the patient ones further down the hall." Elizabeth thanked the nurse and followed the directions, rounding the corner and walking down the hall. She didn't even bother checking the first bathroom. She tried to get a feel for the hospital, and let her eyes roam over the place as she walked. She wasn't picking up anything that seemed particularly interesting or suspicious. She did notice a small, well-lit recreation room with some couches and tables. It was empty save for a copy of the Stately Herald. Elizabeth walked over to take a look.

It was today's edition, which she hadn't looked at yet. She grabbed it to help pass the time. She returned to the main waiting area and pulled out the newspaper, making sure she read every page. It was good to keep in touch with the paper, and stay across the various articles. About halfway through she was interrupted.

"Excuse me, are you Elizabeth?" a kind looking woman with blonde hair asked. Elizabeth paused, folding the newspaper over.

"Yes, and you're Robin?"

"Yes that's me."

"Great. While we're on names, I didn't catch the name of the nurse at the desk."

"Oh that's Delores."

"Thanks I'll note that down," Elizabeth said. Mentally she checked off that Delores had a first initial of D and didn't fit the bill. She stuffed the folded newspaper into her bag, then followed Robin through the corridor and into what looked like the nurse's office. It was packed full of different things, with chairs and desks lumped wherever possible.

Elizabeth smiled and took out her notepad. Robin was friendly and welcoming, which made it easy to ask all the right questions for the article. Once the interview was winding up, Elizabeth threw in a question just for herself.

"So Robin, you've been here so long you must have seen a lot of crazy things. What's been the biggest scandal?" she said.

"Oh, well, I'm not one to gossip," Robin said, reluctant to say any more. Elizabeth put her notepad away deliberately.

"Just for my own curiosity and interest," Elizabeth said.

"Well, one of the doctors was doing the rounds with a few of the nurses, if you know what I mean," Robin said softly, tapping the side of her nose. Elizabeth knew exactly what she meant, and felt disappointed that it was something so run of the mill.

"I see, quite scandalous," she said, sharing a smile with Robin. Then she picked up her bag and rose from the chair.

"Very nice meeting you today. Thank you for your time, I think the article will be published in the next day or two. If you want I can send you a copy," Elizabeth said.

"Oh no don't bother yourself, we get lots of papers through the hospital. It was lovely speaking with you, take care," Robin said with a kindly smile. She walked Elizabeth out and waved as she drove off.

"Lovely lady, but no leads to anything else," Elizabeth thought to herself as she headed back to the office. She would be able to do more digging under the guise of research, but she would have to be careful. George was ever watchful, and would be extremely suspicious and call her out if he saw her over-researching for a simple article.

She took the newspaper and her notepad out of her bag, then typed up and expanded her notes from the interview, filling in extra details that came to mind or seemed important for context. It was pretty good for a first draft, so she printed it and left it on her desk. She could use it as a shield if George came over demanding progress.

She looked up the names of the recent hospital administrators and key medical staff. None of them had the initials CM. She could start digging around for staff lists, but it didn't feel right in her gut. If there was something here, it would require more than brute research. It would require a special finding. She leaned back in her chair, mentally drained. A large man sat on the edge of her desk, rocking it and startling Elizabeth. She looked over in surprise.

"I see you've had a crack at one of my jumbles!" Alan bellowed out in excitement. Elizabeth continued to stare at him, unsure of what to say. She knew Alan, but they rarely spoke and she didn't know what had triggered his excited outburst. Things started to click when he picked up the newspaper she had taken from the hospital.

"I liked this one, it was especially devious, yet simple at the same time. The best kind of jumble. What do we have here; oh Elizabeth this is shameful," Alan said, looking up to give her a reproachful look. She just shrugged at him, letting him finish before she explained that it wasn't her.

"I mean, c'mon you can't just write any letters you want in there. And you didn't even make sensible words out of them. Epic fail," he said, tossing the newspaper over to her. She accepted the paper with a smile and replied.

"Sorry Alan, my mind was elsewhere. I'll take it more seriously next time."

"See that you do. They say that regular mental exercise is the key to a sharp mind, and you should be acing these. Don't disappoint me again!" Alan said. But there was a playfulness to his manner, which she appreciated. The desk groaned in appreciation as he raised his bulk and walked off.

Elizabeth regarded the wrongly completed jumble with interest. It looked like the hand writing was quite deliberate. Maybe there was something more to it, and just maybe it was the lead she needed.

CHAPTER TWO

ROUTINE

"So how are you feeling today, Nathaniel," the doctor said with a cheery tone that was somehow hollow and false.

"Please call me Nathan," he said with a sigh. Another doctor, it was like starting all over again. But he kept his frustration in check.

"So let's see here, you seem to be doing well. But these numbers are still cause for concern. We'll have to keep you for observation a little longer," the doctor said. Nathan looked up and read the identification tag, noting the name.

"Dr Malberg, do you think these observations can be done from home?" Nathan said. It was a question he had pondered often, and occasionally asked.

"Unlikely Mr ... Stenson, things can change so quickly. I will confer with my colleagues, but I'm sure they would have the same response."

"Sure, please ask," he said. But he knew the answer, they always said the same thing. It was almost like they had a script, repeating the same things over and over. He sat through the rest of the visit quietly, not bothering with any more questions. He watched the doctor carefully, noting down what things he did and checked. It was consistent with the rest. Dr Malberg wrote some notes down in a folder, and put it aside.

"Thanks Nathaniel, take care," he said and then walked out. Nathan sat up and looked over at the old clock on the wall. It was seven on the dot, he would be alone for the next three hours. His room was generously sized, containing a sink, bedside table, a large padded chair and a TV on a swivel-arm. There was also a toilet attached to a small room off the side. Everything you could need, close at hand.

But this luxury, if you could call it that, meant that he was alone. Great for sleeping, but tiresome for passing the days. He had lost track of how long he had been in the hospital. Days, weeks, months, they had all merged together. He sat up and then hauled himself out of bed, ensuring that his cables were still connected and not tangled, and sat down in the big chair. The machines beeped away as normal, and he sank down into the cushion. It was time for a nap.

Exactly three hours later the door opened and a nurse eased into the room.

"Good morning Nathan, how are you today?" she said.

"The usual, Robin, thanks for asking. Had a new doctor do the rounds today," he said.

"Really? Let me see here, a Dr Malberg. I don't know him, but there's been a lot of new doctors cycling through here recently."

"Seems about right. What's new with you?"

"Well it's quite exciting, I'm giving an interview today to a reporter from the Stately Herald. It is because of my twenty years here at the hospital."

"Wow that is exciting. It's great that they're recognising your years of service. You've made a big difference to my time here," Nathan said.

"Oh you're a sweetie. Here's your juice, can I get you anything else?"

"How about a newspaper?"

"Sure I'll go pinch the one from the nurse's office. I'll have to collect it at lunch though, is that alright?"

"Perfect."

"Right, well I'll be right back," Robin said and then left the room as she had entered. Nathan waited patiently for her to return and accepted the newspaper with a smile. He tried to read through carefully, as he normally did when he got the paper, but his mind was racing. He had an opportunity here, to make contact with someone outside the hospital. It wasn't just feelings of isolation or loneliness, it was something else. He felt something was wrong, that he shouldn't be there. Nobody spent that long in hospital, it didn't make sense. A reporter would get to the bottom of it, sniff out the story.

"Damn, I didn't ask the reporter's name," he thought to himself. But he realised that it might be for the best. If he managed to get a message through, he had to ensure that it wasn't too obvious and bring himself the wrong kind of attention.

Nathan wrote carefully, paying special attention to ensure that each letter was deliberately and perfectly formed. Once he was done, he looked over the word jumble and admired his handiwork. It was such a long shot, expecting the reporter to see the message in the newspaper. There was no guarantee that she'd even pay any attention to the newspaper. But it was a chance, and he took it. A new energy surged through him, instigated by the possibilities. He was ripe for a change.

He closed the newspaper and left it on the tray table next to his bed. He wanted to make sure that when Robin came back, she would see it and remember to take it back to the nurse's station. The wait was agonising, and Nathan spent every minute wondering when Robin would return, and hoping it was her and not someone else. Robin was predictable, and would unwittingly assist him, but with the other nurses he had no idea.

The knock on the door startled him, and he turned his attention to see who it was. Robin walked in.

"Hello Nathan, how are you going?" Robin said.

"The usual."

"That's not such a bad thing. Let me check a few things," Robin said, as she walked around and took some readings off his equipment.

"Thanks for the paper," Nathan said, reminding her of it.

"You're welcome. Oh I better return that too," Robin said, grabbing the newspaper on her way out.

"I'll be at lunch soon. I'll pop in later after my interview," Robin said.

"Have fun, I'd love to hear about it," Nathan said, and gave her his best grin. She smiled and left the room. Nathan let go a big sigh, and hoped for some luck. Maybe today would be the day.

Robin left the room, made some additional notes on a folder just outside and then strode down the hall. She happened to glance over at one of the recreation areas, and noticed there was no newspaper.

"Oh, somebody's nicked it again," she said to herself with annoyance. So she walked over and placed down the newspaper she had taken back from Nathan. Satisfied by the outcome, she continued on her way.

Nathan patiently waited for the lady to bring around lunch. Today it was rather-too-perfectly sliced meat in gravy, with some steamed vegetables and mashed potato. Accompanying the meal was a small cup of apple juice and a tub of custard.

"And the cycle begins again," Nathan muttered to himself. He had tried every variation of every meal, and had begun to track the order and planning of the meal rotation. He poked around at the food, wishing it would become something else, then finally eating it with some resignation.

He felt a little drowsy and napped after lunch. His sleep was light and dreamless. After a while he noticed a presence in the room and opened one eye. He saw Robin standing over one of his machines.

"It's just me, I'm back," Robin said without turning from what she was doing.

"I was just napping a bit. How was your interview?"

"It was nice, she asked me a lot of questions, but was polite and friendly."

"That's great. Ask you any hard questions?"

"Not really, although she did try and get some gossip out of me at the end. I let slip, off the record, a titbit about one of the doctors dallying with the nurses. But that's old news, and he's no longer here."

"Well that's fine, she's a reporter after all."

"Yeah, but you know it was odd. She was reading her own newspaper. Shouldn't she already know what's in it?" Robin said, pausing from what she was doing and looking over at him. Nathan's eyes lit up. The reporter had been reading a newspaper, there was a chance it was the one he had written in.

"Maybe she's interested in how it turns out?" Nathan said.

"I think you're right. Well I'm done here and my shift is about to end. Marie will be taking care of you this evening."

"Thanks Robin, let me know when your article is published."

"Will do. See you tomorrow," Robin said and left the room. Nathan watched her leave, then felt the surge of excitement from earlier resurface. The reporter had asked lots of questions, tried to find out more juicy information, and had read a newspaper. It was the best he could have hoped for.

"Oh but I still didn't ask the reporter's name," Nathan thought to himself. But then he realised it didn't matter. He had determined from Robin that the reporter was a woman. And if the reporter saw his message, then he wouldn't need a name as she would come looking. Or he'd find out her details when the article was published.

Nathan's enthusiasm was dampened by a beeping sound. The fluid drip attached to him had finished. He pressed the nurse call button and then looked up at the old clock. It was only half an hour past when the nurses changed shift. The new nurses were probably busy, so would be slow responding. He shuffled over to the edge of the bed and sat up. His muscles ached and complained, and he felt exerted by the effort.

"I'm only thirty years old, I shouldn't feel like this," Nathan said to himself. He reached out gingerly to the machine and pressed the silence button. He had seen the nurses do it many times, but it would only buy him a few minutes of peace. He continued sitting up, it was easier than lying down and getting back up in a few minutes time. Right on cue the machine beeped once more. Nathan silenced it and waited for the next round.

Half an hour later a generously sized nurse with black hair and black rimmed glasses bustled through the door and looked around. She looked over at Nathan and assessed the room.

"You called?" she said.

"Yes Marie, my machine has been beeping."

"Oh let me look," she said as she approached. It began to beep again, on cue.

"Yeah, it's empty and needs a change. I'll have to go grab a replacement," Marie said, after pressing the silence button on the machine. Nathan nodded, knowing what her response would be, and patiently waited again. After another ten minutes Marie returned, and completed the replacement of the drip.

"Busy day?" Nathan said

"Oh you know, the usual," Marie said with a sigh, and then rushed off out of the room. That was the extent of the excitement for the afternoon. Nathan whiled the hours away wondering about the reporter, and when he could expect to see her. He then turned his television back on, and watched the afternoon game shows.

Dinner promptly arrived at six, consisting of chicken and rice. It was accompanied by a cup of tea and some yoghurt. Nathan mentally ticked off the meal from his list of potential options, and started trying to predict the next day's menu. After another session of TV he drifted off, awoken by the sound of beeping. The room was dark, and he was quite disoriented by the suddenness of the noise. Once he realised what it was, he dragged himself over to silence the machine, and pressed the nurse call button.

After an age, a nurse burst through the doors.

"Is everything ok?" she said.

"My machine is going off," Nathan said. The machine validated his story by starting off another series of piercing tones.

"Oh, right. Marie is on break, let me take a look," she said. The nurse walked over to the unit, silenced it, and then flicked through Nathan's chart.

"I'm sorry I don't know where they keep this one. You'll have to wait until Marie comes back. I'll let her know. In the meantime you can press this button to silence it."

"Thanks," Nathan said, trying to not let his frustration show.

"Do you know how long until Marie is back?"

"Not sure, probably half an hour. I'll send her over when I see her."

"Great, thanks for that," Nathan said, giving her a smile despite the way he felt. The nurse rushed off and he was alone again. Nathan waited patiently, not wanting to turn on the TV. Having it on was like an admission that he was in for a long wait. Of course that had no effect, and he suffered the long wait just the same.

Eventually Nathan pressed the nurse call button again. He was glad to see Marie, and momentarily forgot his frustration.

"Oh it needs changing again, I'll go sort it out," she said as soon as she walked in. Nathan nodded, and was about to speak but she had already left. So he waited quietly, and within fifteen minutes everything was done. As he moved back into a sleeping position, he felt a large dull pain surge through his back. He knew that he would have to sleep on his other side, even though he hated it.

"Please come tomorrow, I need your help," Nathan said, his thoughts and hopes focused on the reporter. If she didn't come through, what other options did he have?

CHAPTER THREE

DISCOVERY

Elizabeth took the marked newspaper home, so she could examine it in more detail without attracting any unnecessary attention. The deliberate nature of the way the jumble was filled out triggered her curiosity. The answer was so clearly wrong, yet wasn't a proper word.

She left her car at the office and walked home, the fifteen minute trip giving her time to think things over. The jumble was definitely the only thing of interest that had come from the day. Robin was nice, but her idea of a secret was just common gossip. There had to be something else.

Elizabeth couldn't quite put her finger on why she believed the tip so much. But she did, and the only way to move on would be to turn the hospital upside down and examine it from every angle.

When she arrived at her block of apartments, she checked the mailbox and pulled out a fistful of junk mail. She dumped it directly into the recycling bin, and continued on her way. Her apartment was quite spacious but in an older building. Three flights of stairs had to be climbed to reach her front door, the smell of mothballs offending at every turn. She unlocked the door, threw her bag on the couch and then dropped into it herself. She fished out the newspaper, and opened it up to the jumble. There were four words that needed to be unscrambled. The letters in each one were not the ones provided in the jumble puzzle. What was written was as follows:

BRO
SIN
TAPI
SENT

Elizabeth decided to tackle each word individually. She wrote down two options for the first word.

ROB
BOR

Neither made much sense so she moved on. The next word made even less sense.

NIS

INS

The two options she wrote weren't even words, which was a step down from what was already there. She continued on.

PATI
PITA

Those seemed more workable, one could even be a name. Elizabeth tackled the final word.

TENS
ENTS

Again, they didn't mean much in isolation. But she couldn't think of any other ways to transform the words. Once she was sure of that, she looked at other ways to build things. Taking each unscrambled word as a fragment, she could build longer words. Maybe that would work better. She took the first two and tried combining them.

ROBNIS

Which didn't look right, but immediately made her think of the other combination.

ROBINS

Which was definitely a clue, and a very particular one. She quickly analysed the other two fragments and completed the puzzle.

ROBINS PATIENTS

Elizabeth dropped the pen and checked what she had done. It was right, the letters were all there. Someone had left her a message, to talk to Robin's patients. Her mind started racing with the possibilities. However her scepticism jumped in, and prevented her from going wild. She had to entertain the idea that the message was completely unrelated from the mysterious tip she had received about the hospital. But if one of Robin's patients had the initials CM, then that would be something indeed. It was definitely worth investigating.

The next question she had, was who had left her the note? Was it even directed at her? Surely it had to have been left by one of the other nurses. Someone who overheard that a reporter was here and wanted to pass on something a bit juicier than what Robin was willing to give up. That was the assumption she would work with.

However, the clue was also the means to continue her investigation. She could quite easily sell her presence there as follow up interviews with the patients. Her editor wouldn't complain, although he would probably be a little suspicious of her doing proper legwork on what she considered a fluff piece.

But it was decided. She would show her draft article in the morning, and then go to the hospital for more research. Elizabeth stood up from the couch and wandered around her apartment. She had that special feeling, that knowledge that she was on to something. She felt a genuine excitement that had been lacking for so long.

Elizabeth whipped up a quick pasta dish, and ate it with a glass of red wine. As she chewed her mind was turning over, considering the angles she could use to continue her investigation. It would depend on what she unearthed, but she would need a strategy to keep returning there without raising suspicion. It wasn't just her editor she was worried about either, she didn't want to scare off potential leads in the hospital.

The evening flew by, and although she was tired she had trouble sleeping. The promise of a new and interesting investigation had well and truly dug in its hooks, and her brain didn't want to switch off. She eventually slept, dream free.

The next morning Elizabeth continued to think over how she should approach the clue on her walk to the office. Once inside she went straight to her desk and finalised the story on Robin. Then she walked over to George's desk with a printed copy and sat there while he read through it.

"Not your best work, but it's suitable," George said.

"About that, I think I can squeeze a bit more out of it. I'd like to talk to a few of her patients. They can provide a comment to spice up the article," Elizabeth said. George paused, thinking it through.

"I'm not sure, it could add a bit of flavour. You'd need to get permission though."

"Of course. I'd only include them if they wanted to be directly quoted, or I could summarise their thoughts in a more general way. I'm sure they'd love to chime in, she's very well liked there."

"I assume you're asking me because it will affect your deadline?"

"Well yeah, I'd need a day or two extra depending on what I can get."

"You've got today to talk with them and integrate their comments. I want it ready this afternoon so it can go in tomorrow's edition," George said. He gave Elizabeth the 'my decision is final' look and she nodded.

"Sure boss, you'll have it today," Elizabeth said. She gave him a smile, and as she walked off started brainstorming ideas. She didn't necessarily need George to know if she was spending more time at the hospital, but she did need to have a reason to be out of the office frequently on something that wouldn't attract a lot of questions. Today's extension would not be enough. She needed some autonomy while she worked the hospital into a proper story.

But she couldn't get too far ahead of herself. First steps were to meet some patients and get some statements for the article. Then she could worry about how to continue her investigation.

Elizabeth phoned the hospital, spoke to Robin and obtained a verbal agreement that she could come speak to patients. However Robin would have to talk to the patients first and give Elizabeth a shortlist of those who had agreed to take part. That seemed reasonable so Elizabeth agreed. She began to think about how she could get an accurate list of patients. There was a chance that she wouldn't even get to talk to the right ones. If there was any merit to the hospital story, things wouldn't be easy for her. The deeper something is buried, the more effort it takes to dig it out.

After an hour passed, Elizabeth decided it was worth heading back to the hospital. She left the office and walked to her car, feeling an icy wind sweep around her. It left her with a chill, and an ominous feeling. She shrugged it off and continued. Traffic was light, so the drive to the hospital didn't take long. She wasn't in a rush though, as she wanted to ensure Robin had plenty of time to do whatever talking was required.

Robin was waiting for her at the nurse station.

"Hello again Elizabeth," Robin said with a smile.

"I'm back," Elizabeth said.

"It was a very nice surprise for you to return for some additional interviews. I thought reporters usually dismissed these kinds of stories."

"It can't all be bad news," Elizabeth said. She did feel a little bad though, as she initially reacted exactly as Robin said. To make it worse, she was only here to fulfil her own interests, not to help celebrate Robin.

"The second surprise, is that I actually have two volunteers for you to speak with. I'll take you to them."

"Great, lead the way," Elizabeth said. As they walked, she thought of something else.

"How many patients do you normally interact with?"

"Well I only work in this ward, so it really depends on who we have. Currently I'd say around ten."

"Two out of ten is not bad at all," Elizabeth said. What she was really thinking about though, were the eight that she wasn't being introduced to.

"Yeah, one of them is a bit of a favourite of mine. He's a real character, so I'm looking forward to introducing you. Here's our first stop, Tom Norwood," Robin said. She paused outside a door and knocked. After waiting a moment, she opened it slowly and poked her head inside.

"Hi Tom, I have Elizabeth here with me. She's the reporter I mentioned earlier. Is now a good time?" Robin asked. Elizabeth didn't hear the reply, but saw Robin enter the room. Assuming it was a yes, she followed. She saw a very tanned man in his thirties, and it was clear why he was in hospital. His elevated leg encased entirely in a cast told the tale well enough.

"Hi Tom, nice to meet you," Elizabeth said.

"Nice to meet you too. So you're doing an article on her?"

"Yes, I interviewed Robin yesterday, and I just wanted to add some words from her patients."

"Yeah, Robin said if I gave her a good rap, I'd get a nice sponge bath," Tom said, winking at Robin.

"In your dreams maybe," Robin said, unfazed by his comment.

"He's your problem now, come find me when you're done and I'll take you over to the other patient."

"Thanks Robin," Elizabeth said, and watched her leave the room.

"You're like that with all the nurses?"

"Nah just Robin, she's got a good sense of humour. The rest of them, they are way too serious."

"What happened here?" Elizabeth said, pointing to the cast.

"Bike accident. I was cornering a little too aggressively, and the bike tumbled out from under me."

"By 'cornering too aggressively' you mean speeding right?"

"Yeah, that too. Look, nobody else got hurt, and I'm paying for it alright. The isolation and boredom here is just unbearable."

"You don't mingle with the other patients?"

"Nah, I guess I could try. But I never see anyone else, and all the rooms are singles with closed doors in this wing. I'm not exactly mobile enough to roam around looking for friends."

"That's interesting. So you don't know any of Robin's other patients?"

"Nope. She doesn't really mention them either."

"Do the other nurses talk about Robin at all? What's your impression of how they like her," Elizabeth said, changing over to a topic that was more in line with her article. She didn't think that Tom was the person to leave her a coded message, so she didn't want to stray too far from her reason for being there.

"Not really, I get the impression that she's well respected though. She doesn't react to my jokes, but she acts real proper otherwise."

"Yeah I get that feeling too. Is she a good nurse too, not just friendly?"

"She's the best. No fussing around, everything done quickly and without pain. Some of them, you'd think it was their first day. Everything becomes a chore," Tom said, the frustration clearly evident in his tone.

"Does Robin seem discreet to you?"

"Yeah, I think that's why she doesn't talk about other patients at all. Why do you ask?"

"Well I tried to get some gossip out of her, more for context rather than printing, and she didn't really have anything. It's not a problem, just a little surprising. In my experience people are usually keen to appear important or at least hint at having some special knowledge," Elizabeth said.

"Oh you think she's got some goods and isn't sharing?"

"Possibly. I'd expect someone who has been here for twenty years would have a few gems tucked away."

"Yeah, you're probably right. I can imagine Robin sitting on something big. Maybe that's why she's retiring?"

"Let's not get too carried away," Elizabeth said with a laugh. Tom smiled back.

"I'm not really sure what else to add, but she really does make this place bearable," Tom said.

"Thanks Tom, I'll make sure that's in the article. Thanks so much for your help. I'll drop in a copy of the paper when it's published."

"Cheers, you know where to find me!" Tom said, pointing at his leg. Elizabeth gave him a quick wave and left the room. Tom had provided some interesting information, but nothing she could use. She had higher hopes for the next person, based on Robin's description. Within minutes Elizabeth had found her way back to the nurse station. She didn't want to snoop around and raise Robin's suspicions. That would come later.

"He's a good lad isn't he?" Robin said when she saw Elizabeth.

"Yeah, he's a good sort. He likes you too, I got some great quotes for the article."

"That's nice to hear. You ready to see the other patient?"

"Yes, let's go." Robin nodded and stepped out from the nurse station. Elizabeth followed closely, paying attention to where they were going. They walked down the same corridor where she had met Tom, only turned the corner a bit further down.

CHAPTER FOUR

A NEW ASSIGNMENT

Once they stood outside the room Robin began the same ritual as before, poking her head in through the doorway and speaking up.

"Hello Dean, I have Elizabeth with me. She's the reporter I mentioned earlier. Is now a good time?" Again Elizabeth didn't hear the response, but followed Robin into the room.

The layout was exactly the same as Tom's room, but there were more machines clustered around the bed. Dean looked like he was in his sixties, his surprisingly youthful face surrounded by snow-white hair.

"Reporter? What have I done now!" Dean said, looking shocked. Elizabeth froze, surprised by his reaction. After a few tense moments Dean relaxed his face and laughed.

"Always a jokester this one," Robin said.

"So was the last one," Elizabeth said.

"Maybe they send all the funny ones here? Suits me just fine."

"Yeah she's good, she can have a laugh," Dean said, nodding at Robin.

"Well I'd better give you two some privacy so he can say what he really thinks," Robin said and promptly left the room.

"I would say the same thing if she were here," Dean said.

"I believe you. If you don't mind me asking, why all the machines?"

"Ah yeah, I got Cancer. It's terrible, I think I'm near the end."

"Oh, I'm so sorry. Is it really that bad?"

"Yeah, well they're treating me but the doctor says best case scenario I've got is six to twelve months. You've also got those people who seem to live for years and nobody knows why. But not with what I've got."

"Yours is different?"

"Not different, just worse. Stomach cancer, and it's entrenched. They can never really attack it effectively enough."

"Wow, I don't know what to say."

"That's fine, there's nothing to say. When it's your time, it's your time. But enough about me, we're here for Robin today."

"I just want to say it's so great that you can devote your time to other people. Robin seems nice, but she must make a big difference around here."

"Time? I have plenty of it. What else have I got to do around here?" Dean said with a laugh before continuing.

"But yeah, she does make a big difference. She's a real sweetie, and always looks out for you. She's patient, but fast with everything. Some of those other nurses, they don't care. Or they seem to be thinking about something else. But Robin, when she's here it's all she focuses on. You never have to call her back for something she forgot."

"That's great, I'll just make a few notes," Elizabeth said. She scribbled furiously on her pad. Suddenly her fluff piece had taken on extra meaning. She had to make good on it, for this man's sake as much as for Robin.

"I could waffle on for a while, is there anything in particular that you need?"

"I don't know, I had just planned on getting a few quotes to fill out the article," Elizabeth said, puzzled.

"And now the Cancer thing? You want to do it properly."

"Yeah there is that."

"I just had a vibe that you were taking it really seriously. And that maybe you hadn't come here meaning to do that."

"Yeah, you're right."

"Look let me level with you. I don't mean anything by this, I'm just mind mapping with you. And I'm no reporter, so maybe I've got it all wrong. But why did you come back today? Robin is a great nurse, but she was already blown away when you turned up yesterday.

Aren't you busy with other things?" Dean said, looking directly at Elizabeth. She was stunned, and did not expect such a question. He had cut to the heart of the matter, in a way that Robin perhaps was not able to. Elizabeth didn't know how to respond. But she had a feeling that she had to be honest with him.

"Well to level with you, I had another purpose to coming back. Fleshing out Robin's story was nice, but you're right in that I probably wouldn't have done so normally. It's a bit crazy though, so you'll probably laugh."

"I'm listening," Dean said, looking intently at Elizabeth. His eyes lit up and he seemed energised. It was as if he could sense that something important was about to happen.

"I received this note from a trusted informant recently," Elizabeth said, walking over to the bed and handing Dean a piece of paper. He held it up close to his face and scrutinised it.

"Royal Monterey Hospital CM. Doesn't really say much," he said.

"No, but the informant seemed convinced it was something huge. He was skipping town to be safe."

"So you took a story here, to look into it."

"Exactly. I couldn't get anything of interest out of Robin either."

"So you came back today to try her patients?"

"Better than that," Elizabeth said. She fished out the newspaper page with the jumble filled in and handed it to Dean. He accepted it and gave her back the first note.

"I took home a copy of the paper that I found here yesterday. Somebody filled out that jumble."

"What am I looking at here?"

"Look at the letters used. The person who filled out the jumble wasn't even trying to solve it. When I solved the jumble using the letters our mystery person supplied, I got a message. Robin's patients."

"You're joking!" Dean called out in a surprised whisper.

"No, I'm one hundred percent serious. Someone knew I was here and left it for me. It might just be a prank, but it's just too much of a coincidence."

"Hey it wasn't me."

"Ha-ha yeah well I don't think it was Tom either."

"Who's Tom?"

"He's the other one of Robin's patients that volunteered to talk to me."

"If I wrote you that note, I would have made sure that you spoke to me," Dean said.

"Yeah, so maybe the person wrote that note because they knew they wouldn't get the option otherwise?"

"Oh this is exciting. Count me in!"

"Count you in for what?"

"Your investigation."

"It's not really a thing yet, it could still be nothing."

"No, it's definitely something. And nothing is what I have to do right now. I'll even give you an excuse to come back here regularly. I want you to write my story."

"I'm flattered, but I'm not a writer I'm a reporter."

"Even better, you can report about my life."

"I don't know," Elizabeth said, her voice trailing off.

"What's there to know? Just say yes," Dean said. Elizabeth looked at him and realised he wasn't going to take no for an answer. He was also right about it being a good excuse for her to return to the hospital. George would probably be on board with the story as a longer feature, but she wasn't sure how long she'd be able to use it. Was there any harm in letting Dean participate? She had already told him a lot.

"Ok. Fine. Yes."

"Great! Good choice. I smell a conspiracy brewing."

"Let's not get too ahead of ourselves," Elizabeth said. She chuckled to herself, scarcely believing what she had just agreed to.

"Ok let's be serious then. You need to find that patient who left you the jumble clue."

"Yes. It's my best lead so far. I've now eliminated two patients from the running. Not sure how many others there are."

"I don't really get around much. But I'd bet that they're all in this ward somewhere. Whoever contacted you can't be far away, as Robin is their nurse."

"Agreed. I think I'll go find Robin and let her know I'm done today. But that we're thinking of doing a story on you. I don't want to get caught snooping around today."

"Yeah good idea. Take care, see you tomorrow."

"Yeah see you tomorrow," Elizabeth said and walked over to the doorway. She looked back before leaving and noticed Dean looking at her with a serious expression.

"Thanks," he said, and Elizabeth knew exactly what he meant.

Elizabeth counted ten rooms on her way back to the nurse station including Dean's room. Assuming that Robin took care of them all while on shift, that left eight more patients to investigate. More if the ward continued further. It wouldn't take long to check them out without drawing unnecessary attention.

"Hey there, how did it go?" Robin said. Elizabeth looked up in surprise, she had been in her own world. Lucky she hadn't been snooping around.

"Oh great, you're right about Dean. He is a real character."

"Good sort though, true character."

"Yeah, he convinced me to tell his story. Well at least if my editor buys it."

"He can be a charmer when he wants to be," Robin said with a smile.

"I bet I haven't seen half of it! Anyway I got some good quotes today, you should see the article in the next few days. I'll confirm and let you know," Elizabeth said.

"Visiting hours are ten until twelve, and then two until five," Robin said.

"Thanks, I'll play by the rules," Elizabeth said and waved goodbye. As she left the hospital she thought over what she had just done. She had made a contact in Dean, but had also involved him. And she didn't know exactly what that meant yet. It was a moment of weakness, when she was put off balance by his candidness. But her gut told her it was the right thing, that she needed someone on the inside. So for now it would have to do.

Her next step was to get the article about Robin finished. That would have the added benefit of giving her some goodwill with Robin, which would be very valuable. If there was something up with Robin's patients, then any information she gave up would be useful. And Elizabeth needed her trust to enable those small pieces of information.

Elizabeth drove directly to the Herald and went straight to her desk. She pulled out her notes and got straight to work, weaving in some key quotes from Tom and Dean. It came together well, and gave the article a fullness that made the previous version look woefully incomplete.

"I guess I still have some things to learn," Elizabeth thought to herself. Perhaps she had not been putting enough focus on the human factor in her investigations and stories. But that was something to think more on at another time. She printed out the revised article and walked over to George's desk.

He was sitting there, reviewing another story and marking it up with a red pen.

"One award winning fluff article," Elizabeth said, dropping the printed story on his desk. George didn't even turn around.

"See that wasn't so hard right?"

"True, plus it got me another story."

"Another story?" George said with suspicion. He put down the article he was reading and gave her his full attention.

"Yeah one of the patients there has stomach cancer. He's got an interesting story and wants me to tell it for him."

"Doesn't sound like your kind of thing. What's your angle?"

"Honestly I couldn't say no when he asked."

"I can see how that might go down. Well we could do something for one of the weekend editions if it has legs. I hope you didn't promise to publish it?"

"No, I just agreed to write it."

"That's fine, we'll see how it ends up," George said, turning back to his work. Elizabeth started to walk off but heard him speak once more.

"Hang on Liz, I got something else for you," George said, rifling through some papers on his desk. He handed her a page of paper. Elizabeth read it carefully.

"Hang on, a celebrity interview? What the hell George?"

"Mary is sick, I need someone to cover it."

"This is fluffier than the nurse piece."

"Which should make it easier right? Celebrity stories play their part in the success of this newspaper."

"Fine."

"Good, just think of it as an opportunity. You can ask her some hard hitting questions," George said, before dismissing her with his hand. Elizabeth turned and left, clutching the paper in her hand. She grumbled to herself and walked back to her desk.

"I better find out what her latest movie is," Elizabeth said with a sigh and sat down at her computer. The first few posts she found suggested that Lucy Margot was starring in a science fiction epic called Solar Quest. But what really caught her interest was a different story altogether. Lucy was also a Cancer survivor.

"Did George know when he gave me this?" Elizabeth thought. Maybe it was a coincidence, but it was strange that she should tell him about Dean's story and then she gets this interview. She dug a little further into that angle.

There was another nugget of interest. Lucy was treated as an outpatient of Royal Monterey Hospital.

"Now that's intriguing," Elizabeth said softly. It wasn't going to be hard thinking up questions for Lucy, the trick would be weeding out the few she could actually ask.

"Dean is going to laugh when I tell him about this," Elizabeth said to herself and chuckled. She felt better about the interview. There would be a purpose to it and the potential to get a lead on the hospital. She had a feeling that something was going on, and one way or another she'd get answers.

CHAPTER FIVE

MORE ROUTINE

Nathan opened his eyes to see a doctor hovering near the bed, reading a chart. It looked like the same doctor that had visited him yesterday.

"Oh don't mind me Nathaniel, I'm just looking over your observations from last night."

"It's Nathan. How am I doing? Looking good?"

"Nothing bad. But nothing to suggest a change."

"Did you look into my perhaps doing these observations from home, Dr Malberg?" Nathan said, looking directly at the doctor. Dr Malberg stared back at him blankly for a second, before regaining his composure.

"I'm afraid I didn't have an opportunity to do that yesterday. It will have to wait until our next staff review."

"When is the next one?"

"I think next week, I'll check for you."

"Thanks," Nathan said still watching the doctor closely. Dr Malberg resumed reading the chart, returned it and then left the room.

"He never intended to talk to his colleagues," Nathan said to himself with certainty. It was clear that they had no plans of letting him go. That much was obvious. But he couldn't figure out why he had no progress and why he had to stay.

It all started months ago, when he was feeling a bit lethargic and had a reduced appetite. He visited the local medical clinic, and the doctor ordered a routine blood test. When the results had come in, they said he had to see a specialist in the hospital to review his blood test. The doctor couldn't give him any additional information.

So Nathan had turned up to his appointment, and the doctor had given him a long explanation of why he was there with technical terms, but not actually explaining what had them so worked up. What was clear, was that he needed to do another test. So they gave him something to drink, and then he blacked out.

When he awoke, he was in a hospital bed and felt extremely weak and lightheaded. And in a nutshell that had been his experience since. Lots of excuses, lack of explanation and a series of ailments that kept him bedridden. But the thing that rankled the most, was the mind numbing routine. The same irritations on a daily basis. The reporter was a ray of hope.

He thought about whether to ask about her again. But he didn't want to draw unwanted attention. There was a good chance that she got his message, so she would come find him. She had to. Nathan's inner dialogue was interrupted by the door opening.

"Good morning Nathan, how are we today?" Robin said with a smile.

"Better now that you're here."

"You're such a sweetie."

"It's true, the night shift are terrible."

"Don't be so harsh on them, nobody gets a permanent assignment so they moonlight between all the wards. They don't get the luxury of dealing with the same patients all the time," Robin said. Nathan sat up more in the bed, wincing at the effort.

"Sorry, I just get frustrated I guess."

"I can understand. You've been here for a while."

"With no end in sight."

"I'm sure something will come through. Keep your spirits up."

"I'll try. Anything new for you today, got something to cheer me up?" Nathan said. He was fishing for news about the reporter and the article, but trying to keep it low key.

"No not really."

"What about that story in the paper?"

"Oh, I'm not sure. I'll have to check. Maybe you can look for me?"

"Sure, I'd love to."

"Great I'm so flat out. I'll grab you a newspaper," Robin said before leaving the room.

"She's lying," Nathan thought. She had been so excited about the article, he could not believe that she hadn't already combed the paper from cover to cover. But why should she lie about that? His thought process was interrupted by Robin entering once more.

"Here you go love. I'll pop back in at lunchtime. Fingers crossed!"

"I'll let you know if I find it," Nathan said. He smiled at Robin until she left and then turned his attention to the newspaper. He was curious to see if there was an article. Something about Robin's behaviour was off. But he had only just caught it. What if there were other things that he hadn't been paying attention to?

Nathan shook his head, pushing the thought away. He focused on the newspaper, carefully scanning each article. Within five minutes he had looked through the entire paper and there was no article.

"So either she knew it wasn't coming today and lied about it, or she had already looked and lied about it," he said to himself. He had no proof, but he just knew. Now he had to think about her possible motives. But it wasn't clear, he didn't know what she had to gain. So he decided to hold that line of thought and wait until he had more information to work with.

Robin appeared at lunchtime as promised.

"So am I famous?" she said as she entered the room.

"Not yet."

"Maybe tomorrow then."

"Did the reporter mention when it would be ready?"

"Only that it might take a few days."

"Ok well I guess we'll keep checking," Nathan said. He wanted to ask more pointed questions, but held back. He didn't need to alienate his biggest supporter here at the hospital.

Lunch was a piece of lasagne with a few steamed and wilted vegetables. He ate the food mechanically, the broccoli reminding him of rubber. Once done he turned to the small tub of yoghurt, hoping it would save the meal. It was good, but too miniature to make a big impact.

In the afternoon Robin left again and Nathan was left with the night shift. After a thirty minute beeping session from his equipment a young nurse entered the room. She had long blonde hair and didn't look more than twenty years old.

"Hello there, sorry about all the racket," she said. Nathan accepted the apology and the genuine smile on her face.

"That's fine, glad you're here," he said. The nurse walked over and checked the machine. Then she looked over at his left arm, where the drip was connected.

"Hmm that doesn't look good, let me check the notes," she said walking over and picking up his folder.

"You've had that cannula for days now, we need to change it."

"Fair enough. Can I at least have your name before you stick another needle in me?" Nathan said, trying to keep his spirits up.

"Ha-ha good one. Yeah I'm Nancy. I'll turn this off and come back with what I need."

"Thanks Nancy," Nathan said, watching her leave. She had a friendly manner, and had turned off rather than silenced the machine which was a nice touch.

"I shouldn't be so judgemental," Nathan thought to himself. It was easy to get carried away when what should be small things take up a lot of attention. Nancy returned within five minutes with a small tray containing medical supplies.

She carefully removed the current needle, and put a cotton bud over the small dot of blood that surfaced. She then used a piece of tape to secure the cotton and provide pressure.

"Halfway done," Nathan said.

"Yeah that was the easy bit," Nancy said. She walked around to the other side of the bed and inspected his right arm. She examined and felt his arm up and down, judging a good spot to put the needle in. She rubbed the spot with a bit of alcohol and started to insert the needle, but then stopped immediately.

"I didn't get it," she said. Nathan just nodded in response. It was a common thing in his experience, nurses had trouble getting the vein correctly. He waited patiently for her next attempt.

"Sorry," she said as the second attempt also failed. Nathan winced at the pain but said nothing.

"Oops," she said at the third attempt. Nathan looked at her, and could see the nervous concentration on her face. He didn't say anything, for fear of making the situation worse.

The fourth failure really stung, and Nathan let out a little grunt. His arm was becoming tenderer with each successive attempt. He could see Nancy becoming flustered and trying to calm herself.

"Should I say something? Ask for another nurse?" he thought to himself. But with his luck he would get her again, and she was quite young and would probably take it personally. So he steeled himself for the next try.

Half an hour later the cannula was in. Nathan had stopped counting the attempts, happy that he could be left in peace. He felt like his right arm had been beaten soundly. Nancy had apologised on her way out, but Nathan didn't respond. He just wanted to sleep it off. He dozed briefly, not really sleeping.

Dinner came, and he mechanically shovelled down the macaroni and cheese. His right hand was too sore, so he had to use his left. It was a struggle, but he persevered. He tried to savour the custard pudding but his heart wasn't in it. So he put himself to bed, hoping that the day would end.

He was out for a long dreamless sleep. When he awoke it took a moment for him to remember where he was. The pain in his right arm brought back vivid memories of the previous day's events.

His right arm was good enough to handle the porridge for breakfast, and he left the doctor alone and asked no hard questions. He was hanging out to see Robin.

When she finally popped in he saw her clutching a newspaper in her hand. Nathan's spirits lifted when he saw it.

"Are you famous today?" he said.

"You could say that. One of the girls spotted it for me," Robin said, her face beaming. Nathan pondered the probability of any of the nurses seeing that before Robin did.

"Could I take a look?"

"Sure I brought you this copy," Robin said. She left the newspaper on his tray table. Nathan started leafing through it immediately.

"Everything looks good here I'll pop in a bit later," Robin said. Nathan nodded but didn't look up. The newspaper was his key concern. He resisted the urge to rapidly flip through. He methodically scanned each page, making sure he missed nothing. Sure enough, towards the end he spotted the story.

TWENTY YEARS OF SERVICE FOR SUPER NURSE

The first thing he noticed was the name of the reporter: Elizabeth Edmonds. He didn't know her, but committed the name to memory. It was a comfort to put a name to the person who he was pinning his hopes on. It also reinforced that she was real, and had visited the hospital. The details of the story were not of much interest. But it gelled with his experience with Robin. Towards the end of the article were some very intriguing bits.

There were quotes from some of Robin's patients.

"She got my message. She came back!" Nathan said to himself in shock. Well she could have done it all the first day, but it was just too coincidental. And Robin had acted strangely yesterday, surely because she knew that Elizabeth the reporter was coming back.

"They are keeping things from me. Keeping me hidden and not letting me go," Nathan thought to himself. From the article Elizabeth had spoken to two other patients of Robin, called Tom and Dean. He memorised those names too. How many patients had Robin talked to before volunteering those two?

Nathan's mind was running fast, trying to consider all the possibilities. He could deduce that Elizabeth had gotten his message, come back to talk to the patients and been given two names which were not him. Robin had not mentioned to him that Elizabeth was coming back to talk to patients, because she knew that Nathan would ask to be included. It perfectly explained Robin's behaviour and also why he had been left out. It also suggested that he had been left out purposefully.

But then his heart sank - he had missed his chance. He had created an opportunity but not managed to capitalise on it.

"If she's a good reporter, she must know that something else is up. If she got the message, surely the interviews she did weren't satisfactory," Nathan thought. She had to know that neither of the people she interviewed had left her the message. But he was out of options, he couldn't rely on the same trick again.

He scanned the article again, looking for something else that might be of assistance. But that was it. He could confront Robin about not being given the opportunity to talk to the reporter, but she was under obligation to explain herself. The best thing he could do was act on the information he had obtained. Which meant locating either Tom or Dean.

"Since they talked to her, they mustn't have the same restrictions as me. Maybe they could pass on a message. The trick though is getting myself mobile," Nathan said to himself. For all he had been told, there was no reason that he couldn't move around. They were probably counting on his lethargy and the lack of use of his muscles.

"I can't just sit here and wait to be rescued. I need to take action," Nathan thought. It was time to start training.

CHAPTER SIX

THE INTERVIEW

Elizabeth woke just before her alarm and turned it off. It was unusual for her to wake this early, and to beat the alarm as well. It was probably down to her nervousness, or excitement at her interview with Lucy Margot.

Initially she had been rather put out at the task, but through her preparation she had been caught up in it. Lucy was actually a well-spoken person, and would be of interest even without the potentially fruitful link to Royal Monterey Hospital.

"Just don't turn into one of those breathless star struck types," she said to the mirror as she completed her makeup. She had never met a movie star before, and all the articles she had read suggested that Lucy had a very strong presence. Which in itself wasn't an issue, Elizabeth had gone toe to toe with some big personalities like the previous Mayor. But the whole thing was just enough outside her comfort zone that she wasn't as sure of herself.

She had left early enough to skip the worst of the morning traffic, parking underneath The Grand.

"Work can pay for this," Elizabeth thought, balking at the parking rates. The Grand was the oldest and most prestigious hotel in the city. Its aged sandstone was distinctive and made it look like an old castle. There was a story doing the round that it was originally called something else, like 'The Grand Palace' but the last word had been dropped as nobody ever bothered to say it. Elizabeth thought that the story was plausible.

Her interview with Lucy would be held in the penthouse suite, famed for its luxury, antique furniture and elite guest list. Elizabeth had an hour to spare, and her stomach reminded her that she had skipped breakfast. She took the lift up to the main lobby and marvelled at the giant chandelier dominating the space. She crossed the floor and stepped into the hotel restaurant Petit Grand.

She was led to a sun drenched corner and sat down at a table. She ordered a cappuccino and perused the menu. She decided on Eggs Benedict and put the menu aside. Rifling through her bag she retrieved her notes and started leafing through them.

Lucy had finished shooting Solar Quest without incident and at some point after that she was diagnosed with Ovarian Cancer. Her public relations agent had recently announced that she was in remission, which neatly coincided with her promotional tour for the movie. Not only was the timing great, but only three months had passed since news of her diagnosis.

"So she's either very lucky or faking it," Elizabeth thought. But she shelved that line of thinking until she had more to go on. She turned to her other notes about Lucy's career. Lucy had been extremely successful, starring in six blockbuster movies. Her versatility, pretty face and long blonde locks had served her well. She had probably earned enough to never work again. Something else for Elizabeth to ask her about.

Her coffee and food arrived, so Elizabeth shoved her documents aside and dove in. The eggs were poached to perfection and the yolk oozed out immediately. Elizabeth forgot all about the interview until she had finished eating.

"Time to go," she thought looking at her watch. She paid for the meal, kept the receipt and made her way over to the reception desk.

"Hello, how may I be of assistance?" the man behind the counter said. He looked to be in his fifties but had thick locks of dark black hair. Elizabeth couldn't tell if it was dyed or not.

"Hi I'm here to see Lucy Margot. I have an interview at ten-thirty."

"Very good. Your name please?"

"Elizabeth Edmonds," she said. The man picked up a piece of paper and scanned it carefully.

"Please state who you are representing?"

"I'm with the Stately Herald."

"Very good. Finally I'd like to see some identification."

"Oh wow sure, hang on a second," Elizabeth said as she dug through her bag for her wallet and driver's licence.

"Sorry for the security measures, but Miss Margot has many admirers, some of whom need to keep their distance," the man said while looking over the licence. He handed it back to Elizabeth with a smile.

"Leroy will take you up," he said, gesturing to a nearby busboy.

"Thanks," Elizabeth said before walking over. Leroy called one of the lifts, and stepped inside holding the door open. He swiped an access card and then pressed the tenth floor.

"Have a lot of people come up?" Elizabeth said, making conversation.

"Not yet, I think you're the first today."

"Great," Elizabeth said. She waited patiently for the lift to stop and the doors to open. Leroy stood still, ushering her out.

"On your left, you can't miss it. Room 1001," Leroy said.

"Thanks," Elizabeth said and followed his directions. There was only one door to the left, with the room number he had mentioned. Elizabeth walked up to the door and prepared to knock when the door opened. A short woman with brown hair and a clipboard was standing in the doorway.

"Please state your name."

"Elizabeth Edmonds."

"Ok great let's go. Miss Margot is waiting," the woman said, gesturing for Elizabeth to enter. She stepped inside and heard the door close behind her. She walked along a short corridor which opened into a massive room. It was flooded with light from the large ornate windows lining the walls. The furniture looked like it was taken from a throne room over two hundred years ago. Except that it was in immaculate condition.

"Good morning," Lucy said, putting down her cup of tea and rising from the comfortable single seater she was sitting in.

"Good morning, I'm Elizabeth. Nice to meet you."

"I'm Lucy, as you must know. Nice to meet you too," Lucy said, before shaking Elizabeth's hand.

"Please take a seat. Would you like some tea?"

"Sure, whatever you are having would be great," Elizabeth said, sitting down opposite Lucy.

"English breakfast, there's milk and honey on the side," Lucy said as she poured tea for Elizabeth.

"I've never had an interviewee pour me tea before," Elizabeth said as she added milk.

"The mayor didn't pour you tea? How rude! I suppose he was rather furious."

"You heard about that?"

"Yeah it was a good story. Corruption, an exciting investigation by a civilian and success against all odds. Would make a great movie. You think I could play you?" Lucy said. Elizabeth couldn't tell if she was being serious, or having fun.

"I'm sure you could. If anyone asks me I'll recommend you," Elizabeth said with a laugh.

"Great! I'm all about finding interesting roles, and one based on a true story with a strong female character is just what I'm after," Lucy said.

"If you don't mind I'd like to ask you about that. Sorry if I'm just jumping in, but is that what keeps you in the movie business? You must have earned enough already to retire for life."

"Ha-ha that's not a question you get every day. You don't beat around the bush do you?"

"Sorry, old habits. If you would prefer..."

"No it's quite alright, it's a refreshing change," Lucy said, about to launch into an explanation. Elizabeth took out a voice recorder and put it on the table.

"Of course, let's start recording," Lucy said, acknowledging the recorder.

"Thanks," Elizabeth said, flicking a switch on the device.

"So, I'll readily admit that I got into this business for the fame and fortune. It's the lure of movies, and the glamorous lifestyle they promote. I got sucked in. They try and tell you how hard it is, but you never understand until you start."

"It's hard getting that first break?"

"Yes, but it's even harder once you get it. Making movies is long days, with lots of concentration and repetition. But on top of that, you're only as good as your last performance. Once you make it everyone is a critic, and they're watching and waiting for you to screw up."

"Sounds tough. But you keep going back, is it to prove something?"

"It is, but perhaps not in the way you think. The benefits of the fame and recognition are that you can exercise some influence over the industry. You can find whatever it is that you want to work on, or help boost up projects that might not get the light of day otherwise. But there's only so far that will take you, and for some it just ends up as ego inflation."

"How did you avoid that trap?"

"I got Cancer."

"Wow. I guess that's a pretty life altering situation."

"Yes, it sure is. It gives you a whole different perspective on life. It gives you a lens to look through, which filters out everything that isn't important."

"What did you discover?"

"The normal things, the simple things. For me it was primarily family, and just the joy of being. But also a sense of purpose."

"Any purpose in particular?"

"I want to be a positive role model, and use my influence in a constructive way. I want to champion women, such as yourself, who are themselves role models and active leaders in the community. So that younger girls realise that they are only limited by their imagination."

"That's a noble goal, and I think that we could always use more female role models. Did you feel this way previously and never acted on it, or was it a new revelation from your treatment?" Elizabeth asked. She wanted to try and turn the discussion to Lucy's experiences at the hospital, to see if there was anything of interest to her or to Dean.

"Cancer treatment is a full on affair. The effect on your body is so intense, it strips away things that you considered important before like your dignity. The beginning of the treatment is the worst, and you have a lot of time to think."

"Were you hospitalised the entire time?"

"No just at the start. Then I had weekly appointments. I had a variety of treatments, and I felt terrible and they were completely ineffective."

"So this changed your perspective?"

"Yes, I vowed to make changes if I survived. And by some miracle I did. So here I am."

"That's a really inspirational story. I feel like we could talk for hours," Elizabeth said with a smile. She liked Lucy.

"You know, none of the other interviews ever touched on the Cancer properly. They ignored it, like it didn't happen."

"Maybe I have dwelled on it too much. I haven't even asked you about the new movie!" Elizabeth said.

"No, it's fine. I'd like it if your story included more than just promotional material."

"Of course, I wouldn't be able to write it otherwise. So, with your new lens how does the movie stand up?"

"You know, it's actually a great movie. I play Victoria, who is a strong and complex character. It takes a lot to leave your family and everything behind to do something for humankind. "

"You know I haven't actually watched the movie."

"I had assumed as much, since the preview screening was a few weeks ago."

"Well let's use this opportunity to educate our readers too," Elizabeth said, launching into more questions that elicited what was interesting about the movie. After half an hour she turned off the recorder and prepared to leave.

"Thanks for your time today. It was a really interesting interview, especially since I have a friend with Cancer at Royal Monterey Hospital."

"Oh, what kind of Cancer?"

"Stomach Cancer."

"I hear that's pretty bad. I'm not sure how much the treatments differ, but all of mine were terrible. It was only the last one that made a difference."

"What was it?"

"I'm not entirely sure. They injected me with something that they were testing, I had to sign a lot of paperwork. At that point I was ready to try anything. Maybe it was just a coincidence, but that was the point at which I started to get better."

"Wow, I should tell my friend about this. I wonder if they mentioned it to him."

"I don't know much else about it, I really didn't expect anything to change."

"Do you remember the doctor that gave you this treatment?"

"I had a lot of doctors. Maybe a Dr Malburn?"

"Malburn. I'll follow it up, see if they can offer something to my friend."

"Sure, good luck. It was great talking to you, I'll ask for you when we're doing the circuit for the next movie!"

"Great looking forward to it," Elizabeth said and left the room. It had been an interesting interview, but there wasn't much for her to follow up. But at least she had something for Dean to look into. He seemed the type to take a chance on a new treatment. And it was good to keep her work ticking over and George off her back. She knew there was something interesting lurking in that hospital, and she had to find a way to tease it out.

Elizabeth retrieved her car, sighed as she paid the parking fee and dutifully stowed the receipt. She headed straight to the hospital to talk to Dean and fill him in.

When Elizabeth arrived at the ward Dean was in, the doors were closed and there was a note on the door.

"Of course, no visiting during lunchtime," she said to herself, annoyed at forgetting the visiting hours. So she returned to her car, retrieved her laptop and headed to the hospital cafeteria. They had a selection of dubious looking hot food in metal trays, as well as a selection of sandwiches.

Realising that she wasn't that hungry, she walked over to a table and sat down. She pulled out her recorder and plugged in headphones, so she could transcribe the interview on her laptop. She hated listening to her own voice, but it was easier to work with words written down. Budget cuts at the newspaper meant they no longer had staff to transcribe for them.

After an hour, she had done most of the interview and took a break. The sandwiches were starting to look more appetising so she selected one with cheese and salad.

"It can't be that bad," she murmured to herself. She also bought an orange juice to wash it down. The sandwich was a bit soggy, but otherwise inoffensive. She checked the time, packed up her things and made her way back to see Dean.

Elizabeth followed the signs and took a different route. She hoped to find another way into the ward, which might help her gauge the size and locate more of Robin's patients. She took a winding route, going up stairs and down stairs and found a door she didn't recognise. But the sign confirmed she had found the ward.

"Let's see how this goes," she thought. Elizabeth walked through and saw a long corridor with a bend at the end. There were rooms lining the walls. As she walked down she counted ten rooms. She turned the bend, and began to recognise her surroundings. She had traversed down the other end of the corridor and come back to where she had first scouted out. She could see Tom and Dean's rooms, the recreation area and at the end the nurse station.

"So there's about twenty patients," Elizabeth said to herself. And she had only seen two. There was a lot more work to be done. She purposefully opened the door before Dean's and walked inside.

She prepared her response at the intrusion, but there was no accusations. She looked around the room and saw an old woman lying in bed, asleep. Her chest was moving so slowly that Elizabeth couldn't tell at first if she was alive. Elizabeth slowly turned and left the room as quietly as possible.

"That's one down, seventeen to go," she thought to herself. Not wanting to try her luck, she went straight to Dean's door and opened it.

"Back again," Dean said, putting down the newspaper.

"Yeah here I am. Did you read the article?" Elizabeth said.

"Yup, I like it. I don't think it would have been as good without the quotes from the patients."

"Just as well I got them then."

"Just as well. Busy day today?"

"Yes actually. You wouldn't believe who I interviewed."

"Who?"

"Lucy Margot, the actress."

"Hmm don't recognise the name, might recognise the face."

"It doesn't really matter. The exciting thing is that she survived Cancer, and she was treated as an outpatient here."

"I'm happy for her, it happens sometimes. Luck of the draw."

"What if it's not just luck? She said that she was offered a special treatment that was experimental, and she got better after that."

"I'm listening. What is it?"

"I don't know exactly. Some kind of injection. She had to sign a lot of waivers to get a chance to try it."

"I'd be up for that. I'm an old geezer, why don't they try it on me?"

"I don't know. Maybe because you're an old geezer?" Elizabeth said. Dean laughed and nodded.

"Who do I talk to about that?" Dean said.

"Lucy mentioned a Dr Malburn. That's probably a good place to start."

"Good. I'll start quizzing the nurses. Any updates on our investigation?"

"No, not really. I counted twenty rooms in this ward, I think they're all single occupancy. I've visited three, so that leaves seventeen more."

"That shouldn't take too long. If I was more mobile I'd do them all in one day."

"Well sure I could do that, but I want to stay under the radar. If people start complaining to the nurses I'll be kicked out."

"True, you need to be careful. I'll help you."

"How?"

"When you visit I'll make sure I call them over. Then you can quietly check other rooms. If somebody was sending you a message, they'll pipe up if you stumble across them."

"Yeah that's not a bad idea.'

"Then let's get started. I need to ask them about this doctor before I forget the name."

"Sure," Elizabeth said. She watched Dean grab the white cord dangling by his bed and press the big green button. It lit up immediately.

"Off you go, better if they don't see you in here. For multiple reasons."

"Yeah you're probably right. Ok see you later Dean."

"See you tomorrow," Dean said, a big grin on his face. Elizabeth waved and pushed open the door. She didn't see any nurses outside, but didn't stop to look around. She headed away from the nurse station, towards the second entrance.

"I can probably check the last four rooms quickly and quietly without raising suspicion," she said to herself. Elizabeth walked quickly and with purpose down the hallway. She slowed as she approached the door. She sidled up to the first room on her left, and tried to listen in. No noise came from inside the room.

Elizabeth gently pushed open the door and looked in. An old man with sparse white hair and thick glasses was reading the newspaper. He looked up, squinting in Elizabeth's direction.

"So sorry, I must have the wrong room," Elizabeth said. The man nodded and returned to his newspaper. Elizabeth quickly closed the door. She had blurted out her response without thinking, but it had been a reasonable answer. Surely the person looking for her would at least enquire after a stranger just in case. Especially a woman.

"I wonder if the patient read my article?" Elizabeth thought to herself. She repeated the same routine on the next two doors. The blank look she received confirmed that neither were relevant to her. There was one door left before the ward exit, so she ducked in there next.

"Excuse me, who are you?" a woman's voice said with annoyance. Elizabeth looked up at a stern woman in her fifties.

"Oh, wow I've definitely got the wrong room," Elizabeth said. She was surprised at being challenged so strongly, but held her breath in anticipation. Maybe it was the patient she needed to find.

"Indeed. Please make yourself scarce," the woman said, dismissing Elizabeth. She was all too happy to leave, and rushed out. She quickly scanned the corridor and saw nobody else.

"Let's not push my luck," she said to herself, and headed straight for the main doors. She was soon out of the ward and back in the safety of the rest of the hospital.

"Well I've now seen seven patients all up. Thirteen to go," Elizabeth thought. It had been a productive day, but she hadn't uncovered anything significant.

"I need a break on this hospital clue," Elizabeth said quietly. She headed back to the office to continue working on Lucy's interview. It was important to work on it while it was still fresh. And within a few days she should be able to visit the other patients. That should turn up something useful. She just had to find the person who had left her the message, and then things would start clicking into place.

CHAPTER SEVEN

FIRST EXPEDITION

Nathan waited until the afternoon to make his move. He had tried stretching and leaning and testing his muscles. They ached and refused to move and were stubborn. But they weren't completely useless. He had to try.

Robin had said goodbye, and went to hand over to the night shift. He knew from their routine that he would have peace for a while. They were slow even reacting to his nurse calls. He looked over at the various equipment attached to him. The drip was on a stand with wheels, so that was fine. But the rest of the probes were hooked up to machines that were fixed in place. He would have to remove them, and they could be noisy.

"I'll have to take that chance. Maybe they won't notice," he thought to himself. He sat upright in the bed and slowly turned his body so that his legs went off the bed. He kept rotating, slowly, and lowered his legs to the ground. The floor was cold, the harshness of the feeling surprising him. He tried putting some weight on his right foot, and it seemed unsteady.

"Doesn't bode well," he whispered. He tested his other foot, with a similar result. He shrugged his shoulders, the pain and stiffness reminding him that it was a bad idea. But he persevered. He took note of how the probes were attached, and removed them carefully. The first set went without protest, the second set started an insistent beeping. He used the urgency from that noise to spur him on. He removed the third set of probes from his arms and only the drip remained. The pain of the cannula being inserted gave him pause, and he was careful when moving to avoid disrupting it. He slowly eased himself off the bed, leaning more and more on the stand holding the drip. He seemed to be in an equilibrium, and continued his controlled movement. Soon he was at the critical point.

He eased off the bed completely, holding his weight on his legs and throwing his arms onto the stand. It moved a little, but he steadied himself.

"So far so good," Nathan said with effort, hunched over just above the bed. He tried to move forward slightly, leaning more into the metal stand. It moved, but didn't run away from him. He was now away from the bed, if he fell it would be straight onto the floor. He gritted his teeth and moved once more. He felt his body complain, but ignored it. He had to do this. He took another small step, trying to maintain his balance.

Suddenly his right leg gave way, and he crashed to the floor.

"Shit," Nathan called out, the fall taking him by surprise. The floor had smacked him hard, and the ground felt as cold as a tomb. He turned to look up at the bed. It seemed too tall and out of reach. He could probably scramble back up, but it would take the rest of his energy. He looked over to the door. It was a few metres away, but if he could get there he could get a proper look at his surroundings. Maybe he could call out to a fellow patient.

"I've got to try," Nathan thought. The months of frustration needed release. Despite the pain and awkwardness, he felt good using his body. He swallowed hard and then started crawling towards the door. He dragged himself forward, commando style, and then reached back to bring the drip with him. He had poor control over it, and he slammed into his leg.

"I can do this," Nathan whispered. A little voice in his head started to question why he was so weak. But he ignored it, he only had time for his objective. He dragged himself forward again, this time a little further. The floor was smooth, but the friction on his chest still burned. He dragged himself again, willing himself to the door. Each increment was so small he wondered if he was actually getting anywhere. But it did get closer, and after minutes of effort he managed to touch the door. It was his first victory. He pushed against the door, testing it. The door didn't budge.

"Is it locked?" Nathan thought in a panic. He hadn't expected that. If it was, he was screwed. He looked up at the door, wondering if he had been foolish, or unobservant. The door had a cylindrical metal handle, but no obvious signs of a lock.

"I have to get up and try it," he said. He looked around for something to help, and noticed a bench near the door. It was lower than the door handle height, which would help. He took a deep breath and prepared himself. Then he reached up, grasping desperately for the bench. He couldn't reach it from his position on the ground. Nathan grunted then rested. He would need another step in-between.

So Nathan leaned on the door instead, and used his hands to slowly prop himself up into a seated position, hands back to the door. He was sweating profusely, but he managed. With his right hand he pulled the drip closer. Next he turned his attention back to the bench.

With his improved vantage point he was closer, but he could see that he would need an additional boost. Which seemed possible, but he'd only get one try. He didn't trust his body. He calmed himself once more and started reeling his legs in. He bent his knees and got into the foetal position.

"This is it," he whispered, then shot up. He put more pressure on his left leg, hoping it would compensate. It wobbled and strained but held and Nathan got his hands on the bench long enough to shift his stance and lean against it. He had achieved a delicate equilibrium, and was in a semi standing position. It had been harder than he realised, but he felt stronger from the attempt.

After giving himself a minute to recover, he wheeled the drip around with his free hand, then reached for the door handle. This was the key moment, which would potentially determine his fate. He grasped the handle firmly and started turning counter-clockwise. The handle moved slowly, not giving anything away. But it kept turning and with a bit of a pull from Nathan it opened.

The cold air outside his room chilled him. His room wasn't particularly warm or cold, so the sensation surprised him. The next thing he noticed was the silence. He associated hospitals with hustle and bustle and activity. It felt like a tomb out there. Alarmed, he stumbled over to the doorway and leaned against it, to get a view of the corridor. It was well-lit but empty. There were no signs of life. He looked left and right, and all he could see was corridor.

There were what looked like rooms, but the doors were nondescript and looked unused. Looking closer they looked old and forgotten. He turned and looked at his door. It was the same as all the rest, but with one difference. There was a sign on the door.

CM

"What's that?" Nathan thought to himself. But the momentary confusion lead to dread. He was somewhere isolated and by himself. The sign on his door helped the staff find him, the one patient in what must be a deserted ward. The reporter would never see him, even if she talked to every one of Robin's patients. The strength drained from his limbs, and he started to sway. But then a fierce determination flared up within him.

"They mustn't know that I know," he said with defiance. He staggered back to the bench and closed the door. Standing upright, the distance to his bed didn't seem as far as it had on the ground. He made for the bed, the drip stand threatening to run away from him and his feet conspiring against him. But he stayed upright long enough to grab the metal bars on the side of the bed. From there he shimmied across carefully until he could sit on the bed. It was actually a relief climbing back into bed.

But he wasn't finished. He had to reattach the probes, which was tough work and he was already exhausted. The beeping of the machines subsided, and he fell into a deep sleep.

He heard a noise nearby and opened his eyes. A nurse was next to him, pressing buttons on the machines and noting down numbers. Nathan acknowledged it and closed his eyes again. When he opened them again the room was full. There were six doctors crowding around him. One of the doctors, a tall man with white hair and glasses noticed that Nathan was awake and addressed him.

"Nathaniel how are you feeling?" he said. The rest of the doctors fell silent and waited for the response.

"Yeah alright, a bit tired. What's going on here?"

"We noticed some inconsistencies in your vitals."

"Ok. Seems like there's an awful lot of doctors here."

"Well yes, we were conferring on possible causes."

"Oh well, I'm not sure if it means anything, but I turned suddenly and some of my probes came off. It took me a while to put them back on," Nathan explained. That set off a furore of discussion. The same doctor addressed Nathan again.

"If that's the case, why didn't you call the nurse?"

"Well they're so slow responding most of the time, I thought I'd try and fix it myself."

"I see. That would explain the readings," the doctor said. His colleagues nodded along. They conferred amongst themselves and then left. Only the white haired doctor remained. He remained quiet while a nurse entered the room, checked and adjusted the probes attached to Nathan, and also left without saying a word.

"Please don't adjust your probes in the future. We take your wellbeing very seriously Nathaniel," the doctor said.

"Yeah I can see that. I'm hidden away," Nathan thought to himself.

"Well I'm glad I have you looking after me doctor..." Nathan said with a pause, prompting the doctor for his name.

"Sterling. I must be off, take care," he said and then promptly left the room. And like that Nathan was alone again. But it felt different now. He wasn't sure if it was because the room had just been full, or because he knew that he was well and truly alone. Everything started to make sense in this new context. The way that Robin acted, the fact that nurses took so long to see him. He was special in some way, and was not just treated differently, he was placed out of sight.

His plan of finding another patient was now impossible. He needed a way to communicate without leaving his room. Nathan turned on his television and switched his brain off. A game show called Word Boggler came on and he quickly changed the channel. He had to not think for a while.

CHAPTER EIGHT

THE REMAINING THIRTEEN

Elizabeth worked until she had finished a good draft of the interview. She printed it double spaced, stapled the top left corner and left it on George's desk.

"George will freak, I never turn in stories the same day," she thought with a laugh. But it had been interesting work, and she needed a mental break from the hospital. Her brain just kept turning it over and over, and it frustrated her. The message had been clear, but she hadn't managed to find the sender. Her gut said that she wouldn't find the person in the ward she had been searching. But she didn't want to admit that, because then she would have no leads. Either way, she had to eliminate the obvious. And that meant visiting the rest of the patients.

Elizabeth drove home and made herself a quick dinner of spaghetti Bolognese. She found an opened bottle of red wine, and poured herself a glass.

"Better not let it go to waste," she said to herself. After dinner she stretched out on the couch and watched the television. The mental break was a relief, but she got bored quickly.

She was watching a show where people had to guess letters and attempt to solve a word puzzle. It was called Word Boggler. After all her writing and transcribing it was the last thing she wanted to watch. She had worked enough with words for one day. She changed the channel and let the clever wit and dialogue of an action movie wash over her. That was better.

The next morning when Elizabeth arrived at work she headed straight to George's desk. She wanted to see the reaction on his face.

"Elizabeth, just the person I wanted to see," George said without looking up.

"It always creeps me out how you can do that."

"It's a learned skill, gotta listen out for who is skulking around the newsroom. Every person has their own distinct walk, you just need to pay attention. Believe me it was a lot harder back when we had typewriters. Couldn't hear a damn thing."

"So I take it you read the story?"

"Yeah it's good. We'll make a celebrity reporter out of you yet."

"You're joking."

"Yep, you got me. It's a nice feature piece but too in-depth for anything else. Readers want more sex and scandal in their celebrity news."

"But you'll take it?"

"Yeah I'll run it on the weekend, maybe the Sunday edition. I've got something else for you to look at," George said, still not looking at Elizabeth. He pointed at a stack of papers on the end of his desk. Elizabeth walked over and picked them up, leafing through the pages.

"Careful, there's two piles in there. One is reader submissions for story ideas. I figured you earned your pick after covering so well."

"Thanks George. I'm sure there's some amazing stories in there."

"Yeah amazing is the right word. Or is it unbelievable? Anyway trawl away. Don't forget to run it by me first. The other pile in there is stuff that needs editing. I'm swamped."

"You want me to edit them? How and for what?"

"Just obvious errors, and write a summary for me. I don't have time to go through everything in detail."

"Yeah sure. I'll tackle that today."

"That's what I want to hear. Thanks Elizabeth," George said with a wave, his eyes still focused on another document. Elizabeth sighed and hauled the pile of paper over to her desk.

She decided to work through as much as she could in the morning, and then pop over to see Dean in the afternoon. She glanced at the first paper on the pile.

TERRORISTS TO BLOW UP COMMUTER TRAIN

"What the?" Elizabeth said to herself, and then took a closer look. Then she realised that it was a tip from a reader. She wondered if this pile was stuff that George had already discarded as useless.

"Oh well, there will be something good," Elizabeth thought, putting the tantalising tip off to the side and moving the rest of the similar pages with it. She was left with a pile of double spaced printed pages, neatly stapled in the top left corner just as George liked it. Before starting she grabbed her water bottle, filled it and then sat down at her desk.

"Here we go," Elizabeth said under her breath. She turned on her critical mind, the one she used to check her work before serving it up to George. She did two passes over the story, the first looking for spelling and grammar issues and the second reviewing it for factual errors and other potentially problematic parts. She marked up the errors and a dodgy passage, and left a comment at the bottom for George.

"One down, five million to go!" thought Elizabeth. She put the story aside and worked on the next one.

Many stories later, Elizabeth reached for her water bottle and it was empty. She looked at the clock and saw that it was already midday.

"Time flies when you're not having fun right?" a voice said behind her with a chuckle. Elizabeth spun around to see who it was. She saw a tall black man with thin rimmed glasses looking at her with a knowing gaze.

"Was it that obvious Louis?" Elizabeth said.

"No, I just know the feeling. George had me doing that the other day. I think it was because you were covering for Mary."

"Probably. You back on sports now?"

"Yeah it was only a day. You get in the zone so it's not so bad, but it's mind numbing work."

"You're not wrong. I don't think I can finish this today."

"You better not or you'll get more for tomorrow I guarantee it!"

"Ha-ha I think you're right," Elizabeth said and smiled at Louis as he walked off. It was definitely time for a break. She decided to go lunch at the hospital, so she could use the same approach as the day before and check out more hospital rooms. Elizabeth eyed off the pile and considered handing the completed ones over to George. But Louis' comment rung true.

"I better string these out, it will give me some flexibility," Elizabeth thought. She left the pile undisturbed, grabbed her bag and left.

She ran over the numbers during the drive over to the hospital. There were thirteen more patients to visit. She needed a better approach, she didn't want to spend a few more days carefully checking rooms. The lead might go cold.

Elizabeth mechanically chewed her sandwich as she continued to think over the problem. She glanced at the clock and saw the time was already one o'clock.

"No time to stuff around. I'll check a few patients on the way to see Dean and go from there," Elizabeth thought. She threw away the rubbish from her lunch and headed through the maze of corridors that would lead her to the back entrance to Dean's ward. She stepped through the doors, mentally checked off the rooms she had already visited and tried two more. Both had older women snoring soundly. Elizabeth shook her head and proceeded straight to Dean's room.

"Good day to you," Dean said as she entered.

"Hey Dean, how's things?"

"I'm good. Looked for your interview in today's paper but it wasn't there."

"Oh yeah my editor is going to run it on the weekend, probably Sunday."

"That makes sense. Any luck on finding your mystery patient?"

"No, I still have eleven left."

"I have an idea for you. But first I asked about that doctor yesterday."

"Oh great. What did they say?"

"There's nobody here called Dr Malburn. And they don't know about any other special treatments."

"Well I guess that's plausible if only that doctor knows about it. What's your gut feeling?"

"Heh you reporters and your gut feelings. I got a lot of gut feelings, but I don't think you want to hear about 'em. I do reckon there's something the nurses and doctors aren't telling me."

"Well how about I look into the doctor for you?"

"Done, sounds like a plan. When can you report back?"

"Geez you're starting to sound like my editor. When I get something, you'll hear about it."

"Good. I was thinking about your problem, and then it hit me. I had a social worker come visit me today. She was really nice, but wasn't sure if she was in the right room and she even got my condition wrong. Personally I think people should take a bit more responsibility for their work."

"Yeah, but I think I see where you're going with this."

"Be a social worker, nobody will pay you any mind. If they do complain, it'll be about the social worker. And nobody will take that seriously."

"They won't look into it?"

"Nah, everyone's too busy."

"What if a nurse sees me?"

"You'll figure it out."

"Yeah, you're right. It might just work."

"Now I do enjoy the pleasure of your company, but you've got work to do," Dean said with a smile.

"Sure thing boss," Elizabeth said looking around the room before she left. She spotted a clipboard hanging off the end of the bed. She checked it to make sure it wasn't being used then tossed it in her bag.

"Need my prop," she said.

"You'll fit right in," Dean said.

"The way you just described the social workers to me, I'm not so sure that's a good thing," Elizabeth said as she left the room. All she could hear in reply was Dean's laughter.

She decided to be methodical and work her way through the ward. She would only need to be in each room briefly, and working through the rooms would help make her excuse seem more legitimate. She walked up to the first room that she hadn't yet visited, paused and then knocked once. She didn't wait for a reply and headed straight inside.

A bald man in his twenties was in the room, sitting upright in bed and reading a novel. He looked up at her but didn't say anything. Elizabeth pulled out the clipboard and looked at it for inspiration.

"So I'm looking for one of Robin's patients," Elizabeth said, watching the young man's reaction.

"Yes?" the man said, not giving much away. Elizabeth wasn't sure how to respond.

"Let's see here, where's the name?" Elizabeth said, flipping through the blank pages of paper attached to the clipboard.

"Are you a social worker? I didn't ask for one," the man said, his impatience coming through.

"Why yes I am. Well, clearly it's not you I'm after. Sorry for the trouble," Elizabeth said, not having to fake the awkwardness. She stuffed the clipboard back into her bag. As she left the room, she felt annoyed at yourself.

"Just pull it together. That's not the person, you'll get that reaction a lot," Elizabeth told herself. She just had to treat the patients like potentially hostile sources. It just felt different in the hospital. Like she shouldn't be there, bothering these people.

"Businesslike and fast is the key, and I can get this over with and not disturb them," she thought as she approached the next door.

She repeated the same routine over and over. Making sure she said that she was looking for one of Robin's patients. Each time she held her breath as she delivered the message, scrutinising their face for a look of recognition. But none of them reacted. Before she left she made sure that they understood she was a social worker.

The tension in her chest rose after each failure, as the stakes were raised and the chance that she found who she was looking for increased. Finally she was up to the last door. She was almost done. She took a deep breath and steeled herself for anything.

CHAPTER NINE

LINES OF COMMUNICATION

Elizabeth opened the door without knocking, and surveyed the room. Inside was a young woman with long blonde hair, asleep. Elizabeth didn't know what to think.

"This could be it, I can't dismiss her without talking to her," Elizabeth said to herself. But she didn't want to wake the woman. She took a step closer, then stopped. She would have to come back. Elizabeth turned, then heard a voice call out.

"Hey," the woman said. Elizabeth faced her.

"Hello, did I wake you?"

"No, I was half awake."

"Sorry anyway. I'm looking for one of Robin's patients."

"Who is Robin?"

"Oh, well I must be in the wrong place, let me check my paperwork," Elizabeth said, flicking through the empty pages on the clipboard.

"Are you Susan?" Elizabeth said, making up the name.

"Yes," the woman said. Elizabeth cursed herself for picking that name.

"Susan Ambrose?"

"Oh no, I'm Susan Montgomery."

"Oh my mistake. They give us social workers the worst information! Please take care," Elizabeth said, stuffing the clipboard back into her bag and getting out of the room before the woman could reply. She turned and looked for the best way out.

"Can I help you?" an annoyed female voice said behind her. Elizabeth spun to face the voice. It was a squat nurse with short brown hair, one that Elizabeth didn't recognise.

"Oh no, I'm just on my way out," Elizabeth said.

"What were you doing in there?" the nurse said, looking suspicious. Elizabeth had to think quickly.

"Oh well you got me. My friend wanted another pillow, so I ducked in to see if I could find one."

"Really? You should just ask a nurse. There's a linen rack down the hall. Follow me," the nurse said. Elizabeth followed quickly. She just had to see this through and she was done.

"Here," the nurse said, pointing at a metal rack on wheels. The top shelf had various blankets and sheets, the bottom shelf was all pillows. Elizabeth looked through the pillows then selected one.

"Up for the pillowcases," the nurse said. She was still annoyed, but Elizabeth ignored the tone. She took a pillowcase and fumbled the pillow into it. She was surprised that the nurse was still with her, watching and waiting.

"Let's go, take me to the room," the nurse said.

"Sure," Elizabeth said, heading straight for Dean's room.

"He better be switched on," Elizabeth thought to herself. She reached Dean's door and reached out to open it when the nurse stepped in front of her.

"One moment please," she said, opening the door herself.

"Excuse me sir," the nurse said. Dean looked up at her.

"Yes?"

"Did you send for a pillow?"

"No, I don't think so," Dean replied.

"So you definitely didn't request a woman to get a pillow for you?" the nurse said, her voice rising with a feeling of triumph. Dean quickly started to put things together.

"Oh yeah, I sent Elizabeth out to get one. You confused me, I didn't send for a nurse. I'm just an old bloke."

"Of course sir, please in the future call us or get your friends to ask us when you need something."

"No problem, now I know. Can I ask your name? I don't think we've met?"

"We haven't. I'm Annabelle."

"Lovely to meet you today Annabelle," Dean said, giving his best smile. Annabelle did not react, and promptly left the room. She stopped in front of Elizabeth.

"I'm giving you the benefit of the doubt, but if I see you entering that room again you'll be thrown out of this hospital. You must respect the privacy of patients," Annabelle said.

"Absolutely, sorry for any trouble I've caused," Elizabeth said. She watched Annabelle stalk off and then entered Dean's room.

"Here's your pillow," Elizabeth said.

"I didn't even know I needed it," Dean said with a laugh.

"You almost stitched me up there."

"Like I said I'm an old bloke, you gotta cut me some slack!"

"Yeah. I must say though, she was very suspicious and went to great lengths to lecture me and warn me off going into that room."

"That's interesting, you may be on to something there. I've never seen her before, and I've been here a while. It makes you think doesn't it?"

"Another thing to look into. Speaking of which, I've now visited all the rooms on this ward. I'm convinced that whoever left me the message isn't here," Elizabeth said.

"Hang on, so you got a message to look for Robin's patients, but none of the patients here sent it. Does she tend to other wards?"

"I don't remember her saying that, I'll look into it."

"You know, that message might have been more specific than you realised. You were just looking in the wrong place."

"Maybe. I had a hunch that who we were after would not be in plain sight. But I ignored it until I had exhausted all the options. But there's one thing that's confusing."

"What's that?"

"I found the newspaper with the message in this ward. If one of Robin's patients left me the message, then how did it get here if the patient isn't here?"

"That's an easy one. Robin brought it," Dean said. Elizabeth stared at him in amazement. It was so simple, but put everything in a new light.

"Of course. The patient is somewhere else, and has used Robin to get the newspaper message to me. Robin really is the key."

"You going to follow her?"

"Not sure yet, I need to think it over. I got away with today's activities, but I want to be a bit more cautious with this next step."

"I'll have a think too, see what spy stuff I can dream up."

"Great! Hey how are you going anyway?"

"I'm alright, but it's hard. I have some time, but I can't do much with it. I think I'd rather have less time, and be able to do whatever I want. And then I'd drop dead with a beer in my hand and a smile on my face."

"It doesn't work that way does it?"

"Nope. Have you found my doctor yet?"

"No, but I will."

"Alright well that was fun today. I expect another adventure tomorrow."

"Sure. Bye Dean," Elizabeth said and left. She drove back to the office and worked through a few more article edits. She was about halfway through.

"How's my pile going? You done yet?" George said, peering over her shoulder.

"Not quite. I'm probably a third of the way through."

"A third? I expected at least a half. Well bring over the ones you have done," he said and before Elizabeth could respond he had already started back to his desk.

"Bought myself a bit of time," she thought to herself. Elizabeth carefully selected the right amount of papers and left them on his desk. George acknowledged her with a wave and continued what he was doing. Elizabeth stuffed everything else back into her drawers and prepared to go home.

"Any woeful attempts at jumbles to brighten my day today?" Alan said behind her.

"No, I'll admit I haven't tried one since. It's all been a bit manic in here," Elizabeth said, gesturing at the office.

"Yeah sure has. That's why I design the jumbles at home. You need the peace and quiet to enable the proper thinking."

"Don't you have to be here to submit them for the next edition?"

"Yeah I pop into the office around ten each night and do the final bit here. That's why I'm never in early in the morning."

"Oh right."

"Hang on, you never noticed did you?"

"Sorry Alan, I'm usually caught up in other things. Now that you mention it, you do never seem to be here in the morning. I just never processed it that way."

"It's fine, I was just having some fun with you. It must be jumble time!"

"Well I'm heading home myself. Good luck with the jumble tonight."

"Thanks, have a good night," Alan said and left. Elizabeth did one last check of her desk, picked up her bag and also left.

On the drive home she set her mind to think about how to track Robin in the hospital. The problem would be following Robin enough to see where she went, without being obvious about it. There had to be a way to know when to follow Robin.

"Hang on, the newspaper!" Elizabeth said, the idea bouncing around her head and gaining traction. If Robin was the one to bring the newspaper back from the mysterious patient, maybe she was also the one to provide it. Then Elizabeth would only need to follow Robin when she was holding a newspaper.

"It's not foolproof, but it's a start," Elizabeth thought to herself. There was a certain elegance to the idea, that Robin was central to this routine and the key to finding the patient.

Elizabeth continued to tussle with the idea over dinner, this time a Pad Thai from a local Thai restaurant. It was the best she could come up with, and had a decent chance of providing the opportunity that Elizabeth needed. But there was something else about it that she couldn't put her finger on. Something else kept nagging at her.

She lay on the couch after dinner, watching more trashy game shows. Then Word Boggler came back on. Elizabeth was about to change the channel when something on the screen caught her eye. The contestant had successfully guessed the word, and Elizabeth stared at it.

WITCHDOCTOR

"Why is that interesting?" she thought to herself. The word sat there, poking into her brain. Her subconscious or intuition had run ahead, and she was trying to catch up.

"Which Doctor," she sounded out aloud, and let that sink in. It struck her like a bolt of lightning and she leapt up off the couch. That was it! She started pacing the room and talking to herself.

"I ask the patient which doctor is looking after them. I use the word jumble to do that. If I can track Robin when she is taking the paper I could find a location as well as hedge my bets by getting some useful information from the patient," Elizabeth said. She paused to let the thought linger and tried attacking it from different angles.

It relied on Robin taking the newspaper to the patient, and retrieving it. But the fact that she got the initial message meant that there was some sort of routine there. The jumble would have to make sense on its own, so as not to raise suspicion. And she had to convince Alan to run an amended jumble. All those were potential problems, but not deal breakers.

Elizabeth rushed around the house, trying to find a copy of The Stately Herald.

"Why is this so difficult?" she moaned. It was unbelievable that she worked there and couldn't find a copy of the paper. She did eventually find one in the bathroom, in the reading pile. It was from a week ago, but she didn't need something current. She just needed the word jumble format.

It was fairly simple. She just needed to design a question and answer, and then come up with four jumbled words to supply the required letters for the answer. She worked on the question first. It had to mean something to the person she was targeting, but look legitimate to other readers of the newspaper. She racked her brains for a few minutes before writing down a sentence.

What did the confused tribesman reply when asked to point out who had treated him?

And then she wrote underneath.

WITCHDOCTOR

It wasn't bad, and did broach the question she wanted answered. It also incorporated the answer from television that had prompted this approach. But something was missing. It didn't quite work. She had a good think and came up with a new version.

What did the medical students ask the naked tribesman they found lying in a ditch?

And then she wrote a new answer.

WITCHDOCTOR TREATED YOU?

Elizabeth chuckled to herself. It was just bad enough to work. If the patient went to the effort of solving the jumble, then the question became more direct and obvious. Now she just had to come up with the words to match that answer.

An hour later she had the jumble plotted out.

"Alan would be proud," she thought to herself. Which reminded her of Alan's routine. She checked the time and saw that it was only nine o'clock. If she left immediately she should get there before Alan.

Elizabeth ran straight to the car, started the engine and drove to work. She used her security pass to unlock the elevator up to the fourth floor. She used her card again to get in to the Stately Herald. She headed directly to Alan's desk, looking across the office as she went. It was relatively empty, save for the office at the back where the guys worked to prep for the printer. The door was mostly closed, but she could see the glow of light from within.

Elizabeth turned her attention to Alan's desk. It was neat and tidy. Either she had beaten him there, or he had beaten her. She picked up the pace and headed for the back office. She heard voices within, and one of them was Alan. She quickly swung the door open and stepped in.

"Hi guys," Elizabeth said. Alan, and a tall man stopped mid-conversation and looked at her in surprise.

"Last time you burst in here like this, we ran the mayor story," the tall lanky man said.

"Well it's not as exciting as that, but almost Jim."

"What have you got for me?"

"Well, it's more for Alan first. Alan I have a word jumble to go into tomorrow's paper," Elizabeth said. She watched Alan's face carefully. His features went from surprise, to indignation, to curiosity.

"My, that's interesting. Let me see it before you say anything else," Alan said. Jim looked on in interest as Elizabeth handed her jumble to Alan.

"Question has potential. Word jumbling is quite rudimentary," he said while examining the jumble. Shortly after he chuckled and handed it back.

"Decent answer, it's not a bad little jumble overall."

"You solved it already?"

"C'mon Elizabeth, this is what I do. I'll run it tomorrow on two conditions. The first, you let me rearrange the word jumbles. They lack elegance. The second is you tell me why it is so important."

"Well you may certainly rearrange as you wish, as long as the answer is unchanged."

"Of course, it has a certain charm," Alan said.

"And for the reason; I'll fill you in later. It's too risky right now."

"You're risking my patience Elizabeth. I admire your dedication to the jumble but I need something better," Alan said. Elizabeth thought for a moment, then responded.

"I'm using it to contact a source."

"Ha-ha what? No way!"

"Yes, that botched jumble you caught me with the other day? That was actually a message. I'm sending a reply."

"Clever, I like it. A new purpose for the humble jumble. Let's go with it."

"Thanks Alan. You can't breathe a word of this to George. It's too soon."

"That's no problem, he doesn't care much for my puzzles anyway. Leave it with me."

"You're the best Alan," Elizabeth said. She nodded at Jim, who gave her an amused look as she left. She could hear Alan talking him through the required changes as she left.

Elizabeth drove home with a sense of excitement growing within her. The wheels were turning, and tomorrow would be an interesting day.

CHAPTER TEN

A MESSAGE OF HOPE

Nathan awoke to Robin standing over him. He didn't remember falling asleep the night before.

"To be expected, I was pretty exhausted," he thought to himself.

"Good morning Robin."

"Good morning Nathan. I heard you had some excitement yesterday."

"I think the excitement was more for everyone else!"

"True, I guess for you having a bunch of people crowd into your room probably isn't that exciting. Don't mind me, I need to do another check of your probes to see that they are all attached properly," Robin said. She then proceeded to check all the pads and connections to Nathan's body. She was thorough but quick, and it was all over in a few minutes.

"Now that we're so well acquainted, can I get a newspaper?" Nathan said.

"Ha-ha sure. I already brought one with me. It's on your side table," Robin said, pointing to the paper.

"Great, you're always one step ahead."

"Of course honey, that's my job. Well everything looks good here I'll pop in later."

"Thanks Robin, see you later," Nathan said. He pulled his side table closer and swivelled it around so that he could sit up and read the paper. As he flipped though, he wasn't sure what he was looking for. He normally read the paper to stay connected to the world, but there was a fuzzy sensation nagging at him that he should be looking for something. He paused and looked away from the newspaper, wondering what it was.

He thought back over the previous day's expedition, and recalled his solitary position.

"I decided yesterday that I need another way of getting a message out, since I'm physically removed from everyone else. The newspaper was a way before, maybe I should use it again?" Nathan thought. It had to be what his subconscious was telling him. Although he'd want to be more specific this time. It had been days, and while he thought that the message was received, he was still alone and had not been found.

"I wonder if Robin checks the paper after I've used it?" he whispered.

Nathan skipped through until he saw the jumble. It looked like it normally did, but two words caught his attention.

"Medical students," he read out. It was probably a coincidence, and he was looking for messages. But he had time, and was curious so he worked at solving the jumble. A few of the words were quite elusive, but as he solved each one he felt confident that it was the right answer. Once he had all four words he looked at the key to start filling in the letters of the answer. He sat back and looked at the answer.

WITCHDOCTOR TREATED YOU?

Nathan laughed out loud. If that wasn't a message, nothing was. Elizabeth the reporter had sent him a message asking which doctor was treating him. He couldn't believe it. He just stared and stared at it. He even re-checked his answers. But there it was, plain as day.

"Why didn't she ask me where I was?" he thought to himself. But then he realised, had she done so he wouldn't know what to say. He didn't know where he was. And he just so happened to have the name of a doctor etched into his brain: Sterling. But he didn't want to just write the name below the message, which would be too obvious. So he looked at the jumble for inspiration. Within moments he had a solution, so he marked up the jumble to provide his answer.

Nathan chuckled to himself, excited and invigorated by the message in the paper. He was too worked up to read anything, but flicked through the rest of the pages anyway. Once he was done he folded the newspaper and left it on his tray.

The wait until Robin returned was agonising. Not only was he anxious for her to take the newspaper, but the physical activity from the previous day had awakened something in him. He had remembered what it was like to move, and being so still was causing him to feel jittery. When Robin did finally arrive Nathan had to try and calm himself.

"You all good honey?" Robin said.

"Yeah the usual."

"I've been told one of the nurses will be around to take your blood again this afternoon."

"More tests?"

"I guess so, there wasn't any additional information provided."

"Ok I guess."

"You finished with the paper?"

"Yeah you can return it," Nathan said, trying to sound casual.

"Alright then, I'll probably see you later today. Take care."

"You too bye Robin," Nathan said, watching her leave. He wanted to start some sort of exercise routine, so that he was better prepared for when he got a chance to leave. But he expected the lunch lady to come soon, so he had to wait until later. He used the time that he had to inspect the various wires and probes attached to him.

He needed to better understand how they flexed and where they were attached so he could work out what movement was available to him. He wanted to develop a regular routine which would allow him to exercise more without setting off any alarm bells.

Lunch arrived and it was a thin chicken soup with a bread roll and orange juice. Nathan ate mechanically, not enjoying the food. But he finished it, needing the nutrition to fuel his body. He waited patiently for the lunch lady to return for his tray, then he started.

He began by stretching. He spun around so his legs were dangling off the bed, and began by stretching his legs. He could feel them tighten and loosen up. He felt annoyed at himself for wasting so much time.

"How did I imagine things would get better without my direct involvement?" he thought. He had been too passive, and the few actions he had taken in recent days had made him feel a lot better. Mid-stretch he heard one of his machines start beeping and he froze in a panic. He returned to his normal position in the bed, and looked around for the machine. Upon closer inspection he could see that it was a drip that needed changing.

"Phew, all good," he said to himself. He pressed the nurse call button and waited.

A nurse finally arrived. She was stocky and had a surly expression on her face. However she seemed surprised by the beeping once she entered the room.

"Machine is beeping," Nathan said, pointing at it.

"I didn't come here for that, I'm here to take your blood," she said.

"You can do both right? I don't think I know you."

"Annabelle. Let me look at this. Yep fine I'll come back," Annabelle said and promptly left.

"Great, another nurse," Nathan thought. She didn't seem particularly friendly either. But she returned promptly, and changed the drip over quickly.

"Well now we can get on with this," she said in a businesslike manner. She brought a long half cylinder dish with her, full of implements. She swabbed his skin with alcohol, then inserted the needle to draw blood. Five vials of blood later, Nathan felt light-headed.

"That seems like a lot," he said.

"We need to do many tests."

"You never take that much."

"We are trying to do more things at once, it's better. Don't worry we won't take any more this week," the nurse said, no compassion at all entering her voice. Nathan watched her leave weakly, then started to doze.

He opened his eyes and saw a dinner tray in front of him. There was an annoying sound going off, but he couldn't quite place it. He found the nurse call button and pressed it, before dozing off again.

"I'm just changing your drip over," he heard a voice say, and Nathan tried to nod but he was too tired. Later he managed to open his eyes and process his situation. His food was still there, the last puffs of steam leaving the enclosed container. He opened the lid and saw what looked like incredibly processed roast beef with peas, carrots and gravy.

"Another gourmet favourite," he said, before scoffing it down. He was exhausted from the activities of the last day, and also quite hungry. He settled in to watch television, and saw Word Boggler on again.

"I wonder if my message made it through?" he thought. With any luck he would find out in the new edition of the newspaper. But he couldn't stay awake any longer so he slipped into a deep sleep.

Nathan awoke the next morning, to see his breakfast already delivered. This time it was bacon and eggs, only the eggs looked like he could throw them at the wall and have them bounce back into his face.

"Down the hatch," he said and worked his way through the meal. He spent the rest of the morning trying various stretches while he waited for Robin to show up. When she did finally enter he looked for a newspaper and was delighted to see her carrying one.

"How are you today?" Robin said.

"I seem good. Slept a lot."

"Yeah you were completely out of it when I came through this morning."

"I think they took a lot of blood."

"You do look a bit pale. I'll make sure they give you more red meat today," Robin said, checking the machines and making notes on his chart.

"Here's the paper, I'll come collect it later," Robin said.

"You're the best. See you later," Nathan said with a smile, and Robin returned the smile before she left. As soon as the door swung closed Nathan pulled his tray closer and grabbed the paper. He went straight to the jumble and read the question.

What did the parking inspector say to the man driving away without paying?

Nathan chuckled to himself at the potential of the jumble, and set to work solving it. He was getting through it quicker than last time. He wasn't sure if it was the additional motivation, or that he had started to get better at solving them. Within ten minutes he had the answer.

I WILL FINED YOU

And there it was. A cheeky, amusing ray of sunshine. His message was received, and help was coming.

"Thank you Elizabeth. I needed that," Nathan whispered. He thought about trying to leave another message, but decided against it. A reply wasn't required, and he wanted to save further communication for something more important. With great effort he turned the page and hid the jumble. He just wanted to rip out that page, so he could look at it whenever he felt down.

But it was too risky to keep it around. He would just have to remember.

He flicked through the rest of the paper as he always did, but nothing else caught his attention. He just couldn't concentrate. He just felt light and hopeful.

"I should use this feeling," he said to himself, and continued to try stretching and working his muscles. If help was on the way, he had to prepare himself. He needed to be able to walk, or even run.

CHAPTER ELEVEN

THE NEWSPAPER SHUFFLE

Elizabeth's alarm clock started blaring, the noise quite disorientating in the darkness.

"What the hell?" she said looking at it. She thought that maybe it had been set incorrectly, but the time was right. She never got up this early, it felt wrong.

She dragged herself to the shower, her eyes barely open. The initial chill after she undressed was replaced by the gentle warmth of the water.

"More heat," she thought, trying to cook her brain awake. The opposite happened, and she idled under the water in a half-asleep state.

"Go!" a voice inside her head said, and she shook herself awake. She had to focus, today was an important day. She was going to track the newspaper.

Elizabeth quickly got ready, grabbed a breakfast bar and dashed out to the car. She drove directly to the hospital while she munched on her breakfast, wanting to be ahead of the game. She had no idea when the newspaper made it to her patient in the hospital, so the sooner she could track it the better. She parked around the corner on a side street, and walked over to the main hospital entrance. She saw the stack of newspapers neatly bundled together with plastic straps near the main doors.

"I made it in time," she thought, then wandered over to the hospital cafe. It was in a separate small building out the front. The staff were just opening, so she ordered herself a cappuccino and kept an eye on the main entrance. The papers were still there. As she drained the final drops from her cup she saw an orderly fetch the stack of newspapers and drag them inside.

"Here we go," Elizabeth said to herself. She stepped through the main doors and looked out for where the newspapers had travelled. The orderly had them on the main desk, and he was cutting off the plastic straps. Then he divided the newspapers into neat little piles.

"They must be for the different wards," Elizabeth thought. Her guess looked right when she saw the man stick little post-it notes on each pile.

"I better go take a look, I may not recognise who takes the papers for Robin's ward," Elizabeth thought. She sauntered over to the main desk to try and identify which pile she had to follow.

"Hi can I help you?" the orderly asked her, a helpful tone to his voice.

"Oh I was just wondering if you could spare a newspaper?"

"Yeah I think so, just let me finish sorting," the orderly said. While he was looking over the piles Elizabeth scanned them to read the labels. She saw that one on the corner of the bench was labelled 'South 5'. That was the one to follow.

"Great, I'll just be sitting over there," Elizabeth said and pointed to the chairs. The orderly didn't ask any follow-up questions and resumed his job. Elizabeth looked around the room, idling away the time. No one had come to collect any of the newspapers yet.

"Excuse me miss," the orderly said, surprising Elizabeth. He was holding up a newspaper.

"Great, thanks," she said, walking over to retrieve it.

"No worries, just make sure it stays here," he said and then left, taking a pile of newspapers with him. Thankfully they weren't the ones she was after.

Elizabeth first checked the jumble. It was as expected. Alan had adjusted the individual word jumbles but left the question. She set about solving the jumble mentally, which was harder than expected. But she got there, and determined that the answer was correct.

Elizabeth looked up and verified that the pile of newspapers was still there. She kept an eye on them as she leafed through the rest of the newspaper. A few nurses came and went, but none of them touched that particular pile. Finally a bigger nurse with thick black glasses grabbed the newspapers and headed off.

Elizabeth folded her newspaper and left it on the chair she was sitting in. She started to follow the nurse.

Elizabeth could guess the route the nurse was taking, since she knew the destination. That gave Elizabeth the ability to not follow too closely behind. She stepped confidently through the corridors, making sure she was close enough to see the nurse turn the corners as expected. As they neared the ward Elizabeth's pulse quickened and she edged closer and closer. She looked for any odd movements, but the nurse went straight down the corridor, not stopping for anything.

Finally the nurse stopped at the nurse station, and behind the desk.

"She's taking the newspapers into the nurses' office," Elizabeth thought. That made sense too. But now Elizabeth had to find a way to loiter around without looking suspicious. It was still too early for visiting hours, although she could probably sneak into Dean's room. But then she wouldn't have visibility of the nurse station.

Elizabeth realised that she couldn't skulk around so walked directly to the nurse station to assess the situation. She could see Robin at the desk.

"Hi Elizabeth, how are you?" Robin said.

"I'm good, how are you?"

"Great. Hey I really enjoyed your article."

"Oh I'm glad. Those interviews really added a lot, so thanks for the help there. I'm sorry I couldn't catch you sooner, it's been manic the last few days."

"Oh that's no problem, it was nice of you to stop by."

"Yeah, I thought I might have a better chance of catching you before work. While I'm here, can I pop in and see Dean?"

"It's outside visiting hours you know?"

"Yeah, I know."

"Well, I'm sure he's fine, I'll allow it. But you have to at least wait for the doctors to finish their rounds," Robin said. That worked well for Elizabeth, it gave her an excuse to hang around. She looked around the room and saw a young boy with blond hair in jeans and a jacket, seated in the corner of the room. He was kicking his sneakers together and looking bored.

"What's his story?" Elizabeth said to Robin.

"Oh he's the son of one of the patients in this ward. His mum is getting some tests done so he's waiting for her to come back."

"What's his name?"

"Sean."

"He looks pretty young."

"Yeah he's only seven."

"I'll say hello, see if I can cheer him up," Elizabeth said. She had an idea forming in her head as she approached him.

"Hi Sean I'm Elizabeth," she said.

"Hi."

"Robin, that nurse there, said you were waiting around too."

"Yeah."

"I hate waiting, so I invent little games to make it more fun."

"Yeah? Like what?"

"Like spy games or detective games usually. I'd pretend that someone was carrying something important, and see if I could follow them without being noticed. Or I'd try and move things without them noticing."

"Ok. I guess that could be fun."

"Well how about we make up a game. Robin, that nurse there, is a spy. She's going to transport a secret document to a hidden location. Can you follow her and find out where she's going?"

"What is she taking?"

"It's a newspaper."

"Hmm I dunno."

"It'll be fun. I'm pretty sure I know where she will take it, and if you can lead me there I'll give you five dollars to spend on the snack machine. Fun for us both."

"Yeah ok, but only if I'm a detective."

"Sounds great detective Sean. I think that's our spy Robin on the move now," Elizabeth said, pointing at the nurse station. Robin was carrying a single newspaper with her and walking with purpose. Sean stood up and crept over to watch Robin leave. Then he disappeared around the corner.

"I hope this works. She took only one newspaper, it has to be to the mysterious patient," Elizabeth thought. She sat there, impatiently drumming her fingers on the chair. The wait was killing her. Surely Robin wasn't going that far.

Five minutes later she saw Sean poke his head around the corner, then he ran over to her.

"How did you go?"

"I did it! She even went to a hidden location. Cool game," Sean said.

"Awesome! Please take me there."

"Ok follow me," Sean said, his eyes bright with excitement.

"First she went down to the end," he said.

"Shush keep your voice down."

"Ok," Sean said, a lot softer. He then continued.

"She went out through these doors."

"Ok good," Elizabeth said, noting that they had now left the ward.

"She turned right and walked down here," Sean said and Elizabeth nodded. They walked down another corridor and around a bend. They came to a door.

"She went in here and down the stairs," Sean said. He paused for a moment before opening the door. Elizabeth followed him through.

"Wow you followed her this far? I'm impressed."

"Yeah, I was super sneaky. She went through this door," Sean said. They left the stairs and emerged in another hallway.

"She turned right and walked down here. And then she went through this door," Sean said. He stopped in front of the door. Elizabeth read the words on the door.

"Admin only," Elizabeth said, before trying to open the door. It was locked.

"She had a key," Sean said.

"Wow that's pretty interesting. Hey you did a great job Sean. Did you have fun? I had fun."

"Yeah it was pretty cool," Sean said. Then he waited patiently in front of Elizabeth.

"Oh right, yeah you earned your five dollars. Enjoy!" Elizabeth said, opening her wallet and handing the money over to Sean. Sean pumped his fist in the air and then ran off, back the way they had come. Elizabeth started to backtrack herself, then stopped. She noticed a couple of chairs with a good view of the stairs. She walked over and sat down.

"I should keep an eye out for Robin," she thought. It made sense that Robin would return the same way. She didn't expect Robin to have a newspaper with her, but if she did see Robin then she knew this was a good spot to wait. Eventually Robin would retrieve the newspaper, and then Elizabeth could retrieve it.

If nothing else the day had already been a major success. She had determined that the patient was hidden away in a different area. Confirmation would come when she retrieved the newspaper with the jumble message completed. From there it was just a matter of working out how to get in, and who had keys.

"I could just watch that door all day and figure it out," Elizabeth thought. But for now she had to wait for Robin to emerge. It didn't take long. Within a few minutes she saw Robin enter the stairwell at a brisk pace.

"Now I've verified Sean's information, and determined that Robin returns the same way," Elizabeth said to herself. She was very happy with the outcome. She walked back down the corridor to the locked Admin door and looked for another position where she could monitor it better.

Elizabeth spotted a vending machine placed along the corridor near a bend. There was a fair gap between it and the corner, but she couldn't see it from where she was. Elizabeth walked over and looked the space over. It was large enough to stand in, and due to the angle anyone following the route Robin had used wouldn't see you. As long as she was relatively discreet she could monitor the door with relative safety.

Elizabeth walked over to the cafeteria to get herself a sandwich. She opted to go with the cheese and salad option again. She also made sure that she got coins in change from the cashier. Elizabeth then returned to the vending machine, and loitered in her spot. She ate the sandwich too quickly, so that she could concentrate on her stakeout.

Two hours passed, and Elizabeth's legs started to feel sore and uncomfortable. Not a single person had stopped near the door, let alone entered it. She was about to go stretch her legs when she heard footsteps. She peeked around the vending machine and saw Robin dutifully marching towards the Admin door. She pulled out a set of keys from her pocket, unlocked the door and then pulled it closed.

"Here we go," Elizabeth whispered. She had to wait for Robin to emerge again so she could plan her next move. But after waiting this long, a few minutes was no problem. She stepped back slightly, to be less obvious. She heard footsteps approaching from nearby, so she started digging through her wallet looking for coins.

"Excuse me, are you using the machine?" a young man asked her.

"Yeah, but you go ahead I'm finding my coins."

"Cheers, ok thanks," the man said, putting coins into the machine and eyeing off the selection. Elizabeth stepped to the side to look past him and saw Robin walking down the hallway with what looked like a newspaper. Elizabeth threw her wallet back into her bag and set off, leaving the man to his selection.

As expected Robin entered the stairwell so Elizabeth jogged a bit closer, paused outside and then opened the stairwell door. It opened quietly, so she stood still waiting to hear where Robin was. She heard a creaking and a door slam, and then bolted up the stairs. Elizabeth couldn't risk losing the newspaper. When she reached the next level up she carefully opened the door. The coast was clear, but she could see Robin further down turning the corner.

Upping the pace Elizabeth started to catch up, but maintained her distance. Soon they would be in range of Dean's room and then she would have a valid reason to be there if discovered. She saw Robin leave the newspaper in the recreation area and then continue on to the nurse station.

"Almost there," Elizabeth thought as she went directly for the newspaper. She snatched at it and then walked directly to Dean's room. She entered without knocking, and leaned back against the door clutching the newspaper to her chest.

"Winning lotto numbers in there?" Dean said.

"You would not believe the last twenty-four hours. This newspaper could be the key."

"I'm all ears, fill me in."

"Let's see here," Elizabeth said, walking closer to Dean and unfolding the newspaper. She flipped straight to the jumble, saw that it was filled in, and then handed the open newspaper to Dean.

"This is the jumble again," he said.

"Yes, now look at the question and answer."

"Oh nice one. Ha-ha that's fantastic! Hang on, some of these letters are also underlined."

"I bet those are the reply to my message."

"Very clever, I love it. Witchdoctor, dear me. That's too good!"

"Thanks, I like it. So let's see here, the name given is Sterling. Sounds like a real name, I'll have to do some digging."

"That's two doctors you need to look into," Dean said, reminding Elizabeth of her promise.

"I haven't forgotten, don't worry. Oh and I have even better news."

"Hit me."

"I've found where the patient is."

"ROCK! You're on a roll!"

"It's behind a locked door, but that's just details."

"That's something to work with at least. How'd you do it?"

"I followed Robin. I guessed from the earlier message that she takes him a newspaper each morning. And she did!"

"Very clever. I can't believe I didn't think of that."

"I almost didn't. But it was so obvious, it was staring us in the face the whole time."

"That's just how things are. Wow I'm amazed. Brilliant progress. I really needed that today."

"Oh, is there something wrong?"

"I got an update. We're talking weeks rather than months."

"I'm sorry Dean. I..."

"It's ok love. When it's your time, it's your time. I'm really torn though. Part of me wants to just end it now, why drag it out? Another part of me can't let go. It wants to see your investigation out, to try a crazy cure, to find something."

"I promise you Dean, that you will see an end to this investigation and you will have the chance to try a crazy treatment. You just have to hang in there."

"Oh don't you worry about that. I can be a stubborn bastard when I want. But just don't get any silly ideas that you can drag this thing out. The clock is ticking."

"I know, I'm on it," Elizabeth said. She heard a knock and then turned to see a woman dressed in a yellow outfit enter the room. She was pushing a metallic trolley which smelled like chicken soup.

"And here's my lunch. Good day to you," Dean said, addressing the woman.

"Good day Dean. Today is chicken soup."

"My favourite."

"He says that every day," the woman said to Elizabeth, laughing. She pulled out the tray and set it on Dean's tray table.

"Enjoy," the woman said before leaving.

"I better leave too," Elizabeth said.

"Wait a moment. I just had a thought."

"Yes?"

"So you have a problem with a locked door correct?"

"That's the one."

"What's something that a person behind a locked door needs three times a day?"

"Food?"

"Bingo. Do you think the nurses are not so busy that they can wait around to let the lunch lady in?"

"Hang on, so you think she has a key?"

"Yeah I reckon. Sounds like an opportunity to me."

"You could be right. I'm going to go scope out the door for a bit. I'll keep you posted."

"You do that. See you tomorrow," Dean said. Elizabeth left the room, a jumble of emotions tumbling through her head. She was excited at the progress of the investigation, and her contact with the patient. But she was shocked by Dean's news. It was one thing knowing that he had a terminal illness, but it was something else seeing the end come into focus.

It was a big responsibility that she had taken onto herself, and she hadn't even captured any of his story yet. But for now she had to focus on the two things that he wished for: progress updates and an alternate treatment.

"Nothing like a deadline to keep you motivated," Elizabeth thought. It was the mantra of a reporter, but now with an additional layer of grim truth to it. She just had to follow up on her lead, and watch that door like a hawk. Once she understood who had access and when, she could come up with a plan.

But she couldn't spend any more of the day at the hospital. She had to return to work and complete the editing stack that was left to her. Otherwise George would start asking questions, and she didn't have a lot of good answers.

CHAPTER TWELVE

CONTACT

Elizabeth spent the afternoon in a flurry of activity. She needed to finish off George's pile of edits and deliver them by the end of the day. Which she managed, just before five o'clock. She bundled up the pile and took it over to George, triumphantly dumping it on the only spare space on his desk.

"I expected it sooner, but thanks," George said.

"Quality takes time."

"Always with the excuses. Now go find your fun story," George said, waving her off. Elizabeth happily returned to her desk. She could start her research on the doctors at Royal Monterey.

"So did you approve of my changes to the jumble?" Alan said, as she sat down.

"Yeah, and you'll be happy to know I got a response."

"Show me," Alan said, sitting on Elizabeth's desk. She knew that he wouldn't move until he saw it. So she fished out the newspaper and showed him.

"Nice, I like the use of the underlines. Very logical. So where's your reply?"

"What do you mean?"

"Aren't you going to let him know that you received his message?"

"I hadn't really planned on it, but I think you're right."

"Of course I'm right. Well here's the deal: you come up with the question and answer now, and I'll devise the jumble tonight."

"Sure, give me a minute," Elizabeth said, grabbing her notepad. She chewed the end of her pen and stared into space, then scribbled the question and answer on the pad. She looked at it for a minute, then handed the pad over to Alan.

"Ha-ha wow you're getting good at this. Classic! I'll enjoy this jumble. Look for it tomorrow."

"Thanks Alan, will do."

"See you tomorrow," Alan said, ripping the page out of the notepad and then leaving.

"Lucky he reminded me. Oh well, I'll find the patient soon anyway so it won't matter," Elizabeth thought. Now she had to focus on what she had delayed for so long, searching for doctors.

She had two doctors to look into: Malburn and Sterling. Malburn was the harder option, as Lucy hadn't been confident of the name and Dean had gotten nowhere with his questions. So she decided to start with Sterling.

She brought up the Royal Monterey Hospital website on her computer, and navigated to the list of doctors. She searched for Sterling and found an entry.

"Here we go," she whispered. A photo and biography came up for a Doctor Mathew Sterling. He was the head of the Research department at the hospital. Elizabeth looked up the Research department to find out more.

"What are you guys working on?" she thought. But there was nothing specific on the page. But it did have a list of doctors. She scanned through the list looking for anyone familiar.

"Doctor Malberg!" Elizabeth said, slapping the desk with her hand. It was too close of a coincidence. They had been looking for a Dr Malburn, who didn't exist. This had to be the person that Lucy was talking about. She looked at Dr Malberg's profile and saw his picture. She didn't recognise the face, but then she had only really dealt with nurses at the hospital. Nothing on his profile jumped out at her as important.

"It's fine, maybe it'll mean something later. For now I think he's our guy," Elizabeth thought. She was so happy, she had found a proper lead for Dean. She had found Dr Sterling too, the link to her patient. There was nothing actionable immediately, but she at least had a name to investigate. But she might even manage to get herself access to the patient in the near future anyway.

With that win behind her, Elizabeth felt like it was time to head home. It had been a long day, but fruitful. Tomorrow she would need to stake out the secure area in the hospital, and find a way in. But tonight she could rest and plan. Elizabeth grabbed the stack of story tips and shoved them in her bag. She could read through them in the evening and shortlist a few story ideas.

Elizabeth sat in front of the television at home, eating pasta and flicking through the list of story ideas from the public. It was the usual selection of tips: ranging from missing persons, to aliens, to drug trafficking and even police corruption. There were probably some great stories in there, and from the least likely tips too. But she was too tired to process them properly, and put the pile aside. She felt herself falling asleep on the couch, so she went to bed.

The next morning Elizabeth packed all the story ideas into her bag and then went straight to the hospital. She had to observe the routine of who went in and out of that special admin door. If Dean was right then her best bet was targeting the food delivery staff. If they had a key, they were probably the easiest way in. But she wasn't sure exactly how she would approach the problem.

She took up her previous position at the vending machine, and started her stakeout.

"I've probably missed the breakfast delivery, but maybe I'll see them coming back for the tray," Elizabeth thought as she checked the time. Within half an hour her suspicion was confirmed. A woman pushing a metal trolley sidled up to the door, and picked up a bundle of keys off the trolley. She mechanically wound through the keys until she found the correct one, then opened the door. She then pushed against the door, and turned to use her back to leverage it open. Then she used her free hands to grab the trolley and reverse into the secure area.

"Dean was right! I'll have to get a better look at that key," Elizabeth thought. But she had a way in. She glanced at her watch so she could roughly time how long the woman was in the area. That would give her an idea of the distance and the schedule. At the four minute mark she saw movement at the door, and decided to walk closer. The woman opened the door inwards, and then pushed the metal trolley out in front of her. Elizabeth quickly stepped to the side, narrowly avoiding the trolley.

"Sorry," the woman said, and continued moving. Elizabeth said nothing, but used the opportunity to slip into the door before it closed. She felt excited, but also surprised that she had found a way in already. Her success also caused another problem: she had no idea of how much traffic this area had, and when the nurses would return.

"Gotta be quick, in and out this time," Elizabeth said to herself. She looked ahead and saw a fairly normal looking corridor. It ended at a T junction. She rushed down to see what was there. As she reached the junction, she looked left and right to pick a path. It looked like an older disused ward with the same structure as the one she had so thoroughly investigated upstairs. To the right there were a small number of rooms, then big doors. To the left were rooms as far as she could see. She chose left and walked with purpose.

There was a distinct chill in the area, and a feeling of isolation and quiet.

"Definitely seems unused. Well, except for this one patient," Elizabeth thought. She continued down the corridor, looking for signs of life, or that she was on the right track. The plain identical doors gave nothing away. She was about to give up and start randomly opening doors when she noticed one was a bit different. She walked closer, and noticed a piece of paper stuck to the door.

"No way. CM!" Elizabeth whispered, surprise and excitement surging through her. But she felt rooted to the floor, unsure of what lay behind the door. She steeled herself and pushed the door open, just like she had done so many times before.

This time there was a man sitting upright in bed. He appeared to be stretching. He had wild brown hair, which looked like it hadn't been touched in months. But at the same time, there was a thinness to it. In fact there was a thinness to his entire frame.

"Hi I'm..."

"Elizabeth?"

"Yes. How did you know?"

"You said you would find me," Nathan said with a laugh.

"I did. I'm sorry but I don't know your name."

"I'm Nathan. Glad to finally meet you. There's much we need to discuss."

"I know. Nice to meet you Nathan, you're actually the reason I'm at the hospital."

"What do you mean? Didn't you come here to interview Robin?"

"That was an assignment, one that I took begrudgingly. But it allowed me to investigate a tip. One so tightly held, that my informant left me only a slip of paper with a cryptic message on it. That message consisted of the name of this hospital and two letters. CM."

"It says that on my door."

"Yes. I didn't know until today. I was intrigued by your message, and struggled to find you. But that wasn't my reason for being here. Until now."

"I don't have the answers you are after, but I'm sure that I'm being held here for a reason. And it's not for my own safety."

"No, this wing appears to be unused except for you. The door to access it is locked, and I've only spotted food and nurses passing through."

"Doctors too."

"Yeah, I haven't seen them yet though. You mentioned a Dr Sterling in your message. Is he your main doctor?"

"I keep getting different ones. He seems to be a leader amongst them. I also remember a Dr Malberg."

"Hmm that's interesting, he came up somewhere else too. They're both members of the Research department so that makes sense. Look, I can't really stay long, I don't know when a nurse will come through."

"There's usually a gap between breakfast and when Robin comes to check in and take the newspaper."

"Good, but I'm not going to push my luck today. What's your full name?"

"Nathaniel Slade Stenson."

"Anyone who would be looking for you?"

"My mum. Her name is Emma."

"Ok got it. My first order of business is to get myself a key and to establish a better means of communication. We can't keep using jumbles."

"Yeah fair enough."

"I better go. I'll be in touch, I promise."

"Thank you. You're my last hope," Nathan said. Elizabeth couldn't help thinking of the parallels with Dean. They both saw her as their last chance for closure.

"Not your last, just your best bet right now. See you soon," Elizabeth said then left.

As she left the room Elizabeth heard footsteps. She rushed over to the nearest room and tried the door. It opened, so she snuck inside. She was inside another patient room, but it looked like it had been used as a records room. There were a few filing cabinets and shelves with folders. Elizabeth saw the possibilities, but also the liabilities.

"There could be something useful here, but it's not a good hiding place," she thought. She stood beside the door, and tried to listen out. She heard footsteps, but couldn't really place where they were. The footsteps stopped, and her heart also stopped. A moment passed without any action. And then another.

"Maybe they entered Nathan's room," Elizabeth wondered. Then she realised that she finally had a name. He was no longer the mystery patient, but had an identity. She pushed the interesting realisation aside and focused on her current predicament.

It was too risky to enter the hallway without some kind of confirmation that the person who the footsteps belonged to had left. So she kept quiet and listened carefully. A few minutes later she was rewarded by the steady sound of footsteps. She thought that they were heading further away, but it was hard to tell. Once she could hear them no longer, she left the room and looked over the hallway. It was empty.

Elizabeth retraced her steps, trying to be as quiet as possible. Once she reached the T junction she peered around the corner. No one was there. Bolstered by the sight of the clear hallway and the door, she strode out with confidence. She reached the door, opened it and then walked down the corridor as if she belonged. Nobody said anything, and she didn't see anyone around anyway.

Elizabeth kept walking, making her way to Dean's room. She couldn't wait to tell him what she had discovered. There was a lot to discuss and she would value his input. Elizabeth burst through the door, about to speak when she noticed something was off. Robin was in the room too.

"Oh sorry, didn't mean to intrude," Elizabeth said.

"Hi there. No problem was just finishing up here," Robin said, then left the room.

"Is everything alright?" Elizabeth asked.

"Yes, just the normal stuff. No need to go into it."

"I have some good news."

"Please, lay it on me."

"You were right, the lunch lady has a key."

"I knew it. Now we need to work out how to get you a copy."

"We do, but I managed to sneak in today as she was leaving."

"What!"

"Yeah, I found him. His name is Nathan and he's been here for months. He doesn't know why they are keeping him."

"Wow that's unbelievable. You found him," Dean said. His voice sounded almost disappointed. Elizabeth picked up on this and quickly responded.

"Yes, but that's only the first step. I need a way to keep in contact with him, and we need to discover why he's being held here."

"True."

"Also, I did some doctor research last night. There's a man called Dr Malberg that works in the Research department. I think he's your guy."

"Oh yeah?"

"Yeah, the name is really similar, and surely the Research department would be responsible for trialling new treatments."

"You're right. Although I thought the guys specialising in Cancer would be doing it. But it's worth looking into."

"Dean, I know you told me some heavy news yesterday, but I feel like there's something else going on."

"Well, I didn't want to trouble you. It's what Robin was talking to me about. She said that even if there were a trial available, they probably wouldn't bother with me because I'm too advanced."

"Did she come and talk to you because you've been asking around?"

"Yes. I think she's trying to let me down. Get me to focus on other things."

"I see. So she didn't know of any trials and tried to get you to drop it?"

"Yes."

"Don't worry, I'll get to the bottom of it. There's clearly some strange things going on at this hospital."

"There certainly is."

"But look, there's certainly some wisdom in what Robin tried to say. Make the most of these days, and I'll give you updates every day."

"I appreciate that. But that's the question isn't it? What's worth doing at this stage of your life?"

"I don't know. Family? Your story?"

"Yes, they're important. And I forgot about my story. Ok let me tell you a story when I can. It's what we always meant to do right?"

"Of course, let me get out my recorder."

CHAPTER THIRTEEN

A TALE OF CARS

Many years ago when I was a young lad, we didn't have the technology of today. A lot of things were harder, but many were simpler. You knew all the kids on your street, and you would spend the whole day out playing. Running around, exploring, and getting into mischief. Normal kid stuff.

And when we were older, the only difference was the toys that we used. As soon as we were old enough, it was all about driving cars. The freedom of being able to get into a car and drive wherever you wanted was magic. We didn't have the money to buy new cars, so we made do.

My friend Joe was really handy, so we would scour the neighbourhood and newspaper for old bombs. You know, cars that were a few drives away from the scrapyard. And we would fix them up, get them going and drive them into the ground. We'd find old paddocks and tear around, hoon around the streets at night, and generally be well-intentioned nuisances. But we never created any real trouble. We never damaged anyone's property, and we never left a car.

When the cars did give up, we'd try and revive them. We had a pretty good success rate. But eventually they would be too tricky or expensive to repair, so we'd get them to the scrapyard and try again. Find another bomb, get it on the road and be back in action.

They were important years, and set the scene for the rest of our lives.

CHAPTER FOURTEEN

THE MISSING LINK

Elizabeth returned to the office after recording Dean's first story. She was trembling with excitement. There was so much to do, now that she had made the breakthrough and met Nathan. But she couldn't neglect her work, and she needed to get onto a new story before George assigned her one.

It was too soon to broach the investigation that she had been doing. Even though she had found Nathan, there was more to find out. She needed more evidence, and a motive. That would make a story. Going to George with anything less would be incredibly risky and potentially blow the whole thing.

"Nice jumble Alan," she said as she walked through the office. He smiled and nodded, and she gave him a knowing smile in return. She settled down at her desk and pulled out the stack of newspaper story tips she had been given.

"Time to select a winner," she said to herself.

"How's the story lottery coming along?" George said behind her.

"I've looked through, now I'm going to pick one."

"You're lucky that I've got nothing urgent for you today. But I need you to brief me today on whatever it is. And have an alternate story if you think I might veto it."

"Yeah I know the drill. It'll be done."

"Good, you know where to find me," George said as he left. Elizabeth read through the stack again. She was looking for a story that would be nicely publishable, but also time consuming. That way she could burn some time on it, while focusing on the hospital. She noticed the missing persons story again, and read over it in more detail.

"Well if the person is notable, there might be some mileage. And you can waste a lot of time following up with the police and getting a background on the missing person," Elizabeth thought as she looked over it. This particular story said that the police refused to investigate the case, even though the man had been gone for over a month. As she scanned the details something jumped out at her.

"Emma Stenson is the source. Where have I heard that name before?" she thought. And then she remembered. Nathan's surname was Stenson, and he had said his mother's name was Emma. The missing person story was about him, and she had already found him.

"I could work both stories at once. Only I wouldn't reveal that I had found Nathan until the time was right. It could work," Elizabeth thought. It was the perfect excuse to investigate Nathan's background, and build the story that should get him freed. But she also knew George well, and that he might not go for it. So she bottled her excitement, and put the story to the side. She needed another option just in case.

Elizabeth continued searching through the notes.

"Aha, this looks interesting," she said, picking a page out of the stack. There had been a robbery at the museum. An Egyptian piece had been stolen from the collection, but there were no signs of forced entry. She made a few notes about each story on a small notepad and ripped off the page. She stood up and walked over to George's desk.

"Picked something?"

"Yes, I've got my two options here."

"Let me hear the second option."

"There was an Egyptian artefact stolen from the museum a few weeks ago. No signs of forced entry, and nothing on the CCTV footage."

"Hmm. Give me option one."

"Missing person. Hasn't been sighted for three months, has not contacted family and the police refuse to investigate."

"That's your number one? People decide to disappear sometimes, it's not really newsworthy. Unless it's someone notable?"

"I'm not sure, but the tip doesn't suggest that."

"Liz, I swear you love investigating more than actual reporting. Nobody else brings me stories that need the interesting bit dug out of the ground."

"The mayor story? Biggest scoop of the decade."

"I know, which is why I let you bring me these oddballs. Ok how about you get me a decent story out on the museum robbery, I haven't seen it reported yet. You can investigate your missing person in-between other stories."

"Seems fair."

"I'm always fair. You've got to trust me. You seem to have a knack for ferreting out stories, I'll hand it to you. But I can't have you going off by yourself again. You almost died in that fire."

"I do trust you George," Elizabeth said, "I just can't let you in yet," she thought in addition to that statement.

"Ok good, dazzle me," George said and Elizabeth nodded and left. Considering the potential, that had gone alright. She could investigate Nathan's disappearance without raising any red flags. Just as long as she kept her other stories going.

Halfway back to her desk, she remembered her conversation with Dean about Dr Malberg. She returned to George.

"Yes?" he said. His uncanny ability to know who it was still caught her by surprise at times.

"Do we have the contact details for Lucy Margot's PR agent?"

"Yeah, what for?"

"I want to follow up on something. Not for printing."

"Is it going to give me any grief?"

"No, it won't offend her in any way."

"Fine, let me dig up the details," George said, rifling through his contact card filing system. He found the appropriate card and copied the details out on a slip of paper.

"Here you go. Destroy these details after you've made contact. If this number leaks out, they'll change it and go into lockdown mode."

"Thanks George. Don't worry, I'll be responsible."

"I know you will, I'm just reminding you," George said. Elizabeth understood and walked back to her desk. She dialled the number immediately.

"Hello?" a female voice said. Elizabeth did not recognise it.

"Hi, I'm Elizabeth Edmonds. I met with Lucy Margot recently and wanted to leave her a message," Elizabeth said. There was a pause before she heard a response.

"Ok what's the message?"

"She mentioned to me a Dr Malburn, who I followed up for a friend. However there is no Dr Malburn working at that hospital. I did find a Dr Malberg however, and I would like to confirm if that is the doctor that Lucy was thinking of."

"I see. I have taken down your message. How would you like a reply?"

"Please call me on my mobile number," Elizabeth said, before quoting her number.

"Ok I will confirm your request and give you a reply."

"Thanks. Goodbye," Elizabeth said and hung up. She had reached out and needed a reply. She didn't want to approach Dr Malberg directly without a confirmation. Hopefully Lucy got back to her soon so that Elizabeth didn't need to plan another action.

The next thing she had to do was follow up on the missing persons case. George had said to do it in-between other stories, but it wouldn't hurt to make a start. She looked up a phone number for Emma Stenson, and luckily there was one listed. The phone started ringing, and continued to ring for a long time. Elizabeth was about to hang up when she heard a reply.

"Hello?" an older female voice said, unsteady and uncertain.

"Hello is this Emma Stenson?"

"Yes."

"Hi I'm Elizabeth and I'm from the Stately Herald. We got your letter about a missing persons case that's being ignored by the police."

"Oh yes, but that was some time ago. I thought my letter was ignored."

"Dammit George," Elizabeth whispered under her breath.

"I'm sorry, these letters get buried under paperwork sometimes. But I'm looking into it now," Elizabeth said over the phone.

"I'm very worried. He's been gone for three months now. Nobody seems interested in looking into it. I live in hope, but don't know what I should be doing. What can you do?" Emma said. Elizabeth could hear the pain in the woman's voice. She wanted to reach out and comfort her, let her know that she had seen and talked to her son. But something stopped Elizabeth from revealing more. Her gut told her not to raise the woman's hopes unnecessarily.

"It's a tough situation, and I understand the pain you are in. I hope that we can bring some light onto it and get your son's disappearance the attention it deserves."

"What do I need to do?"

"Please let me meet with you and ask some questions. Then I'll start building a story that we can publish."

"Sure, when?"

"This afternoon suits me."

"Ok."

"May I have your address please?" Elizabeth asked, and noted down the address on her pad.

"Thanks Emma, I'll be there around three o'clock."

"Thank you. I will see you then," Emma said and hung up. Elizabeth sat back and thought over the conversation. Emma had written to the newspaper two months ago, but the story had just gone in the slush pile.

If she had not picked it up, it would still be there. Unread and gathering dust. And yet if Elizabeth had not gotten the tip about the hospital and tracked down Nathan, she would not have seen the significance either.

"That's the system I guess. But I can do something about this," Elizabeth thought. But that was for later in the day. First she had to initiate her other story, before George started asking for updates.

She called the Museum of Ancient History to enquire about the theft, and got told that the Director of Egyptian Antiquities was not available and that she should come in tomorrow morning to meet him. Elizabeth accepted the appointment and noted down the details. That suited her fine, she could focus on Dean and Nathan in the afternoon.

Elizabeth arrived at the hospital after lunch and walked directly to Dean's room. She found him by himself, reading the newspaper.

"Hey Dean."

"Hello there Elizabeth. How are you today?"

"Oh I'm fine, the real question is how are you?"

"The usual."

"Is the usual good?"

"It's normal."

"Alright then, I guess as long as it's not worse than normal right?"

"That's one way of looking at it."

"I'm looking into Dr Malberg. Waiting to get confirmation that he's our guy."

"That's good," Dean said, but his voice lacked conviction.

"I talked to Nathan's mum. I'm going to see her this afternoon. I'm going to write an article about his disappearance."

"Oh yeah, did you tell her you met him?"

"No. My gut said not yet."

"That's wise. You gotta listen to your gut."

"What does your gut tell you?"

"That my time is up. There's no escaping it."

"That may be, we don't know."

"I know."

"Jury is still out Dean. You gotta give me a chance."

"Yeah, yeah I know. Sorry, I'm in a bit of a funk today. How about you go interview that woman, even if you can't tell her about her son yet, at least she'll feel better that you're talking to her. Then you can update me tomorrow."

"Yeah sure. Take care."

"You too," Dean said and then Elizabeth left. It was horrible seeing Dean like that. She hadn't known him long, but it felt like she knew him well. And that was not like him at all. She felt a chill run down her spine. She had confronted death herself, but in a different way.

For her it had been the raging fire that swept through the Orphello theatre. She risked her life to ensure that the documents she had obtained would survive the fire. And in another way she had confronted death again, in her dreams after the fire. But they had been a confrontation between two warriors. Toe to toe, face to face.

Dean's struggle was a different one. He was being stalked by death, its stench lingering whenever he turned around, but it was never quite there. It was only slowly creeping closer, and then suddenly it would strike. Not knowing the time he had left, was like a burden slowly chipping away at him. That was a terrible thing to have to deal with.

"I have to do something," Elizabeth told herself. The things she could do seemed hopeless, but she had to try. Nothing ever came from giving up.

She tried cheering herself up on the drive to Mrs Stenson's home. She certainly couldn't look like she had come from a funeral, the poor woman would assume the worst. No, she had to provide some hope to Emma Stenson without revealing everything. And she had to get as much information as possible about Nathan. Both for her article, and also to puzzle out why he was being held.

Elizabeth arrived at the address and looked over the house. It was grey and narrow, with a small paved courtyard out the front and a red door. There was a path leading from the front door to a rusty metal gate. Elizabeth parked the car and walked over to the house. She opened the gate, a loud squeak announcing her presence despite her best effort. As she walked towards the door she could see small tufts of grass breaking through between some of the pavers. Elizabeth knocked on the door and waited.

"Who is it?" a voice called out.

"Elizabeth Edmonds, from the newspaper. We spoke on the phone Mrs Stenson."

"Coming," the voice said. Elizabeth heard the bolt being drawn back and the door opening.

"Please come in," Emma said with a smile. Elizabeth was surprised at how old Emma looked. It wasn't the silvery white hair, but the lines on her face and the bags beneath her eyes.

"Thank you," Elizabeth said, hoping to not betray her initial reaction.

"I aged ten years these past three months," Emma said. Elizabeth realised she had not been successful at masking her face.

"It's a pretty traumatic time I can imagine," Elizabeth said, following Emma into the house. It was quite dark, with lots of old furniture.

"You can't imagine. It's the not knowing that's the worst."

"Maybe I should introduce her to Dean, they sound the same. Actually for that reason maybe not then," Elizabeth thought.

"I'm sure we can bring some clarity. The newspaper is great at bringing things to light."

"I sure hope so," Emma said. She stopped at the end of the house, and sat down at a wooden dining table next to the kitchen. Elizabeth sat down opposite.

"Before I start, do you mind if I record this? Or should I just take notes?"

"Recording is fine," Emma said. Elizabeth retrieved her recorder from her bag, set it on the table and started recording.

"Can you start from the beginning?"

"Nathan is your average son. Calls his mother once a week when he doesn't forget, visits a couple of times a month. I got angry at first when I didn't hear from him. I decided not to call, so that when he finally remembered I could be even angrier at him," Emma said. She paused and shook her head.

"I think I waited three weeks before I called him. I feel terrible about it. Maybe I could have done something if I had known sooner."

"From what you said in your letter, I doubt the police would have helped more if you contacted them sooner."

"Probably. But it doesn't make you feel better. No reasoning can. When it's your child you feel responsible and there's nothing anyone else can say to change that."

"Does Nathan live nearby?"

"Yes, in the next suburb over. In a small apartment by himself. I've had to pay his rent to keep the place for him."

"That's good. Have you been inside?"

"I went in once, I was desperate for answers. But everything seemed normal, like he just left one day and never came back. It didn't feel right digging through his things, so I didn't. Besides, I wouldn't know what to look for."

"Do you have a key?" Elizabeth asked.

"Yes, I do. Do you want to take a look around?"

"Please, if you don't mind. I'm sure there's a clue there as to where Nathan was headed the day he disappeared."

"If it will help, of course. I'll go find it," Emma said and disappeared into another room. She returned soon after with a small gold key.

"Here it is, I'll write the address down too," Emma said.

"Thanks. What date did Nathan disappear?"

"I'm not sure exactly. I've been racking my brain over and over, thinking about when he usually called and when he missed his first call. I think somewhere in the last week of December."

"So after Christmas, but before New Year?"

"Yes."

"Ok good I'll focus on that period. Where did Nathan work?"

"He was an insolvency accountant at a big accounting firm. What was the name? Oh yes, Addensum. When I started to worry I called them to find out if he had gone into work."

"What did they say?"

"They said his manager had left, and that all they knew was that Nathan was on extended leave."

"Ok that's interesting. Do you know his manager's name?"

"I think it was Charles. I don't remember his surname."

"That's fine, I'll look into that too."

"Thank you. It's not just me, it's all very peculiar isn't it?"

"Yes, Emma. It's definitely not you. Something does not add up here, and I promise you that I'll get to the bottom of it."

"Thank you again. I had started to lose hope."

"You're welcome. There's always room for hope. I'll bring you some more next time," Elizabeth said and smiled. She turned off the recorder and went to leave. Emma escorted her out and waited until Elizabeth had left the front gate before closing the front door.

Elizabeth wasn't sure where to go next. She had uncovered two good leads. Nathan's work, and his apartment. She looked at her watch, and saw that it was only four o'clock.

"I don't want to visit his place too late in the day, but I bet the HR department are still around at his work," Elizabeth thought to herself. She looked up the number for Addensum and dialled it on her phone.

"Hello reception, this is Anna," a female voice said.

"Hi Anna, can you please put me through to the HR department please."

"Anyone in particular?"

"No."

"Sure, I'll put you through to Peter then."

"Thanks," Elizabeth said and waited while the phone was on hold. She then heard a click and another voice answered.

"Hello this is Peter."

"Hi Peter, my name is Amy. I'm calling concerning an employee of yours, Nathan Stenson."

"Sure, how can I help?"

"Nothing too crazy, just doing a reference check."

"Has he applied for a new job?" Peter said, his voice tinged with concern.

"Oh no, he has applied for a new rental property. I'm just verifying his reference here. He wrote down a Charles as his manager, but I can't read the surname."

"Oh Charles Manfried? I'm afraid he has left the company. But I can confirm that Nathan is still an employee here."

"Oh ok. I had hoped to talk to Charles."

"I'm sorry we are not allowed to provide any personal contact details."

"Oh no that's fine. I'm sure speaking to you is enough for my boss. Thanks for your assistance Peter."

"No problem. Have a nice day."

"You too. Goodbye," Elizabeth said, hanging up. That wasn't a bad fishing expedition. She had a name for Nathan's manager. Feeling satisfied she drove home. It had been a big day already. She had found Nathan and dug up some important leads. Now she needed to rest and prepare for what was to come.

CHAPTER FIFTEEN

CHASING LEADS

Elizabeth woke in the morning and reviewed the checklist she had written for herself the previous night before going to bed. She had gone from no leads, to an explosion of them, so she needed to make sure she missed nothing.

- *Dr Malberg (confirm?)*
- *Museum Burglary (unrelated)*
- *Charles Manfried (track down)*
- *Nathan's Apartment (have key)*
- *Access to Nathan's Hospital room (need key)*

She had to meet the Director of Egyptian Antiquities first thing to continue that story. The rest of her day however was fair game. She looked through the list to see what made the most sense. She had access to Nathan's apartment, but decided that it was better to go there after she had talked to him again. He might be able to direct her on what to look for. He might also be able to get her in touch with his old manager. She needed that angle to start building a story explaining Nathan's disappearance. Regarding Dr Malberg, she didn't want to investigate him further until she got confirmation from Lucy. Or at least give Lucy a day to respond. So that left her one lead to start with: getting a key to access Nathan's hospital room. It made sense, if she could secure good access to him, then he could assist with the rest of her investigation.

With that decision made, Elizabeth planned out her day. Then she left the apartment and drove to the Museum of Ancient History. It was a bit out of the city, about half an hour's drive from her place. Elizabeth had never been before, but as she approached she understood why they had chosen the location.

The Museum was surrounded by lush grounds, perfectly manicured grass complete with a hedge maze. The building itself looked like a modern replica of an ancient temple. It consisted of a large, domed circular main building, with many wings coming off it. She drove past the property to access the visitor parking, and noticed a few tour buses already parked there.

"Wow I had no idea this place was such an attraction," Elizabeth thought to herself. She had heard of it, but never really paid much attention. If the interior was anything like the exterior, it was worth visiting for the building alone.

As Elizabeth walked through the main doors she let go a small gasp. Polished marble floors reflected an amazing chandelier hanging from the dome above her. The foyer was littered with what looked like precious statues and throngs of people buzzing around. She made her way through the crowd and walked up to the Enquiries Desk.

"Good morning, I have an appointment with the Director of Egyptian Antiquities," Elizabeth said.

"Good morning. Your name please?" a young woman replied, looking up from the computer screen.

"Elizabeth Edmonds."

"Ah yes here we are. I don't think Albert is in yet, but I'll take you to his office," the young woman said. Elizabeth followed closely, as they wound their way through the crowds and out of the foyer. Elizabeth watched with interest as the woman swiped an access card, and took them through a locked door into a completely different environment.

The walls were stark white, and there seemed to be many different rooms along the corridor.

"This place looks state of the art," Elizabeth said.

"It really is. It's a weird blend of the latest technology with some of the oldest things we have."

"Both ends of the spectrum. I guess that these things would have been the latest technology once upon a time."

"Ha-ha you're right," the woman said. She stopped outside one of the doors, and opened it.

"Please take a seat, Albert will be here any minute."

"Thanks," Elizabeth said, and entered the room. It was like she had stepped back in time. The office was unlike the stark, modern corridor. There was an aged, wooden desk with antique sitting chairs on either side. Bookcases ran along the walls of the room, crammed with dusty tomes.

"Excuse my lateness," a male voice said behind her. Elizabeth rose and turned to face the speaker. He was an old man, balding at the front with white wispy tufts circling his ears. He wore a plain grey suit, with a white shirt underneath and a gold pin on his lapel which looked like a pyramid.

"Not a problem, I only just settled in. I'm Elizabeth."

"Albert, nice to meet you. I enjoy the contrast here, stepping into the past from the necessary modern technology."

"Yeah I can see that," Elizabeth replied. Albert motioned to the chair, so she sat back down. He walked around to the other side of the desk and sat down himself.

"I must admit Elizabeth, I'm a little surprised by this visit. We did not publicise the theft."

"We received an anonymous tip, looks like it was on the mark."

"I appreciate that. You were certainly right to act on it. Did you happen to bring the tip with you?"

"Why do you ask?"

"Well, this may be presumptuous of me, but I highly doubt that one of my staff tipped you off. Not many people know of the theft. "

"So you think that maybe the thief did so?"

"It is a theory I've been thinking through. It's the reason why I decided to meet with you."

"You don't want the theft to be public knowledge do you? I take it this is a very expensive security system. Wouldn't be good to have people know that you were compromised."

"I do not appreciate you jumping to conclusions. Actually we do not wish to give the thief the publicity they no doubt crave."

"What was stolen? Surely publicising the theft will make it harder to sell the item?"

"You cannot sell this item to anyone. We gain nothing by releasing this information."

"Look Albert, I think there's an opportunity for us to work together on this."

"There is. Give me the tip, and let me find out what I can from it," Albert said. Elizabeth thought over his offer. She had not noticed anything interesting about it, but once she handed the tip over she could probably kiss it goodbye. But without Albert's cooperation any chance of a story would die, and she really wanted this to work.

"Well how about a compromise. You make me a copy of the tip, you can borrow the original to do whatever you need to do. That way I'll still have a reference in the meantime. You have to share anything you discover, and I'll delay the story until there's more to report on," Elizabeth said. She could see Albert considering the proposal. She reckoned that the delay on the story had tempted him. For some reason he wanted control over the nature of the publicity, and a little delay didn't make a difference for her. It would give her time to dig up something more interesting.

"Ok I think we can work together on those terms. If you give me what you have, I'll go and make you a copy right now."

"Sure, I happen to have it here," Elizabeth said, digging the paper from her bag. Albert looked it over, and then left.

Elizabeth waited for his footsteps to fade from earshot and then stood up. She paced around the room, looking for something of interest. The books were all too dense for her, and too specialised. She walked around to the front of his desk, and looked more closely. There was a computer and monitor, notepads, a stylish metallic pen holder and a few photo frames. Elizabeth looked over the photos, curious to see who might be of importance to this odd man. The first two photos were a man and a woman that she did not recognise. But the third photo made her jaw drop.

It was a photo of a woman and a small boy, standing together in a park. She recognised both faces. The boy was Sean, the kid that helped her tail Robin and the newspaper. The woman was Susan Montgomery, the woman she had stumbled upon when she was exploring Dean's ward.

"Albert is connected to Susan. He must be her father, and Sean must be her son. This just got interesting," Elizabeth thought to herself. She heard footsteps approaching so she quickly rushed back to her seat. She didn't want him to catch her snooping around.

"Here's a photocopy of the tip. Thank you for your cooperation," Albert said. He handed the paper to Elizabeth and sat down behind his desk.

"I'm glad we could come to an arrangement. However I will need to at least gather a few facts before I go today."

"If you must."

"When exactly did the robbery occur?"

"Last Tuesday. We don't have an exact time, but suspect it was during the evening."

"What was stolen?"

"It was a relatively small statue of the god Osiris."

"Have the police been involved?"

"No, we don't believe they have the expertise to be of any use," Albert said, tones of frustration becoming apparent in his voice. Elizabeth picked up on the cues and decided to finish the interview.

"Ok well that's enough of a background for me to brief my editor. I'll hold the story until you can verify more details. I hope you get something useful from that tip, I'd rather report on the recovery of the piece."

"We will keep you informed. Now I must be going, I need to follow up on this."

"Thanks Albert. Talk soon," Elizabeth said. He nodded at her and then rose from his seat. He walked her back to the main foyer, and then disappeared through a locked door. Elizabeth walked out to her car, opened the door and just sat inside. She needed a moment to sort out what had just happened.

"Albert is very suspicious, both in his behaviour and also his approach to the theft. I'm also intrigued by his connection to the hospital. Is it a coincidence that he has a relative in the same ward as Dean?" Elizabeth thought. In her experience there weren't really coincidences. She just had to puzzle out the connection at a later point. At least she had progressed the story, although George wouldn't be happy that she had handed over the original story tip.

Elizabeth turned on the car and headed towards the hospital. Her next job for the day was to figure out how to get herself access to Nathan's room. So far she had noticed that both the nurses and food staff had a key. Perhaps some doctors did too, but she ignored them. Her best bet was targeting the food staff. They were less involved, and would not treat the key as carefully as other staff.

She parked the car and walked through until she reached the right corridor. It was approaching lunch time so she just had to wait until the food delivery came around. After a little while she heard the wheels of the cart rattling along the ground. She looked over and didn't recognise the man delivering the food.

"That's a good sign," she thought. Having different people alternating suggested either multiple keys, or having the keys left in a common location. That gave her more opportunities. As the cart approached she paid close attention. She watched the man bring the cart to a stop, and then reach for the keys. She stepped closer, and walked along the corridor, trying to see which one he picked. She was in luck. He selected a gold key with a round cap. It was an older, traditional style key. The rest of the keys on the ring were more modern keys, with a U shaped set of prongs with jagged teeth.

"Easy to pick out of the rest, but also easily missed," Elizabeth thought. But at least she knew which key to target. She walked over to a nearby bench and sat down. She pulled out a copy of the newspaper and started reading. It was time to wait.

Within a few minutes the man and his cart returned, and Elizabeth waited for him to pass her and get some distance between them. Then she stood and put her newspaper away. She started following him, hoping to find out where he went. With any luck he would be towards the end of his lunch route. It was hard to tell, but it looked like the cart was fairly empty.

He continued down the corridor and then turned right. Elizabeth sped up, not wanting to lose sight of him completely. As she turned the corner she saw him disappear through a set of double doors. Elizabeth kept up her pursuit, and pushed the doors open. Past the doors was a ramp going down, and also going up. She had to choose.

"I'd say kitchen is downstairs," Elizabeth thought to herself and headed down. After following the ramp down one level she had another decision to make. She could keep going, or try the level she had arrived on.

"Let's double down," she whispered and continued down the ramp. As she completed the circuit she saw a set of double doors, instead of a normal door. She turned to look at the ramp and it ended in a wall. She had reached the bottom. She took a deep breath, then pushed through the doors to see what was behind them.

To her right stretched an enormous kitchen, which looked like one big continuous piece of steel. Along its edge was a serving area. To her left she spotted a spare food cart, without any trays in it. Further down the corridor were rooms, which had potential.

"Hopefully one of those is a change room. I'm more likely to find keys there," she thought.

"Let's hear it," a man said to her, his voice gruff and impatient.

"Excuse me?" Elizabeth said, turning to face the man. He was bald and scowled at her like she was trouble.

"Your complaint. Let's hear it. I haven't heard enough complaints today, and I'd hate to miss my quota."

"Oh, well actually I was after your chicken soup recipe. It smelled so delicious, I feel like I can still taste it," Elizabeth said. She carefully studied his reaction, to see if her quip had achieved the intended effect.

"Oh, you're after my secrets eh?" the chef said, a look of suspicion on his face. She could work with that.

"Well, I wouldn't need your secrets necessarily. Maybe you could give me a hint or a pointer?"

"Spices."

"Secret spices? C'mon that's no help to anyone. That is the oldest trick in the book."

"Sweetness. That's all I'll say," the chef said. There was a hint of a smile in his expression, although Elizabeth couldn't be sure.

"I see. That gives me a few ideas. I'm inspired, I'm going to try tonight," Elizabeth said. The chef nodded and went back into the kitchen. Elizabeth turned to leave, but stopped on the spot. Provided the chef wasn't too inquisitive, this was the best time for her to explore the room. So instead of leaving, she crept further into the room.

The first two doors she encountered were bathrooms. The next two were change rooms, one male and one female. The lunch server had been male, and the thought of that reminded her that she had tailed him to this location. He was probably still there somewhere. As if in response she heard a toilet flush from the male bathroom.

Elizabeth had a moment of panic, frozen in inaction. However she recovered herself and decided to head into the female change room. Along one side was a bench with coat hooks above it. Across the other side was a series of lockers. A few were closed and appeared locked, but many were open or just pulled close. Elizabeth walked along the length of the room carefully testing each locker.

The first two were tightly locked. The next one was empty. The one after that was empty save for a stack of metal coat hangers. However the next locker seemed to be full of stuff. That was promising.

So Elizabeth carefully dug through the locker to see what was there. She found a pair of black shoes, a makeup bag, deodorant, coat hangers and small jars that appeared to be different types of hand creams and moisturisers. She almost closed it when she noticed a small pouch nestled in the back corner of the locker. She reached in and took it out, slowly unzipping the pouch. Inside was a key ring, just like the one she had spotted before. And it had the same odd key.

"This has to be for the secure area, where Nathan is," Elizabeth thought with wonder. She had found a key. A whole world of opportunities just opened up. She quickly took the key off the key ring and returned it back into the corner. If she didn't find a way to replace the key in time it would be missed, but at least it might not be considered as urgent if the rest of the keys were intact. At least that was her reasoning.

She slipped the key into her pocket, and made an effort to return the locker to how she had found it. Then she walked over to the door and listened out for any activity. It was all quiet.

Elizabeth crept through the door and then slowly walked through the room. She was trying be quiet without appearing suspicious. It was in her best interests to avoid seeing the chef again. She heard a loud bang from the kitchen and quickened her step. It probably meant she had more time, but the key felt like it was burning a hole in her pocket so she wanted to keep moving.

The first thing she had to do was test if the key worked. As it was around lunchtime she thought that she had a decent window of doing that. The next step would be to then get herself a copy of the key and return the original. Then it would be the perfect crime, and nobody would know that she had access.

CHAPTER SIXTEEN

A KEY PLAY

Elizabeth walked swiftly up the stairs with purpose, trying to maximise her speed without running. She kept a hand in her pocket, feeling the key and reassuring herself that she had it. Despite her speed, the trek back up felt like it took forever. But she remained focused on her task. She continued down the corridor in a business-like fashion, as if she belonged there. As she approached the door, she quickly checked behind her to see if anyone was walking by that she needed to be wary of. She only saw a few people who looked like visitors. Elizabeth took the key from her pocket and inserted it into the door. She carefully turned the key and it moved. The latch clicked open and she shoved the door open, taking care to close it behind her.

Elizabeth quickly strode down the hallway, trying to get to Nathan's as soon as possible. She felt like she had time on her side, but could not be caught at such a crucial stage. She quietened her walk, and kept an ear out for any activity, but heard none. Once she came to the door labelled CM she carefully pushed it open.

Nathan looked up, first surprise and then a smile on his face.

"You returned," he said.

"I did, I found myself a key."

"Great work, that feels like a breakthrough. I'm really glad to see you."

"Thanks, yeah it's a big step forward. But I'm not done yet, and I need to keep moving. If you don't mind I have a few quick questions then I need to leave."

"Sure, fire away."

"First, what is the safest time to visit you?"

"Definitely in the evening. The night shift are overworked, and don't pop in very regularly. After dinner is taken away is the best time."

"Ok thanks that should be easy enough. Works well with my normal routine. Second, just letting you know that I met with your mother. I didn't reveal anything yet, but just that I was investigating your disappearance."

"Ok, how is she?"

"Worried and upset, but seems to be coping alright. She gave me a key to your apartment."

"Ok that's good."

"Is there anything useful there that you can tell me about?"

"I'm not sure. Let me think about it. Do you have anything specific to ask about?"

"I have a name for your old boss. Do you have his contact details written down somewhere?"

"Maybe. I would normally use my phone for that, but they took it when I came in. Actually, there is one place that I can think of. The original contract and letter of offer I received for the job has his name and mobile number on it. Why do you need it?"

"I'd like to get in touch and find out what happened. He has left the company and you are on extended leave and nobody knows why. Somebody is pulling strings here."

"Yeah, alright that's weird. Charles was a good guy, hope they gave him a generous package. This thing is big huh?"

"I'm starting to get that feeling. Each time I discover something new it is almost overwhelming. But I'm nutting this out, and sizing up the beast."

"Yeah, keep it up. You're my only chance."

"Hopefully not your only chance, but I'm acting like it. I better go while I can, I need to get this key back."

"So they don't realise you have it? Sure. Try visiting tonight, we can have a proper chat."

"Will do, don't go anywhere," Elizabeth said with a laugh.

"Promise," Nathan said and gave her a smile. Elizabeth quickly left the room and rushed back down the corridor. She couldn't hear anyone approaching so wanted to get out while it was safe. She reached the door, opened it with care and then ducked out, walking down the hallway as per normal. She stopped by the vending machine and pretended to look at the options and sneaked a peek back. The hallway was fairly clear, but she heard the approach of a trolley in the distance.

"If that's the lunch guy again, I could have been in real trouble," Elizabeth thought. But she had pulled it off. Now she had to focus her attention on getting a copy of that key.

"Better do it now just in case. Can't see Dean anyway," she thought. So Elizabeth walked straight to the nearest exit and emerged at the street. She still felt strange, carrying the stolen key with her. But that would pass soon, as long as she could get her own copy made. The hospital was in a relatively quiet area without a lot of shops. So she hopped in her car and drove down the road to the nearest shopping strip.

She wasn't aware of a key cutting place here, but figured there should be one. While walking down the street looking at the various shops, she spotted a narrow arcade and turned into it immediately.

"These always have a shoe repairer or key cutting service," she said to herself. She passed a dry cleaner, and a tailor at the entrance.

"This bodes well," she thought. The next few shops were a butcher and a tiny convenience store. At the end she found what she was after, a key cutting shop. They also did various repairs and other handy things. But she only cared about the one thing.

There was an old man with a white beard sitting down behind the counter. He was working on something out of sight.

"Hello," Elizabeth said.

"Hi, Bill here. How can I help you today?" the man replied.

"Well Bill, I'd like a key cut please."

"Sure, let me see it," Bill said, putting down what he was working on and wiping his hands on his pants. His hands were large and calloused, and were used to hard work. They were giant as well. When she gave him the key and saw him holding it, the key looked like a child's toy.

"Ok, let me see here. Yeah I can do that, I've got a good template. This design is so classic, but not as popular these days."

"Yeah, but I love that it's classic."

"Yeah, there's a certain charm to it. Is this the original or a copy?"

"I think it's a copy."

"Alright. Just need to let you know that with each copy there's some degradation of the quality and accuracy of the key. You're probably fine, but just make sure you test it properly before you rely on it."

"Ok that sounds like good advice. Thank you."

"No problem, just like to let folks know," Bill said. He took the key and the template he had selected and walked over to his grinder. He placed the two keys in and pulled the lever, the sound quickly filling the room.

He paused and inspected the machine, and then started up again. Within a few minutes he had finished. He took the two keys over to the counter and presented them to Elizabeth.

"This one is the original, this one is the copy," he said. The copy he had given her was silver coloured instead of gold.

"Looks good to me. What do I owe you?"

"Two dollars."

"Here you go. Keep the change," Elizabeth said, handing over five dollars.

"Much appreciated. You have a good day."

"You too Bill," Elizabeth said, pocketing both the keys. She walked off with a spring in her step. Bill's warning about the keys stuck with her though. She knew it was probably a standard concern and warning, but she also knew that it had been a relatively easy job to get the key. And it might not be so easy again. So she resolved to test the copy before she returned the original.

"With my luck, it will be a bad copy if I don't test it," she thought. There was some risk involved, since she would be visiting him in a period where she wasn't sure of the nurses' routine. But it was important. She couldn't wait too long for fear of the key being missed. That was attention she didn't want.

Elizabeth hopped back in her car and drove back to the hospital. She parked as soon as possible, and practically ran back inside. She took the most direct route to Nathan's room, and looked around quickly before pulling out the copied key.

She turned the key nervously, but it didn't move smoothly. In a panic she gave it a bit more force. The key moved all the way and she heard the click of the door unlocking. She opened the door just to double check, and then immediately closed it.

Elizabeth turned and continued down the corridor as if nothing had happened. She glanced around as she walked but nobody was really paying any attention to her.

"That's step one down. Now to return the key," she thought. She had no idea when the next shift started, so increased her walking speed. Her chest felt tight, because she couldn't relax yet. The tension had built up and it would only release once she had returned the original key.

She continued following the route, and then entered the stairwell. She stepped down with pace, holding the handrail to steady herself. Soon she reached the bottom of the stairs and slowed down. It was time to be cautious. She listened out to hear of any signs of activity. The biggest problem would be if she was spotted by the chef. He had already seen her today, and may be suspicious if he saw her again. Her excuse wouldn't work a second time.

As she walked through the door she heard excited shouting coming from the kitchen. She instinctively ducked down, as if she were dodging a thrown plate.

However she immediately realised that being low was probably a benefit, so she crept along staying under the height of the metal bench. That way if the chef didn't come out of the kitchen she would be very hard to see.

As she crept she looked out ahead for any other signs of life. While her current position kept her away from the chef, it would look very suspicious to anyone else. Once she passed the kitchen she slowly straightened until she was upright, but maintained the same speed. She had to focus on being invisible. Elizabeth strained her hears to detect any movement, but heard nothing. So she continued on.

The women's locker room was empty, so Elizabeth rushed over to the locker where she had taken the key. It was a delicate process getting access to the keyring without disturbing the contents. She didn't feel confident enough to remove everything, just in case someone turned up.

Every knock and bang made her wince, but she managed to retrieve the keyring. It was quite sturdy, so she struggled opening it enough to put the key back on. But she did, and swirled the keys around enough so it looked natural. Then she carefully reached back into the locker, to place the keyring back where she had found it.

A whistling sound from the room outside froze her in place. Elizabeth recovered from the scare and released the keys. After a quick glance at the locker, she determined it was good enough. She had to get moving. The whistling was coming closer, so Elizabeth looked around the room. The showers were too risky, but there were toilets. She stepped over to the nearest cubicle as quickly as she dared and closed the door slowly and quietly. She even turned the latch with agonising slowness to keep it soft.

Elizabeth closed the lid and scrambled onto the toilet. She didn't even want her feet to be visible. The whistling became louder still. The whistler had to be nearby, and the sound of footsteps confirmed her fear.

"Gracey is that you in there?" a female voice said. Elizabeth kept deathly quiet, not wishing to give anything away.

"Oh c'mon honey it's ok to respond you know, I don't bite. A little girl talk never hurt anybody. Would you prefer if I was on the can too?" the woman continued. Elizabeth remained silent. She heard the cubicle door next to her close and lock, and the sounds of a woman sitting down.

"Ah, there we go. I'm here, so you comfortable now?" the woman asked.

"No, quite the opposite," Elizabeth thought. Not only was it an awkward situation, she couldn't judge whether the woman suspected anything.

"Honey, don't be embarrassed. We can chit-chat down here, it's different. Nobody else will hear us," the woman said. Elizabeth kept quiet, wondering how she was going to get out of the situation. She heard the toilet flush and the woman leaving the cubicle.

"Not very friendly today are we? Maybe you'll relax when you're done. I'm going to take a shower," the woman said. Elizabeth waited for any sound to acknowledge that the woman was telling the truth. She heard a tap turn on nearby, and the sound of rushing water. But she waited a minute. And then she heard the sound of the shower curtain being pulled closed.

"Now's my best chance," Elizabeth thought. She took a moment to prepare herself, and plan her next move. She wound herself up like a coiled spring, and then unleashed herself. She turned the latch and flung the door open, dashing for the exit of the locker room.

She heard the shower curtain being pulled with force and a voice called out after her.

"Where do you think you're going? So rude! I'm going to give you a dressing down next time I see you!" the woman called out.

"You'll never see me," Elizabeth thought. She didn't even try to be sneaky she just kept running. Out of the room and up the stairs. She kept going until she reached the main corridor a few floors up and then eased into a walk. Her heart was still pumping like mad.

"What a strange encounter," she thought. But the job was done. She had a working key, and the original was back in its rightful place. There would be some confusion when that woman eventually confronted her colleague, but they had nothing to tie it to her. And they wouldn't suspect that the key had been copied and replaced.

Elizabeth slowed down and took a deep breath. Now she could grab a quick bite to eat and then see Dean. After scoffing a sandwich she walked over to Dean's ward. She didn't even knock and entered his room. He looked up and then smiled.

"Elizabeth, nice to see you. How are you today?"

"A bit exhausted actually, it's been a huge day. I have some news though."

"Ooh I'm sitting down."

"I've got myself a copy of the key to where they are holding Nathan."

"Wow, how'd you do that? Was I right about the lunch lady?"

"You sure were. I found the key in the locker of one of the food staff. I got a copy made and returned the original. It was a bit of an adventure, but now I'm set."

"That's amazing. I told you didn't I?"

"You did, you were right on the money."

"Not bad for an old bloke eh?"

"Ha-ha, no you did great."

"Have you seen our mysterious friend again?"

"Just briefly. I confirmed a few details and the best time to visit him. He gave me a lead to follow up too."

"Tell me about it."

"Nothing too crazy, just where I can find contact details for his old boss. I want to approach it from that angle."

"Approach what?"

"Oh my investigation. Turns out Nathan's mother sent a letter to the newspaper, so I can do a proper story on it. Met with her yesterday too."

"Wow, things are really moving."

"Yeah, they need to be. There's something really wrong going on here, and I think the longer it continues the harder it will be to stop."

"I think so too. I just have a feeling that this is big, that's why I want to know all about it. You just can't make this stuff up."

"No you really can't. How are you feeling today?"

"Can't complain. Well I could, but you know apart from the obvious, things are fine. Have you found out about that doctor Malberg?"

"Not yet. I'm waiting on a call-back before I investigate in more detail."

"Ok that's alright. You need to move carefully with that one."

"Yeah that's the feeling I'm getting."

"Good. Well I was thinking of you, and decided that I have another story to share with you."

"Great, I'll grab the recorder and then you can start talking," Elizabeth said. Despite her good news on the investigation, she didn't have anything to report for a treatment for Dean. She felt bad, but didn't want to act too impulsively. But she began to wonder if soon she would have no choice. Even if the program was as established as she hoped and she got Dean onto it, there were no guarantees. And it would take time. But time was against them.

These were the thoughts that ran through her head as Dean related his story. At least while doing so he was distracted from his current situation, and even laughed a little. She could offer him that at least. If all else failed, she would hear and notate his stories. And share them with the world.

CHAPTER SEVENTEEN

AN IMPORTANT CALL

Elizabeth rushed out of the hospital, hoping to get to work as soon as possible. She hadn't progressed her museum story, even though she had done the interview in the morning. She needed some progress to show, otherwise there would be trouble.

She made it into the office and headed straight to her desk. There were a lot of ideas running through her head from the day, but she focused on what was important. First she wrote down detailed notes and a plan of action for the Museum Heist. Even in a normal situation that would be interesting. In fact there was so much going on she probably couldn't give it the full attention that it deserved.

Once she was happy that she had made sufficient progress on that story she switched over to Nathan's disappearance. She had to be careful what she noted down for this one. Obviously she had a lot more information than she could acknowledge. So she decided to stick to the basic stuff and noted down her interview with Nathan's mother and her call to his employer. Charles, Nathan's boss, was one she would leave out for now. If she did manage to contact him, she wouldn't be able to explain how she got his number.

As Elizabeth finished up her notes, her phone started ringing.

"Hello, Elizabeth speaking," she said, answering it as soon as possible.

"Hello Elizabeth, I'm calling you on behalf of Lucy Morgan."

"Great, thanks for getting in touch."

"No problem. I have a message to pass on. She confirmed that Dr Malberg is the one who directed her treatment."

"That's all I needed. Thank you so much."

"There's more. You are not to mention Lucy in any context relating to this matter."

"Sure, I understand. Thank you."

"Glad you understand. Goodbye."

"Bye," Elizabeth said and hung up. That was an intriguing call. She had the confirmation she needed. Doctor Malberg was her next target for investigation. She decided to see what she could find at home and draw up a plan for getting in touch with him. She had the feeling that she might need some leverage before she did so. If they had outright denied any program of treatment to Dean, then they may be quite careful about admitting to her as well. And she couldn't use Lucy as a source.

Elizabeth squared off her notes, and prepared to leave the office.

"How's my museum story going?" George asked.

"Well I met with the Director of Egyptian Antiquities this morning. Very cagey fellow, he only agreed to meet because he wanted to get his hands on the tip we received about the theft."

"Why is that?"

"He thinks there's no value in the item on the black market, and that none of his staff would have told us about it."

"So he thinks the thief gave us the tip to show off?"

"Exactly."

"Did you hand it over?"

"Yeah, I just made sure I got a copy. It's of no further use to us, and it might buy us some cooperation. It all seems very suspicious though."

"Yeah, normally they report these things to the police. You do have a nose for finding these ones."

"What can I say? They stink," Elizabeth said with a laugh.

"Nice one. I'm guessing you also started your pet investigation?"

"It's a real story George."

"Missing persons case for a guy that nobody has heard of and only his mother is looking for? Not really no. But I'm going to let you convince me. Is there anything yet?"

"Not yet, just met with the mother and called his work. Routine checks. But there's a few things of interest there."

"Name one."

"His manager has left and the HR department said that our missing person is on extended leave."

"Oh that's definitely interesting. Why would a person who just disappeared take leave from their work? And not tell their mother?"

"Exactly."

"You've intrigued me Elizabeth. But don't get caught up in this exclusively. You owe me the museum story too."

"Hey, that was the deal. You know me, I honour my side of a deal."

"Can't fault you on that. Last time it almost killed you. Ok keep me posted with your progress. I want something printable soon though, don't drag the museum piece out too long."

"Sure thing boss."

"Good. See you later."

"Bye," Elizabeth said and waved to George. He was a stickler for his rules and merciless over culling nothing stories, but he was fair. If there was some meat in a story he let you have a go at it. But he wouldn't wait forever. Elizabeth packed her things up and got ready to drive home.

However as she walked to the car she had a better idea. She could stop by Nathan's apartment and take a look. She looked up his address and drove there directly. She went straight up the stairs and entered with the key his mother had provided.

Her first impression was that the place had definitely been locked up for a while. It had that stale smell of a place that hadn't been aired.

"If I'm going to spend some time here, may as well make it a bit more pleasant," she thought to herself. Elizabeth walked around the apartment, taking note of the layout and opening windows where possible. There wasn't much airflow, but she felt better immediately. The apartment was fairly compact with only one bedroom and the kitchen, living and dining all combined into the one room. There was also a bathroom and laundry housed in the only other room. But that made things a little easier for her.

Her first thought when looking around the apartment was the same as what Emma had said about it. There didn't seem to be anything suspicious. It was as if he had left one day and not returned. She half expected the place to be ransacked, or show the signs of a struggle. But no, it was just an apartment frozen in time.

Her objective was to find the phone number for Charles, Nathan's former boss. She had neglected to ask Nathan just where he stored his documents, but there wouldn't be that many places. She started off by looking in the bedroom. There was a double bed inside, and a small desk with a computer. She made a mental note to ask him about that next time. There was also a wardrobe along one end of the room with mirrored doors. Elizabeth opened the wardrobe, peering inside. The end she had opened was full of coats and shirts, with shoes at the bottom and a drawer full of clothes. She shifted over to the end of the wardrobe and opened it too.

She had more success. There were stacks of boxes, and tucked away in the corner was a small portable expandable file. She reached in and pulled it out, coughing on the dust that was displaced. She put the file on the bed and clicked it open.

It was a standard type of file, with plastic tabs denoting the various sections. She flicked through until she found one called work. There were all kinds of documents in there, but she eventually found a fairly chunky one. She pulled it out to take a better look.

It was definitely an employment contract, and the front page was a letter with the Addensum logo and address. She scanned through the letter and saw that it was signed by Charles Manfried, and below it was his mobile phone number. Elizabeth pulled out her phone and punched in the number, creating a contact for Charles. With that done, she put the document back in the file, and then put the file back where she had found it.

She felt like it was a good idea to pretend like she was never here. Just in case. She also felt strange disturbing Nathan's things. She had barely met the guy and she was rifling through his things. And the place had a strange sort of feeling to it, like a tomb. She thought that it was because it had been left vacant for so long. That it had developed a different feeling.

With her objective met Elizabeth left the apartment. Partially because she wanted to respect Nathan's privacy, and partially because of the awkward feeling she felt there. She walked straight back to her car and drove home.

Once inside she walked straight to the couch and flopped down onto it. Her day had been quite intense. From the Museum, to the key shenanigans and going through Nathan's apartment. But it was a good kind of intense, much better than the alternative of doing nothing. She felt like she had made real progress. But she had one more item on her list before she had a rest.

She pulled out her phone and looked at Charles Manfried's number. She had it, so she should call it. She hesitated at first, unsure of why. But then dialled it, giving herself no option. The phone rang and rang and she thought that maybe it would ring out. But finally a voice answered.

"Hello," a man said. His voice was nervous and unsteady.

"Hello, is this Charles?"

"Who's asking?"

"I'm Elizabeth. I'm a friend of Nathan and trying to track him down. I thought you might be able to help me."

"Why?"

"Well you were his boss right? Maybe he told you where he was heading for his leave?" Elizabeth asked. Charles already sounded nervous, she didn't want to scare him off too quickly by admitting that she was a journalist and was doing a story on Nathan's disappearance.

"How'd you get my number?"

"From his things, he had your number written down."

"Ok. I don't know anything, you shouldn't have called."

"I'm sorry to have bothered you, I just thought you could help."

"Nope, sorry I can't. Don't contact me again," Charles said and then hung up. Elizabeth stared at the phone. That was a textbook conversation for a scared source. She had had the same conversation many times over when dealing with sources that were too afraid to talk. Her suspicions were right, someone had gotten to Charles and maybe even paid him off.

This was definitely a conspiracy, one designed to remove Nathan from the map and keep anyone from finding him. If she hadn't received the tip and contact from Nathan, she would never have stumbled across him either. It was a very well-constructed disappearing act, one that seemed to have a lot of power and influence behind it.

"This just sounds worse and worse," Elizabeth thought. The enormity of the situation she had gotten herself into weighed on her. But then she remembered her successes and perked up.

"Well despite the effort they have gone to, not only have I found Nathan but I have access to his room. That's gotta count for something," Elizabeth said to herself. She wondered briefly about springing Nathan from the hospital, and dealing with the rest later. But it sounded too risky, and once he was out any evidence would be quickly destroyed. No, as long as it seemed safe they should keep playing along. And she had made a promise to Dean too. It was best for everyone if Nathan stayed put for the time being.

Her next major lead was Dr Malberg. However before she moved on she thought a moment more about Charles Manfried. Because of his behaviour, he was clearly under the influence of someone. But it might not be just because of his situation. Maybe he also knew something vital. Maybe it was worth trying to find him and getting him to talk in a safe location? She decided to leave that thought kicking around to see if she had any good ideas later. But it definitely wasn't something she could act on immediately.

Elizabeth lay down for a while and rested. She watched some television but wasn't really paying attention and didn't notice what was on. She had a good opportunity to see Nathan tonight, but she wasn't sure how to make the most of it. She needed to think about what he could tell her that nobody else could. Of course she could provide him support, but she had to make the visit count. There were no guarantees here, and despite her hard work every visit was still a risk.

Her mind was being rather unhelpful, so she switched it off for a moment. She walked into the kitchen and looked through the cupboards, trying to work out what to eat. Everything fell into the 'too hard' or 'don't have the right ingredients' baskets. So she eventually decided on a sandwich.

"Hey a sandwich is a perfectly acceptable meal," she told herself while assembling it. She sat down to her sandwich and water and watched the news. It was the usual mix of horror stories of attempted kidnappings, shootings and bizarre behaviour. She switched it off in disgust. Those stories were just horrible, and you didn't learn anything from them. They were just a way to scare people with a cheap thrill.

She thought about her own career as a journalist. Sure she had taken on some gruesome stories, but she always strived to find the insight or redeeming feature of the story. The story within the story. She didn't see the point on just reporting all the atrocities that were out there. That only served to kindle people's fears, or worse desensitise them. But she didn't have an answer either. Hiding them was probably worse. Elizabeth put away her plate and glass and decided to have a quick shower.

The length of the day and the stresses washed away with the warm water. She felt renewed after, and ready for the night that lay ahead. She dressed and checked the time. It was almost eight, so dinner service would be well and truly over at the hospital.

"Time to say hello," she said to herself and left. The drive to the hospital was particularly fast, as the peak traffic had died down and most people were already home. She decided to park around the corner from the hospital, to be less conspicuous. She walked through the main entrance as if everything was normal. There weren't many people milling around the hospital, she had never seen it so quiet. Which made sense. She headed directly to the corridor with access to Nathan's area, and quickly looked around. There was nobody in sight.

She retrieved the key and put it into the lock. Remembering her previous experience she used a bit more force to turn the key, and struggled less. The locked turned for her, and she quickly opened the door and stepped inside. She closed the door as quietly as possible and continued walking.

She paused after every few steps, to listen out for signs of movement. The corridor and adjoining area were deathly quiet. She stepped carefully, just in case there was someone around. However she didn't notice anyone, and the area just returned the same silence that she expected. She arrived at Nathan's door and gently pushed it open.

"Hey there," Nathan said once he could see her. He was sitting up in bed and the television was on.

"Hey, I made it."

"Yeah, have any problems?"

"Not that I know of," Elizabeth said with a laugh. Nathan laughed too. He looked tired though.

"How's things here? Rough day?"

"Yeah, the usual I guess. Looking forward to hearing what you are up to. What's happening?"

"I visited your apartment, and don't worry I didn't snoop around."

"I'm not worried."

"Found the number for Charles Manfried. So I gave him a call before I came here."

"How is he?"

"Really spooked. He didn't tell me anything, and couldn't wait to get off the phone. I think somebody got to him, maybe even paid him off. Either way, unless I can get to him in person he won't offer any clues."

"Wow, that's crazy. Charles is a cool guy, generally quite chilled out. That's actually pretty scary."

"Yeah, sorry to hear that. I guess it means that they are serious about this."

"Definitely. Did you want to visit him?"

"It might be helpful. Do you know his address?"

"No, but I remember where his house was. Let me think about it for a minute."

"Take your time," Elizabeth said, watching Nathan stare off into the distance.

"You know, do you have a pen? I'll write down some directions."

"Sure," Elizabeth said, retrieving a notebook and pen from her bag. Nathan started scribbling on the paper, pausing occasionally, before returning to write more.

"Sure beats using a word jumble to communicate huh?" Elizabeth said.

"Yeah, but oddly not as fun," Nathan replied with a chuckle. He returned to the notebook and wrote a few final comments.

"That should do it. No point talking you through, I think you'll just need to give it a go. I hope he's alright," Nathan said.

"I'm sure it is just intimidation tactics. But I'll let you know how I go. So one other question, your computer. Anything I can use on there?"

"I don't think so. I used my phone for anything important like numbers, appointments and messaging. Although I think my phone calendar might be synched up with my computer. You could probably see my appointment on there," Nathan said, his voice raising in excitement as he continued talking.

"Ok, so you made yourself a calendar appointment on your phone for the doctor appointment here, the one which you never returned from?"

"Yes, I'm sure of it. That's proof that I came here and didn't go anywhere else."

"Yeah, that's good. Not enough by itself, but very useful. How do I get into your computer?"

"My username is 'nathan'. The password is 'qwertyiscool' no spaces."

"Great, I'll give that a go. Got my fingers crossed we get something there."

"Yeah me too, damn these bastards. They are going to pay for this."

"Don't worry they will. But remember we need to act cool and use this advantage while we can. They don't know that I know you're here and that we can talk. That's a huge thing."

"Yeah, I get it. It can be really frustrating though."

"I know, I wondered about just getting you out. But it's too risky and we'll blow our chance. Just be patient and trust me."

"Yeah, I trust you."

"Thanks. Now I wanted to ask you about Dr Malberg. Have you seen him again recently?"

"Now and then he turns up for my morning review. Spouts the same old crap about reviewing my case with the other doctors, but you can tell he's not interested in anything other than me staying here indefinitely."

"Has he mentioned anything that you found interesting? He's from the research department you know."

"Research? Maybe they're testing stuff on me. I can't explain it, but I feel tired all the time. This can't be normal. I'm not that old or unwell, I just know they're doing something to me."

"It's possible. Hang on, maybe we can look into that. Do the nurses leave any equipment here?"

"Why?"

"Well, maybe if we can get some of your blood, I can get it tested by someone. That way we will at least get an idea of what they are doing."

"Yeah, that makes sense. I don't think so, they always bring in a little tray full of supplies when they take blood. You would have to find one of their supply cabinets."

"Ok, leave it to me. I'll find something. Because you're in this area by yourself, they probably have something nearby. It's more convenient that way. Let me go have a quick look now, while I'm here."

"Yeah sure. Come back before you go, even if you find nothing."

"Of course," Elizabeth said and left the room. She noticed a definite chill once she left the room. She shook off the shiver and started walking. She had already found one open door on a previous visit, but there had only been old paperwork there, not supplies. So she walked down the length of the corridor and checked all the rooms. But she couldn't find anything useful. As she was leaving the last room she heard footsteps.

CHAPTER EIGHTEEN

THE NOT SO SIMPLE SAMPLE

Elizabeth quickly stepped back into the room and pulled the door shut as quickly and quietly as possible. She leaned back against the wall, next to the door and strained her hearing. She analysed each footstep, trying to judge if they were continuing on as normal, or if they were coming over to investigate her location. She heard the footsteps right outside her door, and tensed herself. Then she heard a door open and the footsteps disappear inside. The person must have entered another door and she had misjudged the noise.

Nathan looked up and started to speak and stopped himself. It was not Elizabeth walking in the door. It was a nurse instead, and his least favourite one. It was Annabelle and she only ever came for one thing: blood. He sighed inwardly and starting mentally preparing himself.

"Surprised to see me?" Annabelle said.

"Yes, I don't think you've come in the evening before," Nathan said, trying to give a reasonable explanation. She was an odd nurse, and had a very suspicious attitude. He didn't want to give her any real ammunition.

"Well yes, but I don't ask questions I just carry out what the doctors ask for."

"Which doctor asked for this?"

"Dr Malberg. It's all above board Nathaniel."

"Yes, I'm sure it is," Nathan said. He didn't have to feign any frustration. Annabelle carried on, readying her implements on the little tray she was carrying. Seeing it made Nathan realise that was exactly what he was after. But maybe he could go one step further, and use Annabelle to help him.

He waited patiently and let her prepare and take the first vial of blood. She put it aside with care and continued. Nathan let her finish, preparing himself. Once she was done and had removed the needle he moved his arm suddenly, pretending that he had a spasm. He managed to knock over the tray containing all the blood and implements she had been using. However he did manage to grasp one of the vials in his hand.

Annabelle reached out to try and catch the tray, but it tipped over and the contents fell onto the floor. The glass vials shattered from the impact and his blood went all over the floor. Nathan used the commotion to hide the vial amongst his sheets. He peered out over the scene, the fact that he had given blood and saw it splashed out below made him feel sick.

"Urgh," he said and tried to lean forward.

"You idiot!" Annabelle said, once she had surveyed the damage.

"What have you done?" she yelled out.

"I don't know what happened," Nathan said.

"You know I'll have to take it again. What a waste."

"I know you need to, I'm not happy about you having to come back either."

"I'll have to talk to the doctor and work out how soon I can return."

"Dr Malberg?"

"Yes. Now be quiet while I clean this up. I am too furious for words," Annabelle said and Nathan took the hint. He didn't want her anger or attention. It was worth wasting his blood, for more reasons than one. He had something for Elizabeth to go test, and he loved seeing Annabelle angry like this. It was like a small revenge for the way he was treated. Ultimately he would pay a price too, but for this one time it was worth it.

Annabelle cleaned up the floor, and moved all the waste into a special bin.

"I'll be back with a mop," she said before leaving.

"I hope Elizabeth is careful," Nathan thought. If she came back while Annabelle was getting a mop, there would be trouble. There would be no way to explain her presence if discovered.

Elizabeth remained perfectly still in the room, listening out for any sounds. She figured that it was most likely a nurse visiting, and that she would not stay long. Elizabeth just had to wait it out. The silence was stifling, as Elizabeth didn't know what to think. All she could do was wait.

She heard a loud crash and was startled by the sound.

"What's going on in there?" she whispered to herself. Surely that was not a normal occurrence.

"Does he need my help?" Elizabeth thought. But she decided that things were probably alright, and the best move was to follow the plan and remain hidden. Once she was spotted in this area, at best they would increase the security and it would be very hard to come back. At worst they may even identify her and make things very difficult.

Suddenly she heard a door open and footsteps stomp out. Elizabeth waited until the footsteps were no longer audible, and then carefully opened the door. She looked out at the corridor, assessing the safety. The corridor was empty and quiet, as it always was. But something didn't feel right. What had happened in Nathan's room wasn't routine, and she sensed the anger in the footsteps of the nurse. Her gut was usually right, and it told her not to venture out yet. So Elizabeth went back into the room and waited some more.

The wait was painful for Nathan. He knew Annabelle was coming back, but he dreaded the door opening. If the door opened and Elizabeth came through, he didn't know what he would do. He had already taken a massive risk, he didn't want to lose their advantage. Despite his best efforts, he kept nervously looking back at the door. He wanted it to open, to see Annabelle there. But he was scared it might be Elizabeth.

After an agonising wait he saw the door opening slowly.

"No, Elizabeth don't come in," he thought. The door inched open and then he noticed a mop bucket coming through the door. He felt such incredible relief, that he had to stop himself from falling out of the bed. The tension had been incredible.

"What are you so happy about?" Annabelle asked when she entered the room.

"Maybe it's the loss of blood making me a bit loopy. But I'm happy that everyone is ok, and that you're helping me out by cleaning this up," Nathan said. He meant every word of it too, not that Annabelle would understand his true meaning. She looked him over suspiciously, but then focused on the mop and bucket.

"You're an odd one Nathaniel," Annabelle said and set about cleaning the floor. First she sprayed something special on the ground, and rubbing that in before mopping. The smell of the chemicals caused Nathan to almost gag. But he resisted.

"Smells great doesn't it?" Annabelle said, as if she had anticipated his reaction. She seemed to enjoy his discomfort, her own revenge.

"I guess she's entitled to that," Nathan thought. He didn't really think that Annabelle was a bad person, just following orders. She certainly didn't make any effort to make his life easier though. Not like some of the others, for example Robin.

Nathan waited patiently while Annabelle worked, and then spoke up as she finished.

"All done? Thanks for cleaning up my mess there."

"You're welcome, had to be done."

"I hope the rest of your night goes a bit better," Nathan said, giving her a big apologetic smile. She returned a look that wasn't a glare.

"I hope so too. Goodnight Nathaniel," Annabelle said. Nathan nodded and watched her leave. He felt relieved once she was out the door, and also hopeful. Things were looking up. He sneaked a glance at the recovered vial of blood. He hated seeing his blood like that, but it also had some potential to get him some answers.

Elizabeth had waited long enough, and was about to leave. Her feelings of impatience and the tension were overcoming her intuition about the danger. She had convinced herself that it was fine, and otherwise she would be sitting in the room all night. She grasped the door handle and began to turn it when she heard a weird sound. She paused and listened further.

It was a familiar squeak that she couldn't place. It irked her that she didn't know what it was. But she knew it was the sound of movement nearby, so she released the door handle and waited. The squeak was also paired with footsteps, probably a nurse. Likely the same one that left in such a whirlwind before. The steps were fast and decisive, the rhythm of their steps echoing through the hallway. However Elizabeth concentrated on the squeaking sound. That was the key.

She heard it again and again, she knew that sound and had heard it before. But she couldn't conjure up the image of what it was. She was even tempted to peek through the door, but restrained herself. Suddenly it clicked.

"That's a mop bucket, and the wheel hasn't been oiled," she whispered to herself. The realisation made her chuckle softly. She started to piece together what she had been hearing. The crash, the footsteps storming out, and the mop bucket returning. Some sort of accident had happened, but it was probably fine.

"Lucky I didn't go back into the room," Elizabeth thought. Once again her instincts had been right. She felt a surge of relief, as her mind imagined what would have happened if she had been in that room when the nurse returned. She discarded the mental image, and waited for the footsteps to end. Once they did, she knew that the nurse was inside.

A few minutes later Elizabeth heard the footsteps and squeak resume once more. This time it would be safe to visit Nathan again, but she would wait a little for safety. Just in case the nurse had forgotten something. The time passed more easily, the fact that she had just avoided a dangerous encounter made her a little more patient.

After five minutes of silence she carefully opened the door and returned to the hallway. She paused to listen again, and then continued on to Nathan's room. Once she arrived she opened the door slowly, so he would know it was her.

"I'm back," she said smiling at Nathan.

"I'm so happy to see you. I was pretty worried, before I thought you would come back too soon."

"I almost did, but luckily I heard the mop bucket. What happened here? Did you make a nuisance of yourself?"

"I certainly did. But for this," Nathan said, pulling back the sheet to reveal the blood vial. Elizabeth quickly walked up to the bed and then picked it up.

"This is your blood?"

"Yeah, I managed to save this one and destroy the rest. They won't even know it is missing," Nathan said. He was grinning from ear to ear.

"That's amazing. Wow, no wonder the nurse stormed off in anger."

"Yeah, it's annoying for them. But I did get a vibe, that it was an unusual annoyance for her. Nurses get frustrated, but over routine matters they just kind of shrug it off. This blood collection for testing is pretty regular. I'm wondering why she was so angry."

"You might be on to something. Which nurse was it?"

"Annabelle."

"Oh I've run into her before. She's very suspicious of people isn't she?"

"That's exactly what I thought. One to look into maybe."

"Yeah, it's a growing list though. Wow, so I have a sample. The next trick will be finding someone I trust to test it. But don't worry, I'll sort that out. It's a good problem to have."

"Yeah, my work here is done."

"Ha-ha, you did great. You have good instincts. Maybe I can make a reporter out of you?"

"If you get me out of here, I'll do whatever job you want."

"When I get you out of here, you won't need to work if you don't want to. They're going to pay for this."

"Sounds good to me. But that's a bonus. Get me out in a way that I can't be taken back here, that's what I need. If you do that, I'll be happy."

"Yeah, I know. That's the main thing. Well I don't want to push my luck, so I think I'll be going. You doing alright?"

"Yeah, it's been the same old story. This routine is wearing me down, but seeing you, and hearing about what's going on, that's keeping me sane. I've got a reason to hope again."

"Good, focus on that. And do whatever you can to try and improve your strength. If we can get more options on getting you out, the better. If I don't have to wheel you out on a bed, I think our chances are much higher."

"I've been thinking the same thing. I'm not convinced that there's any reason why I can't walk right out that door. But being bedridden for so long has taken a toll. Maybe there will be more information in the results from that blood test when you get it done. But for now, all I can do is keep positive and try to exercise a little."

"Take care and don't let them get you down. I'll be in touch again soon," Elizabeth said. She carefully placed the vial in her bag, and turned to leave. Nathan reached out his hand and grabbed her arm.

"You take care too. You can't help me if something happens to you," Nathan said, looking into Elizabeth's eyes.

"You got it boss," Elizabeth said, nodded at Nathan and waited. He released his grasp and sunk back into the bed. Elizabeth waved, gave him a quick smile and headed for the door.

"We've got this," Elizabeth thought as she walked down the corridor. Nathan had proven resourceful many times over, and the useful leads kept piling up. It was only going to be a matter of time until she blew the whole thing wide open. As she left the secure area she looked around the hospital corridor and saw that it was empty.

"Good, now I can get out of here," Elizabeth thought. She was looking forward to going home to rest. It had been another busy day, and she didn't know how many more it would take. She left the hospital via a side exit, and walked the long way around to her car. The streets were poorly lit and quiet, but she wanted to minimise any attention she might get. Things would get ugly if she started to appear on the radar of those behind the conspiracy. From what she had seen that was definitely the right label.

She paused for a moment to adjust her hair, because it was annoying her the way it was hanging. And she heard a footstep that suddenly stopped. It was probably nothing, but put her on alert. She continued walking, trying to appear as normal but listening out for any other noises. Now that she was paying attention, she could hear distant footsteps resuming. She didn't want to turn and look for fear of losing the element of surprise. She turned a corner and then stopped quickly. She slowed her breathing and listened out. The footsteps continued then stopped suddenly.

"Just get to your car," Elizabeth told herself. There was still a chance this was all in her head, with the sneaking around she had been doing. So she continued walking, with a bit more pace and determination. Her heart started pumping faster and faster but she kept a lid on her emotions and just focused on walking. She could still hear the footsteps in the background, which sounded pretty ominous. This was mostly an industrial area, so nobody was around in the evenings. It made her caution and fear more justified.

She spotted her car at the end of the block.

"Ok almost there. Keep it up," she said to herself. Once in the car it didn't matter if there was someone following, she could drive away. She quickened her pace instinctively, trying to get there as soon as possible without running. She heard the footsteps following speed up as well. The chances of there being a random person who just happened to be walking at the same time plunged. She was sure that someone was after her.

Her first thought was about the blood sample. If someone got to her and found that, it was all over. She would lose the sample, Nathan would get moved, and she would be in serious trouble. It would be hard to explain away with so much evidence on her. But if she stashed it, things would be easier.

"Let's play the safe game. Just in case," Elizabeth whispered. She noticed a small garden on the corner of two streets with some bushes in the middle and flowers along the edges. It looked like an initiative to soften the area a little. It was fairly close to her car, so gave her an idea. She pulled her bag off her shoulder and started rummaging through it. She wanted her pursuer to think she was trying to find her keys. What she was doing though, was transferring the blood vial to her makeup bag. That should keep it safe.

Once she approached the garden she fished out her car keys and dropped them to the ground. She bent down to pick up the keys, and in the same movement pushed the makeup bag under the bush. She didn't know how safe it was, but in the dark she couldn't see it well. She scooped up her keys and walked quickly to the car. She unlocked it and rushed forward, heading for the driver's side. She started to open the door and a black hand shoved it closed again. She turned to look, and saw a tall man dressed in black with a balaclava hiding his face.

"Keys," he said, his voice was rough and low. Elizabeth knew to play along. She could ask questions later. But she didn't want to just lay down for them.

"Who are you?" she said as she handed over the keys.

"Nobody. And if you say the right things you'll never see me again."

"I haven't seen you yet," Elizabeth said.

"That's the idea. I have the keys," the man said. She heard footsteps behind her and he was joined by another man, dressed normally but with a black cap pulled down to obscure his face.

"Good. Let's get moving," the man with the cap said. His voice was smoother and more pleasant. He seemed well-spoken. Elizabeth felt her arm grabbed roughly and she followed along as they led her around the corner to a black van. The man with the cap went over to drive, while the other took her to the back of the van, and pushed her inside. Elizabeth shuffled back to get a seat against the wall. The man stepped in, closed the door and sat opposite her.

"Don't try anything, this won't take long," he said to her.

"At least tell me where we are going," Elizabeth said.

"She's definitely a reporter, can't help herself," the man called out to the driver.

"Why don't you help her out then," the driver replied. An ugly grin distorted the fabric of the balaclava and Elizabeth saw a giant gloved fist come down before total blackness enveloped her.

CHAPTER NINETEEN

TAKEN

Elizabeth opened her eyes and took in her surroundings. She was tied to a wooden chair and was sitting in a utility room of some kind. A single neon light lit the room from above.

"You're awake," a voice said behind her. Elizabeth tried to look around, and shuffled the chair around to see who was talking to her.

"Your voice sounds familiar," she said, not recognising the man who sat there. He looked exhausted, his face was pale and sporting stubble. He was also tied up in the same way.

"Charles Manfried."

"Oh right. Now I know why I'm here."

"Why we're both here," Charles said, making it clear who he blamed for his situation.

"Hey, it was a natural thing to call you. I'm sorry but not my fault."

"What are you after anyway?"

"I'm just following up a news story. Clearly I've hit a nerve, but not sure what I have stumbled onto."

"I can't tell you anything."

"Can't or won't?"

"Both."

"Well that's why you're here, they think you might. Who are they?"

"Don't know."

"Fair enough," Elizabeth said. Charles was not being helpful, which was understandable given the circumstances. However, since they were alone she expected a bit more give.

"Maybe we're under surveillance. They're using Charles to see what I know," Elizabeth thought. It was a possibility.

"So what's the story?" Charles asked.

"Is he fishing or just curious?" Elizabeth thought. She decided to answer carefully just in case.

"Not much to it really. Got a tip that a man was missing. Made a few calls, you were the last call I made. Now I'm here. Not ideal."

"So you're a reporter?"

"That's right."

"This is not good."

"Look everything is fine. You don't know anything, I don't know anything. I'm sure this is just a big misunderstanding. Maybe he owes some money or something?"

"I really don't know."

"Yeah, I know. You said that before."

"Stop being smart. You think I want to be here?"

"No, I believe that. Here's an easy question then, did they say you could go home?"

"Yes."

"Ok great, that's a good sign. Now we just play the waiting game," Elizabeth said. She wasn't sure what to make of Charles, although he was clearly scared and uncomfortable. She didn't really feel any anxiety about the situation herself. She wondered why.

"Maybe I have Amy to thank," Elizabeth thought, her mind wandering back to the near-death experience she had had during the Mayor story. Her alter-ego Amy in the dreams had faced up to worse and survived. And oddly those dreams still remained vivid in Elizabeth's memory, like she had lived them herself. An unexpected gift.

Amy had been captured, drugged and left on the street. But she had come back and beaten them all.

"Yes, that's what I'll do. Wait it out, make sure they release me. And solve this puzzle, bringing hell down on them all. They won't get away with this!" Elizabeth said to herself. She felt a warmth run through her, and renewed confidence.

"How long have they left you here?" she said.

"A few hours, I think they're waiting for you to wake up."

"Well I'm awake, maybe they'll be here soon."

"I hope so, I just want to get home. My wife will be terrified."

"Don't worry, we'll be home soon," Elizabeth said.

"One way or another," she thought to herself.

The door clanked open moments later, and balaclava man entered the room.

"You, you're coming with me," he said, pointing at Elizabeth.

"Sorry I'm a little tied up."

"I know," the man said, annoyance in his voice. He pulled out a knife from his boot and sliced the rope cleanly. Elizabeth felt her wrists, rubbing them to ensure everything was alright. Then she stood up and followed the man out of the room.

They were in a dimly lit corridor, with concrete walls. It looked like they were underground. Elizabeth followed closely behind, not wanting to try to escape yet. If at all possible she wanted them to release her. It would make things easier and she wouldn't need to worry about them coming after her again. With any luck.

They soon came to another door, and the man opened it. He stood to the side of the door, and directed Elizabeth to enter. Inside was a similar room, furnished only with a small table and two chairs. Sitting in one was the man with the cap, the smooth talker who seemed to be in charge. She entered the room and sat down on the available chair, resting her wrists on the table. The door slammed shut and she looked at the man across from her.

"Thank you for accepting our invitation for a chat," he said, flashing a wry smile. Even with the cap on she could see his green eyes and they looked dangerous.

"I couldn't refuse," Elizabeth said.

"I'm not at liberty to tell you as much as you may want to hear. But I do need to know what you know about Nathaniel Stenson."

"Why?"

"It's very simple. We want to discover more about his disappearance, and you must have some information if you contacted Charles."

"That's a big assumption. But I'll tell you what I know, so you'll understand where I am coming from," Elizabeth said. She needed to set this guy's expectations, but she didn't buy what he was saying for a second. They were definitely testing her to see what she knew, and if she was any threat to them.

"This story came to my attention via a tip to the newspaper. It was very simple: a mother wanted to know what happened to her son, and the police were not taking notice."

"Why did you pick up this tip?"

"I thought it would be a simple story to solve, and I wanted to help her out. It could be a positive news story to balance the rest out."

"You seem to specialise in big, conspiracy stories. Why go after a simple missing person?"

"Well I recently did a story on a hospital nurse who is retiring soon. It had a really nice tone to it, and the effect it had on people was totally different. I realised that a bit of balance and inclusion of those kinds of stories might be better for everyone."

"I see. Carry on."

"So I met with the mother, and she told me some details. Where he had worked, and roughly when he had disappeared. So my first action was to call his employer," Elizabeth said. She looked over at the man, and he didn't react. He just waited for her to continue.

"They didn't tell me much. Just that Nathan had gone on extended leave and they confirmed his manager's name; Charles Manfried."

"So you called Charles. How did you get his number?"

"I found it in Nathan's apartment."

"You've been in his apartment?"

"Yeah his mother gave me the key. Wasn't really comfortable looking through it to be honest, but she was pretty desperate for answers and I found the number for Charles so it was worth it. Well, so I thought. Here we are," Elizabeth said, looking directly at the man opposite.

"Yes, here we are. Your story makes sense, but aren't you leaving something out?"

"No, that's really it. I made a point of being straight with you."

"I appreciate that. I expected a reporter with your history to have uncovered more information."

"Sorry for disappointing, I'm actually pretty happy with what I've uncovered with such little information to work with. Now that I've explained, do you think you could tell me who you are and what's going to happen next?"

"I can't reveal those details, they are classified. All I can say is that if what you have told me is true, then you have nothing to fear from us. You can continue working on your story, but you can't publish it."

"Why not?"

"Until we find him, we need this matter kept under wraps."

"You can't stop me publishing," Elizabeth said. She didn't expect to have anything worth printing for a while, her focus was on getting Nathan out. But she wanted her captor to see her fight for the story. If she backed down too easily he would get suspicious.

"I absolutely could, if it came to that. But I'd prefer that we have an agreement. It's a very generous offer. I'll let you continue doing what you are doing, but I'll be watching. If you discover anything more about his whereabouts, you must tell me. And you cannot publish anything without my approval."

"That's a lot of conditions. I don't even know who you are? What's your authority?"

"Classified. You can refer to me as Don. My number will be in your phone when you get it back. Text me to get in contact," Don said.

"If that's what it takes, then ok. I'm willing to be pragmatic on this, even though I don't agree."

"Good. I'm glad we are seeing eye to eye. And don't forget, we are always watching."

"I won't. Will it be you or balaclava boy walking me out?"

"It will be my associate. You can call him Nod."

"My pleasure. Can I go now?"

"In a moment. Wait here while I get Nod for you. Goodbye Elizabeth," Don said. He stood up and removed his cap, performed a sarcastic bow and twirl of his cap, before leaving the room. But all Elizabeth really noticed were his eyes. There was a keen intensity to them that never wavered.

Once he had left the room she let out a sigh. She had played tough, and it had worn her down. It was easy because she was angry, but that didn't decrease its toll on her. Things just got a lot harder. She had been careful, but not careful enough.

"That conversation would have been a lot more awkward if they had found the blood sample," Elizabeth thought. She didn't buy his story of looking for Nathan, more like looking for any people looking for Nathan. It was possible he was a government official of some kind, but there was no way to know. What she did know though, was that he had access to people and technology and had tracked her down since she called Charles. And he had gone to great pains to make sure that she understood what he could do. She had to be very careful with her future movements.

Within a few minutes she heard footsteps and saw Nod step through the door. He was still wearing his balaclava.

"Here to escort me out?" Elizabeth said.

"Yes," Nod said in a gruff voice and turned to leave. Elizabeth followed close behind. She was keen to get out of wherever she was.

"Is Charles leaving too?" Elizabeth asked as they walked.

"Already gone."

"Good," Elizabeth said. That made her feel a bit better. It also confirmed her idea that he was just there to get information out of her. They continued to walk up a flight of stairs and down another corridor. Nod stopped in front of a door and waited.

"Blindfold or sleepy time?" he asked. Elizabeth didn't need to ask what sleep time was, she had already experienced it.

"I'll take the blindfold this time."

"Sure," Nod said in what was little more than a grunt. He fished a dirty black cloth from his pocket and walked over to Elizabeth. She closed her eyes and let him wrap it around her head, just leaving a small gap for breathing. He roughly grabbed her arm and guided her through the door.

"Stairs up," he said. And they walked up slowly, one step at a time. Elizabeth could feel the light increasing, as they emerged outdoors. She heard her feet crushing gravel as they walked and then the two beeps of a vehicle as it unlocked. She was guided through a door and then pushed down onto what had to be the back seat. She heard the door close and footsteps walk around the car. She heard another door open and slam shut. Next the car spluttered on and the engine started to hum.

The drive was uncomfortable, as Elizabeth tried hard not to roll off the back seat. She tried to listen out for audio cues, but couldn't really come up with anything useful. After a while she just gave up.

After what felt like an hour, the vehicle slowed and finally stopped. She heard the engine switch off and the door open. The footsteps around to the back of the vehicle sounded cleaner, probably concrete. Elizabeth was gripped by a sudden panic.

"What if they were just lying to me? Maybe this is it?" she thought. But she calmed herself just enough to avoid panic, and decided to see what happened. She felt him roughly pull her into a seated position. Then he started unwrapping the black cloth from her head.

"Ok this is promising," Elizabeth thought. She waited for him to finish and kept her eyes closed for a few seconds more. Gradually she opened them and adjusted to the light. They were parked in a parking lot in an industrial area. But nobody was around, the place looked deserted.

"Out!" Nod said. Elizabeth awkwardly shuffled out of the car and looked around.

"Your car is around the corner. Goodbye," Nod said, pointing Elizabeth to the nearest corner. Then he entered the vehicle and then threw out her bag before driving away. Elizabeth looked for a number plate but it was obscured by something and unreadable.

"That figures," she said to herself. She walked over and picked up her bag, looking inside. Everything seemed to be there, although it was obvious her bag had been searched.

"Well I have my freedom, and my things. Hopefully I also have Nathan's sample," she thought to herself. She walked out of the lot and onto the street. She didn't recognise where she was, so continued walking to the nearest corner. She saw what looked like her car a block away, and started walking.

As she drew closer she recognised the car. She remembered about her keys and rummaged through her bag and found them. Feeling relieved she walked with the keys in her hand, about to open the car. She stopped next to the car and had a think. She was in two minds. She desperately wanted to grab the blood vial to make sure she didn't lose it, but also didn't want to tip off anyone watching.

"It's a low risk, I can't afford to leave it there," Elizabeth thought and kept walking. She approached the bush and garden and had a quick look. She couldn't see anything hidden underneath it, which was probably a good thing. If her makeup bag was still there. She quickly scanned the street to look for people, but nobody was around. So she knelt down and reached under the bush, hoping that her makeup bag was still there. She found it, and stuffed it back into her handbag.

Elizabeth then returned to her car. She didn't dare check the bag yet, deciding to drive home first. It was still very early in the morning, after a hot shower and some breakfast she could pretend it was a normal day.

The drive home felt like it took forever. She kept glancing back at her makeup bag, wondering if the blood vial was still there. But she refrained from checking, even though tempted. When she arrived home, she parked and practically bounded up the steps to her apartment. She fumbled with the keys and opened the front door, locking it behind her and pulling the chain across too. Then she leaned back against the door and let out a big sigh. She was home safe at last.

Elizabeth walked over to her couch, sat down and then opened her bag. She pulled out the makeup bag and looked at it carefully. It appeared to be undisturbed. She slowly unzipped the bag and sifted through the contents. She couldn't find the vial, and a dread feeling crept up from the pit of her stomach to her spine. After thirty seconds of looking she finally found it and a huge wave of relief poured over her.

"This is it, the key to finding out some answers for Nathan. Even if it's as simple as what drug they are feeding him, it's important," Elizabeth thought. She now had the problem of finding someone to test it for her that she trusted. She ruled out the hospital, nobody she could trust there. She didn't have any contacts at blood testing labs, although she did have some contacts in the police. The police did their own lab testing as well.

"I'll have to go with that option. It's my best chance," she decided. She had an excuse to visit the police station as well: the statement from Emma. She said that the police were not interested in the missing persons report. She wouldn't push hard on that angle, because there was no value in it. But it would be good to get a statement for her story, and while she was there she could look up one of her old contacts.

But that still didn't solve the issue of Dr Malberg and Dean's treatment. She had confirmation that he was involved in the program, but hadn't done any investigation yet. It was something that worried her. He didn't have a lot of time, and maybe it was too late. But he wanted closure, and she could understand his frustration. The idea that there might be a treatment out there that he wasn't allowed, it was maddening. How would it feel thinking that you weren't considered worth treating?

Elizabeth fought away the desire for sleep and dragged herself over to her laptop. She opened the lid and did another search for Dr Malberg. She found confirmation of where he got his degree, and his current position. But nothing useful.

"What are you trying to find," she whispered to herself. Searching aimlessly was not likely to hit on anything. But the truth was she didn't know what she was looking for. She paused for a moment, and dug into the problem.

She needed a way to have an honest conversation with Dr Malberg, without mentioning Lucy Margot. She needed to find out about his treatment program, and then provide that information to Dean. Or convince Dr Malberg to take on Dean too.

"I'll just make an appointment with him. If he did it for Lucy, I'll just pretend to be representing a celebrity client," Elizabeth thought. It was as good a plan as any, and it might provide some valuable information.

She shut the laptop and put it away. Then she dragged herself over to her room and flopped on the bed. She had been riding things hard, and her abduction hadn't helped. She felt like she had managed it well, but it had taken a toll. Her body was sluggish and drained, and she needed to rest. So she let herself rest. Tomorrow was another day, and there would be plenty more to do. She needed to be switched on, because there were plans to make. Any and every move she made would be watched.

CHAPTER TWENTY

ANOTHER
CONFRONTATION

Elizabeth woke before her alarm. She felt like she had slept for days, but at the thought of getting up she still craved more sleep.

"No time for that," she told herself. She quickly ate breakfast and showered, getting ready as soon as possible. She had a lot to cram into the day. Not to mention pretending to do her job.

"Going to the police station is my job actually," she thought. She could mention the Museum robbery as well. Once she was prepared she looked up the phone number for Dr Malberg.

"Time to get the ball rolling," she whispered. She dialled the number and waited. It rang out and the call was redirected.

"Royal Monterey Hospital, how can I help you?"

"Hi, I need to make an appointment with Dr Malberg rather urgently. I tried calling his listed number but it rang out."

"Oh yes, Dr Malberg is rarely in his office. There's an assistant that manages his appointments though, if you'd like to talk to her?"

"Yes please that would be great."

"You're welcome. Transferring you through now," the woman said. Elizabeth waited while the call transferred.

"Research Department, this is Emily. How can I help you today?"

"Hi Emily, I need to make an appointment with Dr Malberg today quite urgently."

"What is it about?"

"I'm calling on behalf of a VIP who needs to see Dr Malberg about treatment. It's very urgent."

"I see, what's the treatment for?"

"Stomach Cancer."

"Ok, well urgency is best for that. Can I ask who it is?"

"I'm sorry no, it's confidential. I need to meet with Dr Malberg first to find out more, before the patient reveals himself."

"Certainly, that's not too unusual. I'm looking at his diary now, I can squeeze you in at three. Is that ok?"

"That's perfect. Where do I go?"

"Just come to the research department and I'll direct you. What's your name?"

"Stephanie."

"Thanks Stephanie, we'll see you at three."

"Thanks, see you then," Elizabeth said and hung up the phone. She felt good about finally making a move to help Dean. With any luck she would learn something useful and get him another chance. With that done, she could move on with her next appointment.

Elizabeth drove directly to the Police Station rather than phone ahead. Her contact there was a man named Frank, and she hadn't really talked to him since her work on the Mayor story. She thought it would be better if she just showed up and blindsided him. He might say no if he had time to think about it. It was certainly an awkward request, turning up with a blood sample and asking for analysis under the radar. But he was an older detective with a lot of connections, and she just felt like he would bend the rules a little.

Elizabeth parked around the corner and walked over to the Police Station. It was so busy, she was almost pushed over by people leaving. There were phones ringing, people talking, yelling and complaining, and officers darting around everywhere.

"This could be harder than I realised," Elizabeth thought. She remembered that the detectives were all upstairs, so she tried going straight to the stairwell. A uniformed officer was standing there, sending people back.

"Good morning," Elizabeth said, smiling at the officer. He seemed like he was a fresh recruit.

"No access, sorry," the officer said. Elizabeth didn't notice any hesitation in his voice. Clearly he had been well briefed. She decided to play on his confidence.

"Of course, I understand. I just need to talk to Frank."

"Frank who?"

"Frank Melvillen, the detective."

"Who is asking?"

"I'm a reporter, Elizabeth Edmonds. I've worked with him before."

"He didn't clear you, I can't let anyone upstairs without an escort or prior approval."

"Kid, let her through," Frank said, coming down the stairs. The officer stepped aside and Elizabeth continued up the stairs to meet Frank.

"It's been a while Elizabeth. I'm thinking we should grab a coffee," he said.

"Sure," Elizabeth said. The two of them walked outside and headed to a nearby cafe.

"You know I've been around the block a time or two. I've seen a lot of things. Why is it that I'm anxious when I see you turn up on my doorstop unannounced?"

"Because you've been around the block a time or two, and you've seen a lot of things," Elizabeth said with a laugh.

"So, what do I have to worry about this time?"

"Hold that thought. How do you like your coffee?"

"Black, no sugar."

"I'll be right back," Elizabeth said. She walked up and ordered two coffees, paid for them and took a number back to their table.

"So why am I here? There's the reason I'll say if anyone asks me, and there's the real reason."

"Let's ease in with the reason that won't make me lose sleep at night."

"Sure. I'm investigating a museum robbery, one that they never reported to the police."

"That's the easy one? I should have known. Let me guess, it's that guy over at the Egyptian Antiquities, Albert?"

"How did you know?"

"Not the first time this has happened. He's got a bit of a reputation around the station, very secretive guy. But it's not against the law to not report things missing, so nobody ever looked into it," Frank said. He was interrupted by the waitress delivering their coffees. Elizabeth scooped some foam off her cappuccino before talking.

"Yeah I haven't worked Albert out yet. Thanks for the background info, that helps put things in perspective. Now the real reason I'm here is this," Elizabeth said. She took out a brown paper bag and slid it across the table to Frank. He peeked inside and then looked back up at Elizabeth.

"What have you gotten yourself into this time?" Frank said with a sigh.

"It's complicated, I can't bring you in on it. Let me just say that I need that tested thoroughly. All your drug tests, anything weird. The full package."

"What do you expect to find?"

"I don't know. I just have a guy who's not sure what's going on with him. And there's a reasonable expectation of foul play."

"I gotta tell you Elizabeth, you're playing a dangerous game. Is there any chance of a real case out of this?"

"I think there should be, a massive one."

"Doing this kind of stuff is going to blow your case if it gets out. You should get some help on this, run it through the precinct."

"I don't trust you guys enough, sorry. Not you personally, the rest of them."

"All the more reason to bring it in. If you think it's that sensitive, you can't fly solo."

"Sorry Frank, but it has to be this way. Can you help me?"

"I've got a guy. He's brilliant and owes me a favour."

"Are you sure you can trust him?"

"Yeah, don't worry. If there's anything to find he will find it, and he won't blab to anyone. His work is so specialised that he flies solo, so it's safe."

"Alright, thanks. That makes me feel better, I went through a lot to get this."

"I'm sure you did. I know what your answer will be, but I have to ask: do you need help?"

"Probably, but no. And thanks for asking."

"You're welcome. I really hope we can avoid what happened the last time. At least tell me if it's as big a story."

"As big, might be bigger. I'll let you know."

"Yeah right. I have your number, I'll call when I have something. Is your phone secure?"

"Not sure, I hope so. Just in case, when you call or leave a message reference the museum story."

"Sure, easy. Take care Elizabeth, I'll be in touch."

"Thanks Frank, I'll do my best. Talk soon," Elizabeth said. She stood up and left Frank with the brown paper bag. He watched her leave, then started drinking his coffee.

It was too early for Elizabeth to meet Dr Malberg, so she instead went into the office. She sat down at her desk to start organising her thoughts, and began to write some notes concerning the Museum story.

"Elizabeth do you have a minute?" George said.

"Sure," Elizabeth said, and walked over to George's desk.

"This way," he said, and crossed the office to enter one of the printing offices. This early in the day it was empty.

"So, what's going on?"

"Well I'm continuing my investigation."

"I'm aware of that. Which one?"

"Well like you said, focusing on the Museum story."

"Is that why you were at the Police Station this morning?" George said. Elizabeth was stunned, but managed to recover quickly.

"Yes, I met up with an old contact."

"Frank, was it?"

"Yes, where is this going?"

"I want some explanations. I've got eyes at the Police Station, and you made quite a fuss getting in to see Frank. So enquiring minds followed you, and you know what they saw?"

"No, please tell me."

"They saw you handing him a brown paper bag and then leaving."

"And?"

"Do you know what that looks like? You need to come clean with me Elizabeth."

"Alright fine. That wasn't about the museum story. I was looking into something else connected with the missing person story. Are you happy now?"

"You need to explain yourself right this instant."

"I don't need to tell you anything. Why are you snooping behind my back?"

"It's my responsibility to protect the reputation of this newspaper. I take my responsibility seriously, and I won't have rogue reporters going off and creating problems for the paper."

"Is that what you think I am doing?"

"That's what it looks like. If it's so innocent then just tell me what you were doing there!" George said, his voice increasing in volume.

"I can't, not yet. You need to trust me."

"I do trust you, which is why you still have a job. If you refuse to explain your actions, you have to stop working on that story. I won't suffer another minute on it until you explain yourself."

"Fine. Is that all?"

"No, you can go back to working the Museum story. I haven't seen any more updates. If you can't get anything useful there, I'll assign you something else."

"As you wish."

"Don't be like that Elizabeth. I'm running a paper, and I need my reporters contributing to the success of the paper. You should understand that."

"I do, I just thought we had a different relationship. I got the message, I'll focus on the Museum story," Elizabeth said.

"Good," George said. He said nothing else and watched Elizabeth leave the room.

CHAPTER TWENTY-ONE

THE INCONVENIENT TRUTH

Elizabeth couldn't stay in the office after that clash.

"I can't believe he's keeping tabs on me like that. First that creep Don, and now George!" Elizabeth thought. She was furious. After all she had done for the newspaper, in breaking the Mayor story and keeping that coverage going for weeks, and this was the level of trust she had. She collected her things and left the building. She went down to the car, put everything inside and then just sat at the wheel, thinking.

"I need to be very careful now. I'll work on the Museum story a bit more, meet with Dr Malberg for Dean and then assess where I'm at. I can't visit Nathan at the moment, way too risky," she thought. With her thoughts collected she decided to drive to the hospital and do her work in the cafeteria. She didn't want to see Dean until after her meeting with Dr Malberg.

Elizabeth was distracted during lunch, and didn't do much work on the Museum story. Sure, she had a few interesting ideas based on the information that Frank had given her, but she couldn't focus properly. There were too many things going on, and George's behaviour had thrown her off.

"Have I really misjudged him?" she wondered. She didn't know what to think about him. He had always been a tough customer, but generally fair. In a way he was being fair now, but she felt like she deserved a bit more faith. She always delivered the story.

Time was creeping forward, so she finished the boring sandwich she had purchased, drank some water and packed up her things. It was showtime.

She walked through the hospital leisurely, following the signs to find her way to the Research Department. It wasn't well sign-posted, but she got there eventually. The reception area was fairly compact, with only two chairs and the reception booth. There was a narrow corridor leading off to a series of rooms, most likely offices. Elizabeth walked up to the desk and waited for the woman there to notice her. She had dark brown hair tied up in a bun, and black rimmed glasses.

"Hello how can I help you today?" the woman asked.

"Hi, is it Emily? We spoke on the phone. I'm Stephanie and I have an appointment with Dr Malberg at three today."

"Yes, that's me. I'll just check to see if he's available," Emily said, before disappearing into the corridor. She returned two minutes later.

"I'm sorry, he's not in his office. I'll try paging him," Emily said. Elizabeth nodded and waited patiently. The phone rang within a few minutes and she answered.

"Yes, your next appointment is here. Sure I'll pass that on," Emily said into the phone. She hung up then addressed Elizabeth.

"He's on his way back, he'll only be a few minutes."

"Great, do you mind if I wait in his office, I'm in a bit of a hurry and I need to report back as soon as possible."

"Well, that's not normal, but he will be here soon. I'll show you through," Emily said. Elizabeth smiled and followed her down the corridor. All the doors were closed, and the woman opened the third door on the right. Elizabeth noticed that it wasn't locked.

Inside was a bookshelf, a desk and a computer sitting on it. There was a big lush leather chair behind the desk, and two basic plastic chairs on the other side.

"Please take a seat, he will be with you shortly," Emily said. Elizabeth thanked her and sat down. As soon as Emily had left, Elizabeth stood up and walked around the room. She noticed some papers on his desk and had a closer look. The one that caught her eye looked like a patient file. She didn't want to risk flipping through, but had a peek at the name.

"Susan Ambrose," Elizabeth whispered. That was interesting. She was in the same ward as Dean, and was related to Albert at the Museum. Maybe the Museum story wasn't as irrelevant as first thought. Elizabeth thought she heard something, so sat back down on the chair and started pawing through her bag, as if she were looking for something.

"Hello there, Stephanie?" a man said. Elizabeth stood up and looked him over. He had dark hair and seemed to be in his thirties. Nothing interesting at first glance.

"Yes, nice to meet you Dr Malberg," Elizabeth said.

"Please, sit," he said and then walked around to his desk. He spotted the patient file amongst the papers and swiftly grabbed it, inserting it into a filing cabinet below his desk. Elizabeth noted that with interest.

"Please tell me more about why you are here," he said.

"Well, let me cut to the chase. I'm here on behalf of someone with stomach cancer. I want to see what treatment options are available."

"Why come to me? I'm a researcher not an oncologist."

"Well, how do I put this? The person I'm asking for, is very wealthy and well-connected. So they learned about you and your program. The results are worth investigating."

"I'm intrigued about how you would have come to that conclusion. None of my research has been published, and any patients I have dealt with have strict confidentiality agreements."

"Well, like I said, these things don't matter if you are asking the right questions and have the right connections and influence," Elizabeth said. She wasn't sure where he was going with this, but she knew she had to keep Lucy out of it.

"Of course, I mean no disrespect. I ask because I'm intrigued at how you came to talk to me. The reason I am intrigued is because I've been having quite a few of these meetings. You could say that a queue of well-connected, influential people are lining up to talk to me. And yet I haven't made a single effort to reach out to anyone."

"Well, if you have the right product, people will find you."

"True, true. Well I guess you aren't at liberty to enlighten me more, but that's ok. I will tell you what I have told the others who have come here," Dr Malberg said. He paused for a moment, and then began once more.

"I am trialling a revolutionary new treatment in the fight against Cancer. This treatment is effective against every single type. It is low risk, and very successful in the limited trials so far. However it is a slow process, and manufacturing the required components cannot be sped up at this stage. So while the demand for such a treatment is quite high, the supply is very low."

"So how do you choose?" Elizabeth asked.

"There are many factors. The order in which people came to us, their need..." he said but Elizabeth cut him off.

"Their money," she said. Dr Malberg nodded.

"Of course this program requires funds to continue, so any generous donations will be accepted and would factor into our decision."

"I see, that's good to know. So how would this work?"

"Well, the patient will need to visit me and we can start the enrolment process. However there is a waiting list, with many people on it. Of course I will do what I can, but I can make no promises."

"What about the effectiveness of the treatment? When is too late?"

"To be honest, we have not tried it at the bitter end. But from what I have seen, if the body has enough strength and will to continue, the treatment should help buy enough time to enable further treatment, and eventual remission."

"So the Cancer would be gone completely?"

"If the treatment is successful, then yes. Unlike other treatments this is not a blunt instrument which destroys everything. It is certainly remarkable."

"I see. Are there any plans for making it more available?"

"That would be nice, but for now we need to do more testing. And research on how to increase the supply. Scaling up will be very tricky."

"Ok I understand. Well, thanks for your time. I'll be in touch, and next time will have the patient with me."

"I look forward to being of assistance. Goodbye," Dr Malberg said. Elizabeth stood up and walked out of the office. She waved to Emily on her way out, but didn't stop to talk. She only had one thing going through her mind.

"What a piece of work," she thought. She couldn't get over his arrogance, and self-importance. Clearly he was on to something, but he was profiting from it. Keeping the supply low and working the demand in his favour. There was no way that Dean would get a look in, even though there was a good chance of getting some traction with his Cancer, or even get rid of it for good. If Dr Malberg could even be trusted.

"He was too confident, and Lucy was cured. He knows it works, that's why he's so damn smug," Elizabeth thought. She decided to visit Dean and tell him the news. She didn't want to, but delaying it would make it worse.

Elizabeth took her time walking through the hospital, but eventually she arrived before his door. She just stared at it, frozen. But she forced herself to push it open and step inside.

"Hello there Elizabeth. What's going on?" Dean said. His voice started excited and quickly turned to concern. Elizabeth's face told a grim story.

"I just had a meeting with Dr Malberg, and it's not good news. I had to pretend to be representing a VIP just to get a meeting. He was very cagey and evasive, but did confirm that he is running a treatment program."

"That's good right?"

"Yes that part is good, and is promising. But he's using it as a bargaining chip, says the supply of his treatment is so low he's got a waiting list. One that is heavily influenced by how much you can pay."

"So you're saying there's a possible treatment out there, but I'll never get my hands on it?"

"That's what I'm saying, as much as it pains me to admit it. Although I did discover something strange there. A woman in your ward is being treated by Dr Malberg. I ran into her by accident, and I've even met her father. He doesn't seem that rich or powerful, even though he has a good position."

"Well from what you said he must have something," Dean said. Elizabeth could see the disappointment on his face. But it was also tinged with something else.

"I just can't believe they would do that. Is it just the money? Or am I too far gone?" Dean asked, the pain in his voice touching Elizabeth. She wanted to lie to him, to try and make him feel better. But she couldn't, she had to be honest.

"Obviously it's mainly the money. I think there's a chance for you based on what he said about the treatment, but I can't say for sure. He kept insisting that the supply of the treatment is very low, and that's why there is a waiting list. There's probably some truth to that, but I dare say he's exploiting it."

"Unbelievable! How can people be treated this way? Why isn't this all over the news? Someone has an experimental treatment and people are lining up. Even if it didn't work it would be news. How can they keep this in the dark? It's not right! Without you I wouldn't have even had a clue!" Dean said, his voice rising in anger. His face was red and his eyes bulging.

"I know, I know. I'm going to keep doing what I can. I'll bring this to light Dean, it won't stay hidden. People deserve to know."

"I still can't believe it," Dean said, his voice trailing off. The burst of anger had subsided, and he withdrew into himself.

"Thanks, thanks for telling me. I know it must have been hard, but you did it. It hurts, but it's better to know. Wondering about the possibilities, it gave me hope. But it also consumed all my thoughts. Maybe I can focus now on what's important, in the time I have left."

"Dean, it's not the end."

"Yes it is. It's been staring me in the face for so long, and I haven't noticed. I'm scared Elizabeth. I don't know what's going to happen. I'm not ready, and maybe I'll never be."

"You don't have to say that. Yes, things are bad. But you can't give up hope."

"For a cure, yes I can. It's too late now. I'll save my hope for something else. Listen, I think I need some time. If you don't mind."

"Of course. Take care Dean, I'll be back tomorrow," Elizabeth said and left. Before she had closed the door she had tears in her eyes. At first they were little droplets, and she wiped them away quickly. But once they started, the pent up emotion flowed out and she couldn't stop. She rushed to her car as quickly as possible and once she was inside just bawled and bawled.

She had been dreading this moment, for a long time. She just hadn't realised it. Her delays and inaction in researching a cure for Dean had been purposeful. She feared this result, having to tell him that he couldn't be cured. Or wouldn't be. But she had done the investigation, she had spoken to Dr Malberg and knew the truth. Dean wasn't going to get any better, and they weren't going to treat him. And this wasn't something she could just fix.

She let the tears run their course, and then she turned on the car and drove home. She just needed to get there and crash. It had been an emotional day, and she needed for it to be over.

CHAPTER TWENTY-TWO

A WARNING

Elizabeth turned off the car and sat back in the seat for a moment. She was finally home, and could rest up. She turned to get out of the car and jumped back in fright. There was a face pressed up against the driver's side window. The balaclava gave away who it was immediately.

"Hello in there," Nod said. Elizabeth wound down the window, forcing him to step back.

"What are you doing here?"

"Boss needs to talk to you."

"Right, is this really necessary?"

"I'm here, so yes. Please step out and come with me," Nod said. Elizabeth sighed, removed her keys and opened the car door.

"This way," he said, and started walking down the street. Elizabeth looked back at her apartment, wondering if she should just make a break for it.

"No, they let you go last time and they're not being violent. It's alright just get this over with," she told herself. Nod stopped around the corner next to a black van.

"In the back," he said and opened the back doors. Elizabeth climbed up and turned only to see the doors being slammed shut. She leaned back and tried to sit down comfortably. The van jerked suddenly and then started driving away. She had to cling to the wall, but then relaxed once the van settled down.

"At least I'm awake this time, that's an improvement," she thought. She needed to figure out what Don wanted. She had been careful to not visit Nathan just in case. So at least they couldn't use that against her. Maybe her visit to the police station had tipped them off, but she could explain that away easily enough. It all depended on what they were after.

As much as she hated to admit it, she was rattled. She knew it was the response they wanted, and that they were trying to break her down and find out what she knew. But knowing didn't help, they were still quite obvious in their communication. They had just proved that they knew where she lived, and could come after her at any time. She would not be safe until this was all over.

After half an hour the van slowed at a gentle pace, and then finally stopped. She heard footsteps on gravel, and then the rear doors of the van swung open. She tried to look out, but Nod jumped in and blocked her view.

"Wear this," he said, thrusting a black T-shirt at her. Elizabeth wrapped it around her head comfortably, but making sure that she couldn't see.

"Rather I do it nicely, than he does it," she thought. Nod checked and seemed happy, so he grabbed her hand and led her outside. They walked slowly, the gravel crunching under their shoes.

"This is probably the same place. Interesting that it's within half an hour of my apartment," Elizabeth thought. They went down stairs, and then along a concrete corridor. She heard a door open, and then she was roughly guided down into a chair.

"You can take it off now," Don said. She removed the shirt and let her eyes adjust. They were sitting in the same room at the same table, and Don was across from her.

"Here we are again," Elizabeth said.

"I told you we would be watching. And you will be back here as many times as I need you to be."

"Good to know."

"Yes, I want you to know this. There is nothing you can do without our noticing. Do not forget."

"I won't."

"Good. Now I have some questions. Why were you at the Police Station?"

"I was following up on a story," Elizabeth said. She was relieved that the questioning had started on a point she was strong on. She was prepared.

"Which story?"

"A Museum robbery. It wasn't reported to the police, so I wanted to follow up and see if there was a history of that or if they had any leads I could follow."

"How did you come across the Museum robbery story?"

"It was a newspaper tip from a reader."

"I see. And that was your only business there?"

"Yes, I spoke to an old contact. He told me there's been rumours of robberies happening there and never being reported. It was an interesting lead."

"Ok, well we will validate your statement, but it sounds alright. Next question," Don said, before pausing. Elizabeth wondered what he would be asking. It couldn't be this easy.

"What is your interest in the hospital? You've been there a lot. Is it connected to your search for Nathan? You can't tell me the hospital is connected to your robbery," he said. Elizabeth tried to keep her face expressionless. She needed to give him something good, that would eliminate further questions. But she didn't have much.

"I was doing a story there before, about a nurse. I met a patient there during that story and I've been visiting him."

"Who is this patient?"

"His name is Dean. Just a regular guy, he's got it rough. Cancer."

"And what's your interest in this man?"

"Nothing, I just met him and felt bad."

"Really? That's it?"

"Yeah, he got me at a moment of weakness. He asked me to write down some of his stories so he would have a legacy."

"I didn't realise you were such a philanthropist."

"It's not a situation you find yourself in every day. Why do you care so much?" Elizabeth said, throwing it back at Don. She didn't like his questioning.

"Let me be crystal clear with you. I like you, and I like your story. It's plausible, which gives me an out. But the thing is, I know what you are like. I've seen you operate, and I don't trust you."

"Why not?"

"Don't interrupt. Imagine a line like this," Don said, moving his arm horizontally in the air between them.

"This is the line of believability. Your story of why you are doing things is right on the line. Plausible, but convenient. Any additional flag would send you over the line," he said, and demonstrated by moving his arm up.

"And for people like our friend Charles, I would accept such a situation. He doesn't have it in him to lie, or hide things from me. He's an open book. But you, you're driven and you pry and you open every door," Don said. He paused and watched Elizabeth. She looked him in the eye and waited, unsure if he was continuing.

"So, I don't buy your stories, they're too convenient. They may even have some elements of truth, in fact I expect it. They wouldn't be good stories otherwise," Don said. He stood up and started pacing the room.

"I know you're up to something. Don't say anything, I know you are. And I'm going to catch you. And I'm even going to tell you how. I'll be watching every move you make, every action, every place you visit. Don't bother looking for me, because it might not be me. But there will be someone watching, and they will come tell me everything. And when you slip up, when you make that fatal mistake I will bring you back here. And we will have another conversation, but it won't be as friendly as this one," Don said. His voice had turned to ice, and the look he gave Elizabeth gave her chills. He clearly had a stake in this, or someone had made sure he did, and he was serious.

Elizabeth didn't know what to say. He was right that there was no point trying to deny his claims, or lead him astray. He was set on his path, and had made it clear to her.

"Are we done here?" Elizabeth said, trying to sound as nonchalant and confident as possible.

"Do you understand me?"

"Yes."

"Then we're done," Don said, dismissing her with a wave of his hand. She stood up and walked to the door, feeling like she was back in school. She opened the door, and saw Nod waiting outside in the corridor. Once he noticed her, he started walking and she followed.

Elizabeth's heart was racing, and her adrenaline was pumping. She hadn't expected that. She wasn't sure how to react, so she didn't and left it for later. She just focused on following instructions so she could get home. Once they reached the end of the corridor, Nod handed her the t-shirt and she wrapped her head again. He led her up the stairs, and she heard the familiar crunching of gravel as they walked to the van. He helped her up and then closed the doors.

Elizabeth removed the t-shirt, and let the tears fall. Things were beginning to unravel, and this was the last thing she needed, at the end of an emotional day. She let the emotion continue, and left the planning and decision making until later. The van started up and she felt relief as it drove away.

The trip home went fast, and she was in a holding pattern. So much had happened, that she didn't let herself react any further. When the van came to a stop, she waited patiently until Nod came around to open the doors. She stepped out, handed him the t-shirt and kept walking without a word. She could hear the van doors slam behind her, Nod walking back to the driver's seat and the van driving away. But she didn't look back, she just focused on the walk home.

She was around the corner from her apartment, so the walk was short. She didn't notice any people at all, although that didn't mean the streets were deserted. She was just focused on her goal, getting home. She fumbled her keys once before opening the door, and then staggered over to the couch and collapsed onto it. She thought briefly that her bed would be more comfortable, but that was the last thought she had.

***

Nod drove back to the complex with care, not rushing. If he returned too quickly, Don would chew him out for speeding and potentially drawing attention. He didn't really feel like another lecture. He parked the van in the usual spot, and went down the stairs. He found Don reading a book, in the small room that doubled as a kitchen and dining area.

"Job's done. Not a peep out of her," Nod said.

"Good, now we wait."

"You think that worked?"

"Yes, definitely. She got the message, we just need to be vigilant just in case."

"If she's as crafty as you said, then I don't see how you can be so confident that she will play along."

"She's resourceful and talented, but I've seen her kind many times before. She's a solo operator. The way you close them down is to make them feel like they can't do it themselves. Then, they give up."

"Alright then, I hope you're right."

"I'm right, you'll see. She's right where I want her, and I've got insurance in place should she cause more trouble."

"Alright then," Nod said, and walked off. He thought Don was making a mistake, but it wasn't his problem. He was just the muscle, not the brains. He half wanted her to stitch Don up, just to see the look on his face. He chuckled at the thought.

CHAPTER TWENTY-THREE

THE STORY

Elizabeth woke up on the couch, feeling incredibly disoriented. It took her a few moments to work out why she was there.

"Yes, that happened," she thought, recalling the previous day's events. It had been pretty eventful, and she'd had confrontations with George and Don. And had to break the news to Dean.

"Best not to think it over too much," she thought and stretched out into a seated position. She did have something to think about though: what do to next.

Don had made himself clear, that she would be watched and hauled back there. She didn't want to see him again, she had a pretty good idea of how it would go down. She couldn't afford to bring anyone in to help her though. She needed a way to move forward by herself.

It would take Frank days to get the results of the blood test, that wouldn't help her. There was a possible link to the museum, with Frank's mention of the rumours of unreported robberies. But it was a weak link, and she couldn't afford to waste time. There was another option, but it didn't feel right.

She could go to George, and bring him in. Tell him enough to get his backing to run the story as it was, or find out what he needed. If she could get the story out, public pressure would release Nathan and get Don off her back. There would be no secret to Nathan's whereabouts at all.

It was a compromise. She could bring in someone who was already connected, and still own the investigation. With George's backing she could get the story up so fast, that Don would not be able to do anything about it. It wouldn't be the slam dunk she was hoping for, but it was enough to blow it wide open. Then she could continue her work in safety, to ferret out the final few details.

"He'll go for it, he's dying for a big story," Elizabeth said to herself. And if she was right, she should have enough bargaining power to get what she wanted. It was all coming together. Pleased that she had a firm plan in place, Elizabeth stood up from the couch and paced the apartment, working through the details in her mind. There was a spring back in her step, after the deflation she had felt over the past day.

She headed into the office early, and started working on the notes for her story. Nothing sensitive, just the framework in broad strokes. Once she had a skeleton, she printed it off and went to find George. He was sitting at his desk, doing three things at once as usual.

"Yes, Elizabeth. What updates have you got for me?"

"Good ones. On the other story."

"I thought you weren't working on that."

"That's what I want to discuss."

"I've been quite clear, I'm not sure what there is to discuss."

"I need your help."

"Why do you need my help on a story you shouldn't be working on?"

"Because I'm willing to tell you the details."

"Ah, my weakness. You want to spill your secrets. Ok fine, let's go have a chat. But I doubt I will change my mind."

"It's a risk I'm willing to take," Elizabeth said. They both walked off to one of the printing rooms and George closed the door.

"Start talking and make it good."

"Let me sum this up: I found the missing person."

"Oh, that's interesting. What else?"

"What do you mean what else? I cracked the case."

"Depends on where he is."

"Royal Monterey Hospital."

"Hardly a news story. What did he have an accident or something?"

"No, I think he's being held against his will."

"Why would you think that? Have you actually met the guy?" George said. It was a valid question, but

Elizabeth felt uncomfortable answering it. Her gut told her to lie.

"Nah, just a hunch. Why hasn't he called his mother if he's in hospital?"

"We don't know. It's a pretty serious thing, messing with hospital patients. I think you should leave it alone."

"Really? That's not the reaction I expected from you."

"Well do we even know if there's a story here? Could blow up in our faces. We can't afford that."

"A man is missing and might be being held in a hospital and you don't want to look into it?" Elizabeth said, her voice full of amazement.

"I'm just saying that we need some hard evidence. If you don't have any, then it's too risky. What were you handing that police officer?"

"Oh, that was just a personal thing. Unrelated, sorry to burst your bubble."

"Still not happy, but let's park that particular argument for a second. What about the HR manager you mentioned? Charles was his name?" George said. Elizabeth started to reply, but stopped. Something was off about that last statement.

"Charles, you called him Charles."

"Yes, did I get it wrong?"

"I never mentioned his name to you. Oh my god. George," Elizabeth said, stepping back. There was only one way he could have gained that information. And she didn't like it one bit.

"What do you mean? Of course you told me you just forgot."

"Oh no, I can't believe it. They got to you didn't they?"

"I don't know what you are talking about."

"You slime ball. What did they promise you?"

"Elizabeth, you are being delusional. Just calm down."

"You should be the gold standard. You should be the one that doesn't take crap from anyone. Otherwise this newspaper may as well be made out of toilet paper."

"I don't appreciate you making those kinds of statements."

"Even if they're true? You used to care about the truth George. You can drop the game, I know they got to you. Just tell me why."

"I don't know what you're referring to. But I will say that I will do anything to keep this paper afloat."

"There's no point doing that, if you've failed the people reading it. What's the purpose of this newspaper? It's to inform the people. As soon as you stop doing that you're worthless."

"Look Elizabeth, let's just agree to disagree. But you have to drop the story, there's no two ways about it. Because I won't print it."

"And there we go. You think you're doing the right thing, but you're making a big mistake. I quit George. I can't work here another moment."

"Don't be rash Elizabeth, just take some time off. We'll work this out. "

"Nothing you can say can convince me to stay. Be happy that you served your masters and I'm off the story. I just hope you can sleep at night!" Elizabeth said, before storming out of the room in a fury.

As she walked away, her anger was joined by horror as she thought about what that encounter meant. Setting aside her career and identity, it meant that George was working with Don, and who knows how long they had been in touch.

"I could have spilled the beans completely," she thought. Only her instincts had stopped her from sharing key details with George. Had she done so, Nathan would have vanished in an instant never to be found again. She had come so close to losing it all.

However as she thought more about it, she had pretty much lost it all. Her job was gone, and even if she went back hat in hand and begged for it, things would never be the same. She would never trust George again, and wouldn't be able to do a proper job of investigating anything. So her job was done.

Her whole identity was wrapped up in it. As she packed her things, she realised that she had nothing else. Her whole life had been angled towards being a reporter, and her entire focus since had been going after that big breaking story. Now, that was all over. She didn't say anything to her colleagues, she just couldn't handle the questions. So she just took a few things of importance, and went on her way. Nobody stopped her or said a thing. Maybe they didn't realise, or didn't care.

"Don't know who I can trust anyway," Elizabeth thought. She put her box of things into the back seat, and then went behind the wheel. As she pulled out she looked back at the building, wondering what her future would be like without it.

The drive home was over in a flash, her brain was otherwise preoccupied. She still had trouble processing what had happened. Everything was going so well. And then bang she had just run into a wall. Once she stepped inside the apartment, she opened a bottle of red wine and poured a glass. She sat down on the couch and swished the wine around, thinking about what to do next.

Don was following her every move, and he had gotten to George. Don had wanted to make an impression on her, and it had worked. Every idea she came up with had to be dropped immediately. If she went straight back to Nathan she would get stopped in her tracks. She had no-one to run the story, so publicity was out of the question. If she wasn't careful she would lose the blood test results as well.

"Even if those results come back, what can I do with them?" she wondered. Her whole plan had been built around using the story as leverage, and it had been compromised. And with all the surveillance she was hamstrung from any action. There was nothing she could do.

There was only one person left that she could help.

"Dean, he needs a friend. I should spend time with him. That would be meaningful, and would give this whole episode some value," Elizabeth thought. It sounded right, spending some quality time with a man who had almost run out. Maybe she could even write more of his story. That would be a nice tribute, and a story that could be told.

Elizabeth felt a bit better about herself and the situation, so cleaned herself up, left her wine unfinished and prepared to go to the hospital. She wasn't worried about being followed, if they were that diligent they would only see her visiting Dean. Maybe then they would get the hint and leave her alone.

Elizabeth left the apartment and walked back down to the car. She felt a bit lighter, although there was still a cloud hanging over her. She was still not happy about how things had transpired with George. The betrayal was something else, something she had never expected. But the whole thing just felt wrong, as her investigation had suddenly had the rug pulled out from underneath. However she tried to dismiss those thoughts, and focused on Dean instead. She had helped him a little, but there was a lot more she could do.

The drive over to the hospital was like being wrapped up in a blanket. She was safe and warm and felt like she was doing the right thing. The angst of her struggles to find and free Nathan were somewhere else, not haunting her right now. She could feel them still there, in a corner of her mind. But she just chose not to look there. She focused on the good that she could do.

She had left Dean on such a poor note before, she was glad to be going back. Hopefully she could make a meaningful difference for him, and make sure his story was not forgotten.

Elizabeth walked through the hospital in no rush, but not looking out for anything. She was completely focused on getting to Dean's room. She almost missed her phone ringing and managed to take it out and see who was calling. It was Frank, no doubt he had some information for her.

"I don't want to have that conversation right now," she thought. So she let the call ring out, and then continued on until she reached Dean's door. It was closed. She knocked briefly, and then stepped in without waiting for an answer.

Dean looked terrible, he was quite pale and his face was more drawn than before. He looked at her with effort, the energy and vitality she was used to was gone.

"Dean what's going on?" Elizabeth said with concern. She ran forward to the side of his bed.

"This could be it, the beginning of the end. I've felt a change, and I'm not as strong as I was," he said, trying to shuffle up in the bed. Elizabeth stepped over and helped him sit more upright.

"Thanks. Yeah, it's funny you know how things can change so quickly."

"I know," Elizabeth said.

"Yeah, sorry about yesterday. It was a tough conversation. I hope I didn't make you feel bad."

"No, it wasn't you. I felt terrible giving you that information."

"The reality of the situation can be hard. Even when you think you have confronted it, there's still that hope lurking in the background. You tell yourself that you're being realistic, but you cling to that hope. You hold on tight, and you believe with all your heart. That you will be the one that's different, that you will be the one to survive against all the odds."

"Of course you do. It's your story, you should be the hero and survive."

"Well the hero doesn't always survive you know, not that I'm the hero. But some of the best stories end in tragedy."

"Tragedy is just a perspective. I'll make sure your story has a happy ending," Elizabeth said. Dean laughed, the effort curbed by his pain.

"You going to make up the ending huh?" he said.

"No, but I'm going to end it in triumph. It's all about perspective."

"Well, good luck with that. But enough about my woes, let's hear about your other story. How's that guy going? Got him out yet?"

"It's not good, I'm in over my head," Elizabeth said. Dean laughed again, not even the pain reigning it in this time.

"I never thought I'd ever hear you say that. Didn't think you knew the words. What's got you all worked up?"

"There's this guy, says he's a government agent. He's following my every move, restricting what I can do. I tried to push things with my editor, a bit prematurely, and then discovered my editor is in on it. Or at least he's been approached and bought off."

"Oh wow. Government conspiracy, and the newspaper editor is complicit. That's a pretty rocking story."

"There's no story, because the editor won't run it. And I quit."

"You quit? The newspaper?"

"Yes."

"Why?"

"I can't work for that guy anymore. You need to stand for what's right, not bow to government or corporate pressure."

"Well I did peg you as an idealist. But that's a pretty rash decision. What are you going to do now?"

"Well, I'll find something else. Maybe another paper, maybe something totally different. But for now, I can spend more time with you. Make sure we can get that story down."

"Well I do enjoy spending time with you, and I do like the idea of my story being told. But I'm not where you should be spending your time."

"Why not? Your time is limited, we should make the most of it."

"You're right, my time is limited. Soon I'll be gone. But you will still be here, and so will that man in the hospital. What are you going to do then?"

"I don't know."

"You're giving up on him, aren't you?"

"No, just putting it on hold."

"Listen here," Dean said, his voice rising in volume. He attempted to sit up further and waved away any help from Elizabeth.

"You do not put that man's freedom on hold. That's as good as giving up. You and I both know that as soon as the urgency is gone, it'll be easy to start making more excuses. And then conveniently forget. And then he will be lost, and you'll have to deal with that."

"It's not my problem."

"Yes it is, you made it your problem. And you did great things. But now you're throwing in the towel. All because you got some pressure from the government?"

"It's not like that. I can't do it myself."

"Aren't you the one that took down the corrupt mayor? They pulled you out of a burning building. And you survived, and you went back there to get the evidence."

"Yes," Elizabeth said, defensively.

"So why are you stopping now? Because you can't do it alone."

"Yes, I've got no more avenues to investigate. I'm being watched constantly. My hands are tied."

"Either you are a complete coward, or you have the biggest blind spot I've ever seen."

"What do you mean?"

"Get some help. If everyone is watching you, play that to your advantage and use someone else to do the legwork for you. This is a dangerous game you are playing, there's teams of people against you. Why not even the playing field?"

"Who can I trust? I don't want to get anyone else in the line of fire."

"Only you can answer that. But don't take people's choices away from them. If someone wants to help, let them. We're all adults here, and you can't take everyone on yourself."

"I'll think about it."

"Think about it? You know what, let me make this easier for you. I won't say another word to you until you come to me to say that he is free."

"What?"

"I mean it. And if you want us to talk again, you better get moving. The clock is ticking and we both know death waits for no man," Dean said with a wry smile. He enjoyed the look of bewilderment on Elizabeth's face, and her inability to respond. After a moment of looking down, and then looking up again Elizabeth spoke.

"You're a hard taskmaster Dean, but I think I needed to hear that. I'll be back," she said. Dean just nodded and watched her leave.

"Save him, for us both," Dean thought. He had found Elizabeth's investigation interesting, but now it had become a purpose for him. His last stamp on the world, however small. He smiled again, and settled back into a nap. Sleep was always so close by these days.

CHAPTER TWENTY-FOUR

REGROUPING

Elizabeth left the hospital room in a daze. Dean had completely blindsided her. She had expected that to play out completely differently, with her being the comforting supporter that Dean needed. But he had seen through her, and told her off for giving up. He was right too, she was not looking at it properly. She was letting the events of the past day loom too large in her mind. As she left the hospital she remembered Frank's call. It was time to take action.

Elizabeth sat in her car and called Frank back.

"Hey, how are you going?" Frank said.

"Not great, but I just got a pep talk."

"Ha-ha, they're always useful. My guy came through in record time, and I've got some results for you."

"Is it something we should discuss in person?"

"Definitely. They are strange."

"I'm going to need some help with that. I'm under surveillance and got hauled in by some shady characters just for going to the Police Station. Got any ideas?"

"Yeah don't worry I've dealt with this kind of thing before with informants. No doubt you have seen your fair share with your own leads. I'll text you an address to visit tonight. It's in the Black Jungle."

"Is that safe at night for a woman alone?"

"Nope, but you've gotta manage it. At least until we can meet. I'll include a few instructions."

"Alright Frank, I'm putting my trust in you. Don't let me down."

"Wouldn't dream of it. See you soon, and take care."

"Will do. See you," Elizabeth said. She hung up the phone and waited for Frank's message.

"How funny, this whole thing started at the Black Jungle," she thought. It really wasn't a place she was looking forward to revisiting, especially at night. But she had to take a chance, so that she could get the information from Nathan's blood test. She knew that would be key.

Frank's message came through within a few minutes. He provided an address, and mentioned that there were night markets. The markets were so popular that a large and varied crowd ventured into the Black Jungle, so it was a bit safer and easier to blend in.

"Off I go, back into the jungle. At least it's moving forward, I can figure out the rest later," Elizabeth thought. She started driving so that she could think. She wanted a few ideas before she met Frank, but mostly she would need to take the information he had and find the best way to use it.

Elizabeth parked a few suburbs away, in a safer location.

"No way am I leaving my car there," she thought. The Black Jungle was way too risky, anything could happen to it. She walked to the nearest train station and bought a ticket. That was the best way to get there, and she would blend in with the others travelling the same way.

The train pulled up and it was absolutely packed. Hordes of people streamed out of the train, but there were so many that the guards blew the whistle before anyone had a chance to get on. This caused a surge of panic as the passengers on the platform forced their way onto the train. Elizabeth was swept along with it.

She couldn't move at all on the train.

"At least it's only a few stops," she thought to herself. The air-conditioning was running, but it just couldn't cope with the masses of people so the temperature was constantly rising. At each stop she got a breath of fresh air, but not enough people left the train to make a difference to her comfort.

Finally they arrived at Grunford station. Which was the suburb's actual name, even though nobody called it that. She would have to look up how it got the name Black Jungle.

"Probably a good story in that," she thought. But either way, it had stuck and there was nothing anyone could do now. The train emptied as she disembarked, which worked in her favour. The large number of people had to be going to the markets. There was no other reason to visit. But it helped her blend in, just one more amongst the crowd. If she was still being followed, they were going to have trouble. Elizabeth laughed to herself at the thought.

She followed the crowd, curious as to where they were going and enjoying the relative safety. She wasn't completely sure of the route she needed to take, so also wanted to see if the crowd knew. There were so many people everywhere, it started to give the area a different feeling than before. Maybe part of its problem was the general isolation. A place was much more dangerous and scary if there was nobody around to help you.

The wisdom of the crowd won out, and she started to notice the beginning of the markets. The main street was blocked off from cars, and there were stalls lining each side of it with a fairly wide passage down the middle for foot traffic. The variety of stalls was interesting as well, ranging from tarot card reading to wax hand castings and home-made jewellery. However she was looking for a bookshop.

She found it about halfway down the street. It was a simple stall, with second-hand books covering the available table space. Her instructions had ended there, so she browsed what was available.

"There's a wider selection available inside the shop," an older man said, pointing to the back of the stall. Elizabeth looked up and saw that there was an actual bookshop behind the stall. She looked over at the man, sussing him out. He looked fairly normal, with a clean blue shirt on and dark pants with a brown belt. She was here to play along, so she decided to see what happened.

"Thanks, I'll take a look," she said. She stepped around the stall and entered the shop behind. Inside it looked like an ordinary bookshop, with rows of books lined up in the main floor space and also on the walls in shelves. She walked through the rows, not sure what she was after. At the end she noticed a room off the side, and decided to take a look. After she stepped through the door it slammed shut and she turned around nervously.

"Come down quick, it's alright," a familiar voice said. Elizabeth turned around, looking for Frank. She couldn't see him, but did notice a trap door in the floor and a ladder going down. She rushed over and peered inside.

"Quick, and close the cover behind you," Frank said. Elizabeth started to climb down the ladder, and after a few steps reached up and pulled the trap door closed. As she reached the bottom she noticed they were in a dark room with a single light hanging from the ceiling.

"This is a quiet room I can think in private," Frank said with a laugh. He was seated at a table in the middle of the room.

"Very intimate," Elizabeth said, and sat down opposite him. Frank pushed over a manila folder, and Elizabeth opened it.

"Results are in there, first page is the human readable summary for us."

"Ok thanks, I'll have a read."

"Hopefully it makes more sense for you, I don't have much context here."

"Yeah, sorry about that. But I'll make up for it," Elizabeth said, reading through the front page. She gasped and looked up at Frank.

"This is starting to make sense."

"Talk me through it."

"As you read, there are a few key things which caused concern for your friend. In the blood sample was a sedative, anti-nausea medication and here's the kicker: a form of chemotherapy drug. I'm no doctor, but it sounds like Nathan is being treated for Cancer."

"Well that's what I figured from the results, the sedative sure sounds suspicious though."

"Yeah it does, and let me give you some background. This guy has been held in hospital for months with no proper explanation for his being there, and no offer of release. They're holding him there for some reason."

"You think for a reason other than treatment?"

"Yeah, what would you think if I said that one of his doctors is running a research team that is testing a new Cancer treatment?"

"I'd say that he's got himself a live guinea pig. No offence to your friend."

"Exactly! There's still something missing, but this is enough. We can nail them with this. If we use it the right way."

"Well what's the right way? Are you going to write a story about it?"

"No, I can't. I left the newspaper."

"What?"

"Yeah, long story. I guess I should fill you in."

"Yes, you should."

"Don't worry, I won't hold out on you. But I need to know something: where is the line?"

"What do you mean?"

"Well you're a cop. You've done me a huge favour here, but I know your hands are tied. There's only so much you can do. So I need to know how far I can depend on your support."

"Elizabeth, I've seen my fair share of troubles. I've seen the law bring justice, I've seen the law protect rich criminals. I've done my time. I still believe in the law, but I won't be bound by it if I think justice won't be served. If the situation warrants it."

"Wow, well I think this one does. We've got a lot to discuss. Is this location safe?"

"For a time, but we shouldn't linger just in case. It connects to a discreet backstreet so we can travel freely."

"Well let's move on to a safer place. I need you to understand everything. We can't gamble with Nathan's life, and without your help this could get ugly."

CHAPTER TWENTY-FIVE

RADIO SILENCE

The morning after he smuggled the blood sample to Elizabeth, Nathan awoke with a smile on his face. Life was good. He had defied the hospital and used Annabelle against it, claiming the sample and destroying hers. It was his first major victory. One to be celebrated.

He did a few stretches, with care, not wanting to set off any alarms. He had to be extra careful because his additional enthusiasm had given him extra energy.

"Elizabeth will get me out of here with those blood test results, I need to be ready," Nathan thought. But he had to pace himself, both for his own development and also to stay under the radar. They had to think he was still unable to walk by himself. Although, he didn't really know how effective his training would be. He would have to find a way to test himself safely.

The morning rounds came, and Nathan was ready for them. He saw Dr Malberg again, and decided to try talking to him.

"Hello again Dr Malberg," Nathan said. The doctor looked up at him, surprised to be addressed.

"Oh yes hello again Nathaniel. How are you feeling today?"

"The usual."

"Ok good. I can see here you had a bit of an accident last night. Has this loss of motor control been a consistent problem?"

"I don't think so, at least not that I have noticed."

"Hmm, alright that's fine. Please take care and let a nurse know if they reoccur. Also, we may need to schedule another blood sample sooner than normal, it's very important."

"Won't that be dangerous?"

"If consistently done, yes, but I see no problem this time. The nurses will let you know."

"Fair enough. Hey, so any update on when I can continue the treatment from home?" Nathan said. This statement caused Dr Malberg to stop what he was doing and look up at Nathan.

"I'm sorry that you got that impression. With your condition, we can't possibly send you home with a clear conscience. I'm afraid for the time being you will need to remain here, so we can provide you with the best and most appropriate care."

"What is my condition?"

"I'm sorry I don't have time to go over this again. Take care Nathaniel," Dr Malberg said and left. Nathan watched him go and chuckled to himself. In other circumstances he would have been annoyed, but he knew that help was on its way. It didn't matter what their reason was for keeping him, he just had to play along until he could leave.

He waited for the food staff to come and take away his breakfast tray and then he did some more exercises. Stretching mostly, but also a little bit of strengthening his arms. He could do that in the bed without causing any alarms. He couldn't ignore his legs, but it would be wiser to wait until the evening when there was less chance of disruptions.

Lunch came and went without any sign of Elizabeth.

"Well, I shouldn't expect her here all the time. She must be coming later today," he thought. He was a little disappointed, but it made perfect sense. They had to play the long game, and make sure that they made the most of their current advantage. As long as the hospital didn't know that Elizabeth had access to him, the better. It kept their options open.

He did a few more exercises in the afternoon, and watched the television. The same old shows, which was tiring.

"How is watching television tiring, I don't even do anything," he wondered. It was a funny thought. It should be relaxing, but was the opposite.

"Maybe for someone who doesn't do much it's a lot of effort. Or maybe I'm just so over it my brain can't take any more," he thought. It had been months of the same routine, and he was already over it a long time ago. But Elizabeth's intervention had given him hope. Hope to be free, and walk on his own once more.

Dinner arrived, and it was lasagne, with rice pudding and orange juice.

"Now this is a decent meal, smells good," Nathan said to himself. He unwrapped his cutlery and begin to dig in when one of his machines started beeping.

"Seriously? Can't you see I'm trying to eat?" he said, looking at the machine. It only beeped at him in response. Nathan pressed the nurse call button and started eating. The lasagne was hot and cheesy, which hit the spot. However after only a few mouthfuls the door opened. He saw Annabelle rushing in.

"Just my machine," Nathan said.

"Ok, that should be fine," she said. Annabelle walked over to the machine and checked the indicator.

"Needs a refill I'll be back."

"Sure," Nathan said and returned to his food. He forgot about the machine and started enjoying the food. The machine beeped again.

"Again? Whatever," Nathan said. His annoyance was rising, but he pushed it aside with thoughts of freedom. He needed to eat, to build his strength. Then he could get out of here, and be free of all the machines and prodding and blood sampling.

Annabelle returned within a few minutes, and started attaching a new package to the drip.

"Here we go, this should do the trick," she said and reset the machine. She waited a minute until she was satisfied it was working correctly, then turned to leave.

"Annabelle, Dr Malberg said you would tell me when my blood test would be rescheduled?"

"Oh yes, probably tomorrow," she said.

"Ok thanks, see you later."

"Bye Nathaniel," she said and left. Nathan thought over their encounter, it was pretty normal.

"I think she's warming to me a bit, she doesn't seem as surly," he thought. Although he was a bit surprised that she had come when he buzzed, she usually only came to take blood. Not that it mattered. His stay would be over soon. He finished his dinner and set the tray aside. He left the television on, but didn't really watch it. There was nothing to watch. After his dinner tray was taken Nathan waited patiently for Elizabeth to show. He didn't have much to share with her, but was keen to see what updates she had for him.

Hours passed, and Elizabeth did not show.

"What's keeping her?" Nathan thought. He had been putting off his exercise until after she came, but decided to push ahead anyway. He leaned over to the side of the bed and with an effort swung his legs over the edge. It was time to test his strength a little.

He lowered his left foot to the floor and tried putting some weight on it. It felt alright, but it was hard to tell.

He tried the same with the other foot, still sitting on the bed but letting some weight be borne by his right foot too. It was a similar sensation, but after his previous expedition he felt nervous. He didn't feel like trying again so just sat there for a few minutes, flexing his legs and trying to remember what it felt like to walk properly.

Nathan started to feel very tired, so he swung himself back into the bed and made himself more comfortable. Sleep found him soon after.

He awoke to a stinging sensation. He opened his eyes quickly and looked around. The room was still dark, but there was a shape standing over him. As his eyes adjusted he saw it was a nurse, probably Annabelle. They were taking blood from him.

"What?" he managed to say.

"Relax, we are just finishing the blood sample."

"While I'm asleep?"

"After the last episode it seemed like the best option," Annabelle said. Nathan slumped back into the bed, he didn't have the energy to argue any further. He felt Annabelle finishing up, and wrapping a bandage around the entry point.

"There we go, all done. Back to sleep," she said, her voice attempting to be sweet. Nathan wanted to laugh at that but felt too tired. He even wanted to stay awake to rebel. But he couldn't.

Nathan awoke feeling terribly weak. It was a struggle to sit up properly. He remembered his night-time visit, and looked over at his arm. The bandage was still there, and it felt sore.

"Great," he said. Elizabeth had not visited him last night, and the blood they had taken had taken its toll on him. He moved his arms, trying to see if some exercise could shake off his fatigue. But it was no trick, his body was genuinely tired and sore. He felt like he had gone backwards, after all his progress.

"It's alright, Elizabeth will come through," he thought. He held onto that thought, clung to it like nothing else. He needed to be rescued, he couldn't save himself.

A different doctor did the rounds, but Nathan didn't bother asking any questions. He knew the answers, and wanted to save his energy. When the newspaper arrived he eagerly flipped through, hoping to see a message from Elizabeth. There was nothing obvious, so he had a go at the word jumble. It occupied him for a while, but there was no hidden message. He threw the newspaper down in disgust.

"It's only been one day, everything's fine," he told himself. It was the voice of reason, but he had trouble believing it. He looked at the facts and things weren't that bad. One bad night and a crummy morning, and he felt like he had been abandoned. It didn't make sense. But he couldn't shake the feeling. Something was not right.

Lunch came and it was chicken noodle soup. He ate it reluctantly, but didn't enjoy it. He kept looking up at the door, half expecting Elizabeth to sneak through at any moment. But nobody came, except to retrieve his lunch tray.

Nathan dozed throughout the afternoon. The television was on, but he couldn't concentrate. His spark and energy were gone, and he didn't know how to get them back. So he just tried to rest, allowing his body to do what it wanted. As the afternoon became evening, and dinner was served, Nathan was starting to really worry. It wasn't just his intuition, it had been too long. Elizabeth had a key and could visit him anytime. But she hadn't even sent a message. He had to resign himself to the possibility that she had given up. The overwhelming routine of the hospital was getting to him, and as much as he hated it he was starting to accept it.

"Is this my life now?" he thought. He knew that he was being irrational, but he couldn't shake the belief. He lifted the lid and his dinner looked like slices of roast pork with vegetables. He replaced the lid and left it there for a time, while he thought about his predicament.

CHAPTER TWENTY-SIX

THE SHOWDOWN

After a long night of talking and planning, Frank escorted Elizabeth back to her car. She had delighted in finally sharing all the details of her investigation with someone, and Frank was very interested in all of it.

"So are you comfortable with this?" Elizabeth said.

"Yes, don't worry about me. I'm more worried about you."

"I can handle it."

"I'm a believer. Drive safe and call me later to let me know how you are tracking."

"Will do. No matter how this ends, I just want to say thanks. I didn't realise how much help I needed."

"No thanks required, just stick to the plan," Frank said, before waving at Elizabeth and disappearing back into the night.

She drove home slowly, knowing that her mind was not completely focused on the road. It was the first time she had brought someone into her investigation before it was done, and it was a new feeling. But it was positive, and she felt like a weight had been lifted from her shoulders.

"Someone else is part of this now, I don't have to deal with the burden alone," she thought. And she hadn't realised until now what a burden it had been. She felt foolish for giving up so easily when George betrayed her, but luckily Dean had put the boot in and turned her around. She couldn't let him down either.

She was anxious to get the plan in motion, but it was too soon. She would ruin things if she rushed. So she purposefully took her time getting home, and then took a long shower. She dressed and prepared for bed, having an early night. It was the best thing she could do for now.

Surprisingly she slept easily. Her worries and concerns drifted away and were silenced by her desire to rest. She awoke the next morning refreshed, and ready to go. As she did her morning routine she almost left to go to work, then remembered she had left.

"Some habits die hard," she thought with a laugh. The distance of sleep had given her a bit more perspective on the previous day. She still felt hurt by George, but it was less biting and less personal. She could understand him, and his fears. He saw her story as a risk, one that he couldn't protect the paper from. He chose to put his head in the sand and take the easy option. And that was perfectly understandable. He didn't have to look Nathan or Dean in the eye. But she did, and she would have to live with herself. She would do anything to get the right outcome, story be damned. And that's where they were different.

She went out for coffee, walking to her local cafe. The owner greeted her with surprise, as Elizabeth hadn't visited on a weekday in years.

"Day off," Elizabeth said and didn't offer any more information. She drank her cappuccino slowly and deliberately, drawing out the experience. She knew herself well, and she had to pace herself. The plan required precise timing.

Elizabeth finished her meal, paid and walked home. She looked at her watch as she entered her apartment and decided that it was time to get to work. She opened her phone and dialled the Research department at Royal Monterey Hospital.

"Hello, you've reached the Research department," a woman said over the phone. Elizabeth didn't recognise the voice.

"Hello, I came in earlier to see Dr Malberg. I need to speak with him urgently."

"I'm sorry Dr Malberg is currently unavailable. Can I take a message?"

"Yes, please tell him that I'm calling about Nathan and we need to meet. He will know what I mean. Here's my number," Elizabeth said and then related her number over the phone.

"Of course, I'll pass on the message as soon as possible," the woman said and hung up. Elizabeth put down the phone and waited.

"Now, I wonder if that will get his attention?" Elizabeth thought. It was a purposefully vague message, but surely dropping in Nathan's name would get the right reaction from him.

Within ten minutes her phone rang, this time an unlisted number.

"Bingo," Elizabeth whispered before answering.

"Hello," Elizabeth said into the phone.

"Hello, this is Dr Malberg returning your call. You are?"

"My name is Elizabeth and thanks for so promptly responding. I would like to meet you in person and discuss a few things."

"Such as?"

"I think you know what. I won't do this over the phone. Can you meet tonight?"

"Yes, I am available. Where should I meet you?"

"Come at eight," Elizabeth said before relaying the address to him. It was an abandoned office space that Frank knew about.

"Ok I have the address, I'll see you tonight."

"Come alone," Elizabeth said.

"As you wish," Dr Malberg said before hanging up. She sighed and put her phone down. The call had gone exactly as she had planned. He had taken the bait and agreed to meet her. He would definitely call Don, so she had to get moving before they came looking for her. If they couldn't bring her in they would have to meet her on her terms.

Elizabeth left the apartment and rushed over to her car. She started it and started driving. She didn't have a destination in mind, just focused on places to avoid. Nod would be looking for her soon, if not already. She had to make sure that she wasn't easy to find.

She drove through the Black Jungle first. It was relatively safe to drive through during the day, if you stuck to the main roads. And wouldn't be expected. She continued through some industrial areas until she was in the suburbs. She had never really visited the area before, so she felt like it was safe. The streets were wide, and lined with trees. There was a peaceful atmosphere. She parked the car outside a park and retrieved her phone. She sent a message to Frank to confirm the meeting was set for eight.

Elizabeth put down the phone and then left the car. She walked over to the park and sat down at a bench. It was nice to take a moment, and also a necessity. She had to wait it out, until their meeting tonight. There was no other preparation she could do. All the places she would want to go were out of bounds. She couldn't visit Nathan for fear of tipping them off. The longer they were in the dark about how much she knew, the better. She had purposefully only thrown his name around to let their imaginations run wild.

It was still a gamble, they could do a lot to hamper her efforts. But she had Dr Malberg and Don figured out. They were confident and arrogant. Once they compared notes and worked out who she was, they would dismiss her as being able to be handled. But she would show them.

Elizabeth's blood started to boil at the thought of Don and Dr Malberg, so she tried to think about other things. But her mind kept going back to the plan and those two, so she gave up and returned to the car. She turned on the engine, and just started driving.

She whiled away the afternoon that way, only stopping occasionally to get some food. And finally it was time to get moving, this time with purpose. She drove to the meeting place, parked her car around the corner and then started to walk up. They had picked an abandoned office space in a dodgy neighbourhood. There was less chance of any surveillance and less chance of interruptions. But it was still a risk.

On the third floor of the condemned building, there were two apartments. One was the designated meeting spot, however Elizabeth was waiting in the other. She was two hours early, but didn't want to be surprised Dr Malberg or Don pulling a trick. The wait was agonising, and she nearly jumped at any sound, but she kept her cool. At five minutes to eight she heard footsteps coming up the stairs, and a knock on the apartment next door. There was another knock, and a pause, and finally she heard the door open. She only heard one set of footsteps so she felt like it was safe.

Before she emerged, she walked over to the balcony and stepped outside. The balcony door was open in the other apartment, so she tried to listen in to hear anything useful. She heard Dr Malberg talking.

"I'm here, no sign of her yet. Stay back, if she spots you she'll get spooked. I'll let you know when I have what we need," he said. There was no reply, so Elizabeth assumed he was on the phone. She had heard enough, so walked back through the apartment, opened the door quietly and then entered the other apartment. She saw Dr Malberg standing in the middle of the room with a phone to his head.

"I better go, talk soon," he said and immediately closed his phone.

"Dr Malberg, thanks for coming," Elizabeth said. She put on her game face and exuded confidence. This was it.

"Ah, we meet again. I know your name was fake, but did you really have a celebrity patient with cancer?"

"No, I was just testing you."

"Interesting. Did I pass?"

"You could say that."

"So, why am I here?"

"Well, I've been doing an investigation. And I'm going to blow this thing wide open, but I wanted to give you an opportunity to get in front of it, and explain yourself. Maybe we can limit the damage to your reputation and career," Elizabeth said. Dr Malberg laughed, a dark shrieking sound that was very off-putting.

"Oh that's marvellous. Is that a threat? And how are you going to blow this thing wide open, when you are no longer a reporter?"

"There's more than one way to go about this."

"Yet your most effective avenue is closed. So what exactly are you blowing wide open?"

"I know you have been holding Nathan Stenson against his will in the hospital for over three months."

"Why would I be doing that? And where's your proof of that?"

"He's part of your research program," Elizabeth said, watching Dr Malberg's reaction. His smirk had disappeared but he still appeared confident.

"There's no proof of that, and even if you could prove he was in fact at the hospital for the time you are claiming, how could you demonstrate it wasn't for a just cause?"

"Well, testimony from Nathan is a pretty strong piece of evidence, and he's got lots of stories to share."

"Oh so you've met Nathan then?" Dr Malberg said. Elizabeth knew she was getting somewhere, although she was concerned with Dr Malberg's change in tone.

"Yes, he's fully cooperative with my investigation and will give testimony that will damn you all."

"Well, if that's the cornerstone of your evidence, I'm afraid you have called me here for nothing. Nathan is a sick man, and his testimony is not something that will stand up. He's an unreliable witness."

"Only if you make him so. But I have something else. I have this," Elizabeth said. She removed a photocopy of the blood test results. She handed the copies over to Dr Malberg.

"Third party lab testing has confirmed the cocktail of things you are injecting into him. This coupled with his testimony is enough to send you all away for a long time," Elizabeth said. She saw Dr Malberg's eyebrow twitch as he read the report, and his lips pursed. He was clearly annoyed at the report.

"So what do you think this proves?" he said very quietly. He was looking at Elizabeth with an intense gaze, trying to pry the answer out of her. This was her moment, this was her time to reveal the answer.

"I know you're keeping him as a guinea pig to test out your new Cancer treatment. I don't know why him, but that will come out. You and your career are finished Dr Malberg," Elizabeth said, emphasising the last few words. She watched his reaction with interest. His face went from showing concern, and then puzzlement and finally he started laughing.

"You really don't get it, do you? Oh wow, I can't believe this. You went to all this trouble, and called me here, and you still don't know!" Dr Malberg said.

"What do you mean?"

"Oh I'm not giving you anything. Whatever you think you have here, we can deal with that. You have failed," Dr Malberg said, reaching for his phone. Elizabeth ran over and knocked it out of his hand. Dr Malberg stepped back in surprise. Then he regained his composure.

"Call or no call, they will come eventually. And this whole episode will be over," Dr Malberg said. Elizabeth looked at her phone, no messages or calls.

"Maybe it's all over. Did I lose?" Elizabeth thought to herself.

CHAPTER TWENTY-SEVEN

GOING ROGUE

Frank removed his police badge and gun, and put them in the drawer of his bedside table.

"It's been a while since you acted so rashly. Why now?" he asked himself. The story about Nathan was quite compelling, but he thought it was something else. Years of dealing with procedure had been weighing on him, and he saw an opportunity to act. To do the right thing.

Frank changed into plain clothes and packed a few tools into his pockets. Tools he shouldn't really have, but would prove useful. He had scoped out the hospital earlier in the day, and knew what he had to do. But if he was caught it had to be as a private citizen, not as a policeman. Even though he was still a policeman. The distinction would not matter to most if he did get caught, but it mattered to him.

He left the house, locked the door behind him and stepped into his car. It was an older style wagon, with many years of reliable service behind it.

"Just like me," he thought with a laugh. He drove with care, taking his time. He parked in a quiet area a few blocks from the hospital. It was nice and secluded, but the distance could be a problem. But he would deal with that as the situation required. He removed his backpack from the car and started walking.

He expected to be nervous, but he wasn't. It was more excitement than anything else. He hadn't seen a lot of field activity lately, and he hadn't realised how much he missed it. Making a difference used to be a hands on activity, but not so much anymore. Lots of paperwork and phone calls and meetings. An old dog operating in a new landscape.

"But I've got a few old tricks up my sleeve," he thought. He entered the hospital grounds and went down a level, walking with confidence. He headed straight for the janitorial rooms. The door wasn't locked, which he had confirmed earlier. Inside were cleaning supplies, a few trollies already loaded and some spare uniforms.

"Everything I need," Frank whispered. He removed his backpack and shoved it under the trolley. Then he threw over the coveralls and interchanged a few of the cleaning products. Once he was happy, he pushed the trolley out of the room.

"First things first," he thought. He headed down the corridor and kept an eye out for other hospital staff. He spotted the woman delivering dinner and made a beeline for her. As he closed in he looked at how full her trolley was where she was heading. Based on the information he had received from Elizabeth, his timing was perfect. He tried to push past her with his trolley, the two knocking into each other.

"I'm so sorry," Frank said. He used the disruption to slip a folded piece of paper under the plate on the uppermost dinner tray.

"You should be more careful!" the woman said.

"I know, rushing too much. Too much to do," Frank said. The woman's face softened.

"Isn't that always the case? Just take more care next time."

"Sure thing, I don't want to make your night harder as well," Frank said, before smiling and taking off. She returned his smile. Once he reached the end of the hallway he turned back to look at her progress. She had unlocked the door to Nathan's area and was heading inside.

"Job done, time to move on," Frank thought. He quickly turned around and headed back the way he had come. He had to get to his next destination as quickly as possible. He followed the network of passages until he had reached the Research Department. He pushed his trolley in, pretending to ignore the people inside. A woman in the reception booth called out to him.

"Hey, hold up there," she said. Frank waited a second before stopping, then turned to look at her with a puzzled expression.

"Look, we're still working. Can you come back a bit later?" the woman said.

"Sure, but I want to finish up soon. When will you be done?"

"The last doctor inside will be leaving at seven thirty. Please don't return before then."

"Alright, that's going to be tough. I'll shift my order around and come back then."

"Sorry, but he can't be disturbed."

"I understand. I'll be back," Frank said and waved at her. Then he turned the trolley around and left the room. Things were proceeding as expected. It would have to be Dr Malberg staying back, and his leaving at seven-thirty would give him just enough time to reach Elizabeth's meeting on time. It was only a short window for Frank, but he could make it work. But it also meant he had to lie low for about an hour without getting spotted by the other cleaning staff. They would definitely have questions, and suspicions.

He did a lap of the hospital, making a shot at rearranging his supplies or trying to restock dispensers of paper towels. Whenever he saw anyone remotely resembling a hospital worker he changed course and tried to avoid them without attracting attention. He regularly checked his watch, to make sure he was on track to return on time.

When it was seven twenty he decided to head back. It wouldn't hurt to get back a bit early, and he could loiter nearby to observe Dr Malberg leaving. Seeing things with his own eyes was always the best action. It helped diffuse that voice of doubt or worry which could pop up at the worst times. He sat around the corner from the research department, looking through his supplies. He noticed a man leaving the room in a hurry, which matched Dr Malberg's appearance.

The doctor stopped in front of Frank and waited to get his attention.

"Can I help you doctor?" Frank said.

"Yes actually. My carpet is filthy, can you make sure you clean it properly for once?"

"Of course, for you I will take extra care."

"Good, if it's not better tomorrow I will be making a formal complaint."

"Don't worry doctor, you will be pleasantly surprised," Frank said. Dr Malberg gave him a look of disbelief and annoyance and then walked off.

"Oh you'll be surprised alright," Frank said. He waited for Dr Malberg to turn the corner and then pushed his trolley back into the Research Department.

The foyers was now empty, which was a good sign. He pushed the trolley through and checked each of the doctor's offices. Each one was empty. He decided to start in Dr Malberg's office. He pushed his trolley inside and closed the door behind him. The warning from Dr Malberg actually gave Frank a good idea for his cover.

He left the room and walked back to a nearby janitorial supply cabinet. He removed a vacuum cleaner and returned to Dr Malberg's office. He turned it on and left it running. The noise would signal he was there, and also mask what he was doing.

Frank walked straight over to the metal filing cabinet and dropped to his knees. He pulled out one of his trusty tools, a lock pick.

"Let's see if I've still got it," he whispered, having some fun. He inserted the lock pick into the lock and started trying to open it. At first he had no luck, not getting any traction. But he slowed down and focused, making his movements more precise and defined. He started to open the tumblers, fuelling his confidence. Within a few minutes he had the lock open, and he paused for a moment to drink in his success. Then he pocketed his tools and yanked open the filing cabinet.

There was a lot of paperwork in there. He started leafing through it. He noticed what looked like payment advices, financial statements as well as medical reports.

"Can't judge this now, gotta grab the lot," he thought. So he reached in and pulled out all the documents into a neat stack. Just before he closed the drawer he noticed a USB stick at the bottom.

"Jackpot," he said and retrieved the USB. He shoved the drawer back in close and made sure it was locked. He stuffed the documents into his backpack below the trolley and turned to face the door. He saw an Asian man in a janitor's uniform standing in the doorway, looking annoyed.

Frank walked over to the vacuum cleaner and turned it off.

"Hey what's up?" he asked the man.

"I should be asking you. What are you doing here?"

"Oh hey, the doctor pulled me aside and said that he wasn't happy with the floor. I was searching the trolley to see if I had any, you know powders or stuff to help with the vacuuming," Frank said casually. He watched the man carefully, to see his reaction.

"You don't normally use this vacuum do you?"

"Honestly, no."

"Look I better do it. He's complained before, don't want it to happen again. Just get out of here."

"Sure thing boss. Thanks for helping me out."

"Alright. Just get moving," the man said. Frank didn't waste any time, and pushed the trolley out of the room as quickly as possible. He walked out of the Research Department quickly, without running. He needed to get out of the area, but also look like he was meant to be there. Once he had rounded a few corners he slowed down and allowed himself to relax.

"Wow that was close. Almost caught with my hand in the cookie jar," he thought. But he had gotten away with it. His janitor disguise was no longer useful, so he had to return all his kit and change back. He looked at his watch and noticed that fifteen minutes had passed since Dr Malberg left. That meant he would be arriving at the meeting point soon.

"Better keep moving," Frank said to himself. He made his way to the janitor's room and took off his coveralls, throwing them in the corner. Then he retrieved his backpack and slung it over his back. It was time for the next phase. He walked back into the hallway, and continued along. The corridor leading to Nathan's room was empty, which was a good sign. He walked up to the restricted door, and tried his key. As Elizabeth had said, it was a bit stiff, so he used a bit of force and it opened first try. He stepped down the ensuing hallway carefully, listening out for any sounds. He didn't hear anything. He continued his walk, looking at each door. Once he reached the door marked 'CM' he stopped and adjusted the backpack.

"Here we go. Hopefully he's alone," Frank thought. He pushed the door open slowly and then stepped inside.

CHAPTER TWENTY-EIGHT

THE LONG WALK

Nathan looked at his dinner a bit longer. He didn't feel like eating, but staring it at wasn't doing anything. So he shuffled the plate around on the tray, rearranging things to see if that made the meal more appealing. As he did so he noticed something sticking out from under the plate. He reached under and tugged it out. It was a folded white piece of paper. He scrambled to unfold it quickly, curious about what it said.

Tonight. Prepare yourself and limit what they're pumping into you.

Nathan stared at the paper, hardly believing what it said. Was it a trick? There was no signature and he didn't know the handwriting. But the last time he saw Elizabeth she had taken away the blood sample. It was consistent, and it meant that he was getting out. Tonight.

"Is this really happening?" Nathan thought. He tried to shake himself out of the daze he was in. In the end it didn't matter if it was real. He had to prepare himself just in case. He had to hope again.

"It has to be her. I can't mess this up," Nathan said to himself. The first thing he did was start eating his food. He needed his strength. He mopped up all of the food, drank all the juice and ate his dessert as well. He scrunched the note up into a little ball and stuffed it into the disposable container his juice was in. They wouldn't look twice before disposing of it.

Then he did some light arm stretches while he waited for the lady to come back for his dinner tray. He smiled at her when she came in, and waited anxiously for her to leave. A few minutes after she had left, he considered it safe and got to work.

He looked at his machines, and isolated the ones that were pumping stuff into him. There were two different drips. The thing was though, he was always the one that had to get the nurse to change them. So it was safe to say they weren't monitored the same way as the rest of his probes. He turned the machines off, best as he could. They still seemed to be on, but the rate of flow had dropped. He watched them with curiosity, trying to tell if they were still doing something. It would be easier to just unplug them completely, but he wanted to pass a casual inspection if a nurse did come in. With his luck, one would.

Once he was satisfied, he resumed his stretching routine. Next he worked on his legs, stretching them and making minor movements in the bed. Once he had warmed up he sat on the edge of the bed again, and swung his feet down to the floor. He resumed his previous exercise of putting some weight on each foot. Again it was hard to tell, but he felt like his legs were improving. But he couldn't risk taking the steps that would tell him for sure.

He set about a routine that meant every five to ten minutes he would get back into the bed and rest. This was to give himself a break, and also to help mask what he was doing. If the nurse caught him half out of bed, it would raise alarm bells and suspicious questioning. Especially if Annabelle was the one to catch him.

After three sets of his routine he decided to have a longer break. But no sooner did he swing into bed, than he noticed the door opening. He looked over, unsure of who would be there.

Annabelle came through the door, looking business-like as usual. Nathan suppressed his disappointment, and tried to act normal. He remembered his feeling earlier in the day and decided to channel that. It would be super suspicious if he was all perked up and excited.

"How are we feeling today Nathaniel?"

"I'll be honest, not great. Whatever happened yesterday hit me hard."

"I'm sorry about that, but we had to move quickly. How's your arm feeling?"

"It's a bit sore, but more normal now," he said. She walked over and inspected his arm.

"Good thing I left the drip connected," Nathan thought to himself. She looked like she was heading over to review the machine, so Nathan quickly piped up again.

"Was that normal to take so much blood again so soon?" he said. Annabelle paused and came back to address him directly.

"No, it was not normal. But you left us no choice, with your behaviour the other day."

"It was an accident. I'm clearly suffering because of it."

"I know, and hopefully this won't happen again."

"Please let me know next time, it was really disorienting having it done in the middle of the night," Nathan said. He needed to try and get her sympathy, and reinforce that he was going to be here for a while.

"Don't worry. You and I will get along fine, we'll find a way to make this work well. I understand the inconvenience you must feel."

"I'm so glad to hear you say that," Nathan lied. There was no way she could understand, and she just took it for granted that he would be here for a while. But he suppressed his anger and gave her a smile. He had to focus on happy thoughts.

"She's buying what I'm saying, and wants to foster a better relationship. That's good," Nathan said to himself. Annabelle walked over and picked up a clipboard, reviewing his stats and making a few notes. Then she turned to leave.

"Goodnight Nathaniel."

"Goodnight Annabelle," Nathan said. He watched her leave.

"Won't be seeing you," he thought with hope. He looked at the clock and noticed that it was approaching eight o'clock.

"So when is this prison break going to start?" he wondered. He had no idea, so he waited a few minutes in case Annabelle returned and then swung his legs over the side of the bed again. He watched the door open in horror, he couldn't move. He was frozen in place, waiting to see who came through the door. It was an older man, with greying hair and a hard frame. Nathan didn't recognise the man, and immediately panicked.

"You're in the right position, ready to go?" Frank said. He tried to use a light tone to not scare Nathan. He was shocked at how skinny and frail Nathan looked, but managed to hide his reaction well.

"Sorry, I should introduce myself. My name is Frank and Elizabeth sent me. We gotta get moving though, or the plan will be ruined."

"Frank, sorry I'm just a bit surprised. But happy to hear you say that. I'm not sure what condition I'm in, and if I remove these probes it'll set some alarms off."

"Don't worry, it's the night shift. We'll get a few minutes lead time, and that's all we need," Frank said.

He walked over and opened up his backpack, throwing some clothes on the bed.

"Got a fresh shirt for you, some pants and a coat. Do you need help?"

"Yeah, definitely," Nathan said. Frank walked over and watched Nathan carefully adjust his hospital gown to avoid tampering with the probes.

"Want to buy us a few extra minutes," he said, explaining his actions.

"Sure, but we can't be too delayed. Everything is really time sensitive," Frank said. He helped Nathan remove his gown, and handed him the shirt. He helped stabilise Nathan while he pulled the pants on.

"Ok try standing up," Frank said.

"Alright, but last time was a disaster."

"I'm here, lean on me," Frank said. He helped Nathan up and supported the frail man's weight. Nathan's weight shifted suddenly, but Frank handled it. After a few wobbles, Nathan grew steadier.

"Not too bad," Nathan said. He paused and then started removing his probes.

"Clock starts now," he said.

"Yeah, but you seem steady enough, we can work with that. Throw this on," Frank said, handing Nathan a brown coat. Nathan kept one arm leaning on Frank and slipped the other through the coat. They shuffled around so he could put the other arm in, all while keeping a grasp on Frank.

"That will do," Frank said.

"Let's hope so."

"We need to keep moving. Let's take a step, easy does it," Frank said. Nathan took a step, wobbling a little but remaining firm. He took another, slowly but surely.

"Good, we just need to make it out of the door, and you can graduate to something more dignified," Frank said. Nathan laughed and took another step. He gained a little more confidence and strength with each step. Frank slung the backpack on and guided him to the door. Frank opened the door and stepped out first, holding it open for Nathan. The corridor was exactly as he remembered, and it still had that strange empty cold feeling. But there was one new thing: a walking stick.

"Very dignified. I can channel old geezer," Nathan said.

"Yeah, you would kill it," Frank said. He handed Nathan a blue baseball cap as well. Nathan put it on and also accepted the walking stick. He kept a hand on Frank's shoulder and started leaning on the stick too. Then he gradually let go, and put all his weight on the stick.

"So far so good," he said.

"Yeah, this is promising. But I'm going to have to point out that we need to keep moving. Time is not our friend."

"Yeah, I get it. Let's take a few steps," Nathan said. He took the first step, keeping his weight on the stick. He felt a bit unsteady, but he didn't fall or stumble. He took another step, and it felt better.

"Well, I won't be doing any hurdles, but I can do this."

"Good, let's make a start," Frank said. He stayed next to Nathan, but walked slightly ahead, looking for any signs of entry. He needed to act quickly if anyone came through the doors as there was nowhere to hide.

Frank opened the door and quickly glanced around the corridor. It was empty, so he waved Nathan through. Nathan stepped through as quickly as he could, which wasn't too bad. He was improving with the walking stick.

"This way," Frank said, turning right down the corridor. He had memorised the route they needed, which would lead them to a less popular exit. There shouldn't be anything to worry about, since Elizabeth was acting as bait. But he didn't want to push his luck, so kept Nathan moving as swiftly as possible. They made slow but steady progress down the corridor. Frank just hoped that anybody who saw them thought nothing of it. A close examination would reveal flaws however. For example, Nathan's bare feet. But they didn't have time for that, and it was a hassle they couldn't afford.

There were two possible scenarios that Frank worried about. One was that the hospital staff were really remotely monitoring all of Nathan's vitals. They could mount a response immediately if that was the case, and once they found the room empty the hospital would go into lockdown.

The other was that the goons that Elizabeth described came to the hospital instead to secure Nathan. Similar scenario, although he hoped that it was less likely. If the plan worked properly.

"What do they say about plans? Even the best plan only lasts until the first arrow is fired?" Frank thought. He let it linger a moment, and then pushed it aside. He had to focus on the task at hand.

Nathan stopped, and leaned against the wall.

"What's wrong?"

"Just need a short break, my legs are on fire."

"We're still in the first corridor. We're sitting ducks, we need to keep moving."

"Alright, I'll push on," Nathan said. He stretched his legs tenderly, and then started walking again. Frank thought about the path ahead, and wondered whether he should alter it. But he didn't think it would add much safety and would only delay their trip. Nathan didn't seem to be in a state to take on any extra distance. And they already had a long walk ahead of them. The hospital was just the first part. But at least it was the riskiest. Their chances improved vastly if they could get out of the hospital grounds.

Nathan put one foot in front of the other. He wasn't as fast as he had been, but he worked up a steady rhythm.

"This is crazy. Walking should be something I take for granted," he thought. Yet here he was, struggling with each step. But they were the best steps he had ever taken. Each one was taking him closer to freedom. A future where walking would be frequent and easy.

"I never thought I would long for that," Nathan thought. He almost laughed. Their course took them around a corner and into another corridor. Nathan looked over at Frank, and saw the concern on his face relax a little.

"What does he know that he's not letting on?" Nathan wondered. But he bit his tongue and kept walking. That was his only job, and it was very important for both their sakes.

They continued on in silence. They only passed a few visitors or patients on their walk, no hospital staff. Nathan felt self-conscious, but they didn't even give him a second look.

"The clothes must be enough to blend in," Nathan decided. It certainly would have been odd to have a man in his hospital gown stumbling around. And he didn't want people to think to ask any questions or take it upon themselves to get help. He would rather that they just kept on without paying him any mind.

Frank did relax a bit more with each turn they made. Although they weren't on a secret path, each step and each turn took them further from the likely search area and closer to escaping the hospital grounds. He had been watching and listening out for any rapid response from the hospital but hadn't noticed anything.

"If they are remotely monitoring him, it's not something they are doing constantly. Otherwise we would have been swarmed by now," Frank thought. But he didn't know for sure. So he kept his eyes and ears open.

As they rounded another corner they could see an exit at the end of it. An automatic door separated them from the outside.

"So close," Nathan said.

"Don't falter now," Frank said. Nathan nodded and picked up the pace a little. Frank noticed some movement up ahead, so he motioned for Nathan to move closer to the wall.

"Make some space," Frank said, and he walked in front of Nathan to make them single file. Two men jogged through the entrance. One was slim and tall, the other one was stockier. The way they moved had purpose and a hint of aggression. He didn't want to draw attention by looking too closely, but he thought they matched the description provided by Elizabeth. He had considered this a possibility, but was still a bit surprised.

"I don't like it, this could be trouble," Frank thought. He considered getting the jump on them. With the element of surprise he could probably take them down, or at least injure them significantly. But it would give the game away, and there was a chance he was wrong.

"Too risky," he decided and kept going, keeping them in his vision but not looking at them directly.

Nathan also noticed the movement up ahead, but didn't pay much attention. He was completely absorbed in walking as normally as possible. It was imperative that he not look like a man who had been bed-ridden for months. He wasn't sure who would be looking for him and when, but didn't want to provide them an easy target. He noticed the speed with which the men ran past, and turned to look at them with curiosity.

Frank noticed Nathan slowing and watching the two men run past.

"Keep moving," Frank whispered and Nathan stopped looking. Frank snuck a last glance at them and followed his own advice. If the two men hadn't stopped, then they weren't sure of Nathan's whereabouts. Which bought him a few minutes. If he was lucky they would be stumped. If he was unlucky, they would remember passing a man with a cane and go on the hunt.

Frank increased his speed without thinking, and looked back to see how Nathan was faring.

"We're almost there," he said, offering some encouragement.

"Oh, did you park close?"

"We're almost outside. Car isn't far," Frank said, stretching the truth a little. He didn't want Nathan to be distracted or lose his momentum. Nathan continued at the same pace, only pausing to make sure he gave the doors enough space to walk through safely.

There was a slight breeze, and it hit Nathan in the face. He had missed the sensation so much and stopped to savour it. He hadn't been outside for months, and had missed it. He knew it probably wasn't a particularly fresh breeze, but it felt so light, cool and delightful. He breathed deeply, for the first time in a long time. The air just felt lighter, and full of promise.

"Plenty of time for deep breathing if we can make it clear of the hospital," Frank said.

"Alright, fair enough," Nathan said. He knew it was too early to celebrate, so started walking again. Frank looked behind them again, but couldn't see anything. Perhaps they would make it clear without any incident.

CHAPTER TWENTY-NINE

A CHANGE OF PLANS

Don and Nod sat in the van. Nod was looking at traffic, staring aimlessly while Don was staring at his phone intently.

"So what's the plan?" Nod said.

"The doc is meeting with her any minute now. He's supposed to call once he's found out what she knows. We can go pick her up if he gives the signal."

"Shouldn't we be there then?"

"He doesn't need our help with her, and I've got a bad feeling. Something isn't right."

"You reckon it's a setup?"

"It could be, my gut doesn't like it and I'm never wrong."

"Well, you said she would give up. If she hasn't there could be something funny going on."

"Yeah, well she should have. Something must have happened, that changed things. Hmm I can't just sit here. Let's go back to the hospital and scope it out."

"Sure thing boss," Nod said, starting up the engine. He didn't care as long as they were going somewhere, he was bored just waiting around. He had a quiet respect for the journalist, and he hoped she had kept things interesting.

Nod parked the van and Don jumped out.

"We better scope things out here, just in case," Don said.

"Wait a second," Nod said, making sure the van was parked and secure. Don was on the phone, calling Dr Malberg.

"No answer?" Nod asked.

"Nope, keeps ringing out. He should at least be responding. Something is up, we better check on our guy," Don said. He started walking, but soon upped it to a jog. Nod ran after him, surprised at the rush.

"Wow he's really worried," Nod thought. The two of them ran towards a smaller entry for the hospital. It was less used, and a great direct route through to the area reserved for Nathan. They hadn't visited in a while, but Don still remembered the layout. As they rushed in they noticed a pair of people walking out of the hospital. An older man leading a young man with a cane.

"Probably a sports injury," Don thought as they ran. He didn't give them another thought, his concern was ensuring that the patient was still secure. Nod didn't even notice the pair, he was concerned with keeping up with Don. There generally wasn't running in his line of work, he saw to that.

The two of them continued down the corridor, winding their way through the hospital. They didn't see anyone else on their way, and reached the door within a few minutes. Don pulled out his key ring, and jiggled the keys until he found the right one. He opened the door, pushed it open and started running again. Nod stopped it from slamming him in the face and then followed. They rounded the corner, passed a few doors and then stopped in front of the door labelled 'CM'.

"Never seen the guy before, this will be interesting," Nod thought. He waited for Don to push the door open and followed after.

The bed was empty, a pile of wires laying on the bed. Something was not right.

"Shit, how'd he do it?" Don said.

"He must have had help, it can't have been long," Nod said. Don thought it over quickly.

"Hey did you notice that pair of people leaving?"

"No, not really."

"Seemed innocent enough, but it's too late to be discharging people. It could be him. You backtrack and find those two. I need to check something else," Don said.

"Sure thing boss," Nod said, but he wasn't enthused with running back. He was definitely surprised by what had happened. Things were getting interesting. He started jogging to make a show for Don, and after a few turns slowed to a fast walk. He didn't really know who he was looking for, but there wouldn't be many people around at this time. Two people together would be enough. He navigated the corridors, working his way back to the exit. He didn't see anyone inside, but chances were the people he was after would be outside.

He picked up the pace as he reached the doors and jogged outside. He saw the odd person in the distance, but not two people together. He decided to do a lap of the grounds to make sure he was thorough. But he didn't have a good feeling.

Don was stunned by the hospital bed. Part of him was glad that he was right, that something was up. But he started to worry. If the reporter had gotten him out, then all was lost. They had to find Nathan. But there was also one other thing weighing on his mind.

She had shown her hand by contacting Dr Malberg. Clearly it had been part of a plan to distract them. But Don worried about the potential for one other problem. He left the room quickly, and ran down the corridor. He burst through the door and continued on his way.

Don tried to keep quiet, but speed was his goal. He almost bumped into corners as he skirted around them. He had to know how bad it was. He saw the sign for the Research Department and increased his speed even further. As he was about to enter he saw a janitor leaving.

"Stop. What are you doing?"

"Just vacuuming the floor sir. Is there a problem."

"Just wait here, don't go anywhere."

"Sure, what's this about?"

"Just wait, I'll be back in a minute," Don said. He rushed through the doors and along the corridor. He entered Dr Malberg's office and walked over to the single height filing cabinet. The lock appeared intact. Don allowed himself to relax a little, but still wasn't convinced. He removed some tools from his pocket and started picking the lock. It didn't take long, and he shoved the drawer open. It was completely empty. There wasn't a single thing left.

"Shit!" he said, staring at the empty cabinet. He slammed it shut and ran out to confront the janitor.

"Did you touch anything in there?" he asked, looking over the janitor. The Asian man was carrying nothing except the vacuum cleaner.

"No, I heard the other cleaner in there and went to check on him. He was doing a terrible job with the cleaning, so I took over and did the rest of the offices for good measure."

"Who was the other janitor?"

"Not sure, never seen him before. Had all the right kit, even had the right vacuum but didn't seem to be doing a proper job. I sent him away probably twenty minutes ago."

"Ok, thanks. Don't speak a word of this to anyone else. What's your name?"

"Chew."

"Ok Chew, here's my card. Call me if you remember anything else," Don said. He walked off in a fury. They had been played. They let their guard down, and got fooled by a reporter. He called Dr Malberg and it rung out. As he walked out of the hospital he kept ringing.

"Answer the damn phone!" Don said in frustration. If they couldn't recover Nathan they had to get the reporter. Elizabeth was the key now. If Dr Malberg let her go, then they had nothing.

Nod finished his lap of the building, and didn't find the two men that Don had mentioned. To be fair, he didn't get a good look at them himself. But he didn't see anyone that he recognised, and there certainly weren't two people together. So he decided to wait outside the exit, preparing himself for Don's wrath.

***

After they had properly cleared the hospital exit doors Frank pushed forward a bit further and then stopped. Nathan stopped right behind him.

"Why are we stopping?"

"I think those two men that rushed in are looking for us. I need you to head in that direction. It's the most direct way to the main street. Once you reach the street turn left and keep walking. I'll go another way and meet you there."

"Why? I'll be a sitting duck without you."

"They'll be looking for two of us, and it's dark. Get moving and keep moving. Trust me, you'll make it,"

Frank said. He didn't even give Nathan a chance to argue, running off in a different direction. Nathan watched Frank go and decided he had to keep going too.

"I hope he knows what he's doing," Nathan said to himself. It sounded like a decent plan, but he was sceptical. He also felt incredibly exposed. But he had no other ideas, so started off again.

His legs were more than just complaining now. Each step was painful and forced. He wanted to stop constantly, but kept forcing himself to make that one more step. He tricked his mind, by promising to stop soon. Just a few more steps. But he kept changing the goal posts, and keeping his momentum.

As he passed a rubbish bin he tossed in his hat. He was outside now, and there was less chance of being recognised. Wearing a hat might bring himself more attention. He didn't break stride, and watched his hat sail into the open bin.

"Ha-ha, good shot," he thought. He used the good feeling to push through a few more steps. He heard the sound of a man walking, and turned slowly to take a look. He recognised the man as one of those who had run past him as he had left the hospital doors.

"Shit, maybe that's the guy. Just take it easy, play cool," Nathan told himself. He wanted to change direction, his pace or go hide somewhere. But decided to act normal. Surely he would attract more attention by changing his behaviour. He kept walking, trying not to look behind him. He heard the footsteps loudly, like they were closing in. But he couldn't tell where they were. So he just kept walking, hoping that he didn't suddenly get tackled out of nowhere.

He saw the gates that Frank had mentioned, and the footpath on the main street. Nathan got a renewed surge of energy, and made for the main exit. Once he was out there, he was almost free. Freedom was so close, he could feel it. The pain in his legs was forgotten and he pushed forward. The loud footsteps of his pursuer were distant now, clearly the man had not spotted what he was looking for. The exit was getting closer, only steps away.

And like that he stepped out of the hospital grounds and onto a main street. He turned left as Frank had suggested and looked behind him. The hospital looked large and imposing, but he was finally leaving. The pain and anguish of the past few months started to leave him with every step. Like he was leaving it there.

That pain was replaced by the fire in his legs. The surge of adrenalin that got him out, had been exhausted. Now his legs were giving up too. The initial danger seemed to be over, and they were threatening to collapse on him. But Nathan had come too far to give up now. He slowed, but kept moving. Frank would find him, in time. Until then, he knew what to do.

CHAPTER THIRTY

THE SECRET

Elizabeth looked at Dr Malberg. Her mind was filled with doubt. Had she done the right thing? Had she missed something?

"Why don't you just let him go and we will forget about this," she said, using a bluff to buy more time.

"You don't get it do you? You don't have anything useful, certainly not a bargaining chip. Why would I cave in to your demands?" Dr Malberg said, taking the bait. Elizabeth needed to keep him on the hook longer. She didn't know how this would play out, but until she heard something to suggest that Nathan was free she had to keep playing along.

"You keep saying that, but don't explain why I'm wrong and why the information I have is not a threat to you," Elizabeth said.

"Look, I'll admit you are resourceful and definitely clever. You have made it this far, and you've tried to bluff me. But I know the game. If you knew more you would lead with it, not keep it in reserve."

"So it's that bad huh?"

"Keep trying, you won't succeed. I will repeat myself: I am not giving you anything. You are just wasting time here. My colleagues will arrive soon and they can deal with you," Dr Malberg said. Elizabeth wondered about that. If Don and Nod were going to take her again, why was Dr Malberg threatening her with it? Was that some sort of signal? Her train of thought was interrupted by Dr Malberg's phone ringing on the floor.

"I should answer that," he said, looking over at it. Elizabeth ran over and picked up the phone, looking at the number dialling. It was Don.

"This is your backup?"

"I don't know what you are talking about. I do make a habit of answering my phone though," Dr Malberg said. His reply frustrated her, but she ignored him. If Don was calling Dr Malberg it meant one of two things. Either they had succeeded, or they had failed. But which was it?

Elizabeth held onto Dr Malberg's phone and pulled hers out. No calls or messages.

"Why have I heard nothing?" she wondered, staring at the phone. They had a plan, and it should have worked. She had clearly missed something, that much was clear due to Dr Malberg's frustrating smugness. But it shouldn't matter if they could get Nathan clear. That was what mattered the most.

"How long are you going to hold my phone hostage? I thought this was a negotiation?"

"As long as I need to think this through," Elizabeth said. It was the truth, she needed to figure out the best path out. If someone was coming, she had to leave. But if Frank had failed, she needed to get something useful from Dr Malberg. Which way did she go?

Elizabeth felt a vibration, and looked at her phone again. There was a single message.

Go

She didn't know if it was success or failure, but she couldn't waste time processing it. She had to trust Frank. She returned her phone and threw Dr Malberg's phone at him.

"Catch," she said. It was ringing again, and he was focused on catching the phone. Elizabeth turned and ran, heading straight for the door. She had no idea what was coming, so sped down the stairs as fast as possible. She didn't look back once, just focused on moving ahead. She burst out from the building and rounded the corner, heading for her car. As she closed in, she retrieved her keys and opened the door, jumped in and turned on the engine. Within moments she was away, driving.

"Well, that's done. I don't feel great about that though," she thought. In her mind she had built up a big confrontation between her and Dr Malberg. She would batter him with evidence and he would confess and give up everything in exchange for telling his story. It was all neat and perfect, her investigation solving the day. But the reality was that she had no story, he laughed at her, and her every hope was pinned to Frank getting Nathan out of there. It was completely different to her last big story.

"At least I haven't been hospitalised yet," she said and laughed. There were certainly drawbacks to how she had done things in the past. And if she was honest, that approach would have failed here. Well she may have failed anyway, she wouldn't know until she reached the meeting point.

Elizabeth drove on for another hour, until she reached an old run-down house. It was out of town, and the front garden was completely overgrown. She parked the car across the road, and walked up to it. The rusted gate was closed but not locked, so she unlatched it and walked down the pebbled path. It was a cute little house, but had certainly seen better days. But it would be safe. She knocked on the white front door three times, and waited. There was no response. She noticed some movement in the curtains from a nearby room, and then heard footsteps. The door opened, and Frank was standing there.

"Come in," he said, giving nothing else away. Elizabeth walked in and followed him down the hallway. At the back was a kitchen, with a dining table opposite. Seated at the table was Nathan. He smiled at Elizabeth.

"Forgive me for not getting up, I've had quite a night."

"I'll bet. I can't believe it," Elizabeth said, running over and giving Nathan a hug.

"Easy there, everything hurts," Nathan said.

"But you're here. Great work Frank."

"It was a team effort, we all played our part. How'd you go with Dr Malberg?" Frank said.

"He was a tough one. Didn't crack no matter what I threw at him, even laughed me off. I missed something crucial. There's still a mystery to be solved here."

"This might help," Frank said, emptying the contents of his backpack onto the table. Paper spilled out everywhere, and at the end a USB stick bounced out.

"Is that what I think it is?"

"If you're thinking the contents of Dr Malberg's files then yes."

"I wasn't sure you could get these. This is incredible. He's going to freak out when he discovers they are gone."

"Well I employed a few of my lesser known skills to liberate these documents. I hope they prove useful."

"Whatever we need will be in here somewhere."

"Well, as curious as I am I don't think I can keep my eyes open any longer. Besides, this was your invention, your story. You get the honours," Nathan said, pointing to the pile of paperwork.

"Thanks, although why do I get the suspicion that you hate paperwork?"

"No reason," Nathan said with a smile. "I've got a room set up for you Nathan, I'll take you over," Frank said. He helped Nathan stand up and the two of them walked out of the room.

"Just me and the paperwork. Just you wait Dr Malberg," Elizabeth said. She grabbed all the paperwork and started sorting it out. From flicking through she could see that there were different types of records. Patient records, payment information and letters. The patient records she sorted into many different patients. However she focused on just two piles: Nathan and Susan.

Nathan's records were not all that interesting. Records of his medication, which she already knew from the blood test information. His vital readings were noted, but that didn't seem to be too telling. Another interesting thing to note though, was the fact that they took blood from him regularly. And recently they did so again right after the botched attempt where he had smuggled her out a sample.

"Interesting," Elizabeth thought. She noted that for future reference.

Next she scanned through Susan Montgomery's records. She was on a similar list of medication, which made sense with Elizabeth's theory that they were using Nathan as a guinea pig for treatments. But apart from the fact that she knew something was missing, there was another thing to note. Susan didn't get anywhere near the same number of blood tests, and she even received regular transfusions.

"They are taking blood from Nathan regularly, and giving blood to Susan. Let me look at the dates," Elizabeth said to herself. She compared the dates and noticed a pattern. The blood transfusion always followed the blood samples from Nathan by a day, without fail.

"So, if I'm right they were putting Nathan's blood in Susan? Why?" Elizabeth wondered.

"Turn up anything yet?" Frank asked as he entered the room.

"Maybe, some odd correlations between blood samples taken from Nathan and blood transfusions to one of the patients that Dr Malberg was treating."

"That sounds like something."

"Possibly. But what I'm most concerned about is trying to find out about Nathan's condition and health. I'm no doctor, but the vital charts they have recorded seem within the normal levels. But since he's not monitored and not receiving treatment I want to make sure that we're not being irresponsible by having him here."

"You think he might need to go back to hospital?"

"I hope not, but I'd rather find that out now than later."

"Makes sense. I'm sure the last thing he wants is to go back to a hospital, but we should do our best to eliminate that as an option," Frank said.

"Why don't you help me read through this stuff? How are you with financial statements and payment ledgers?"

"Not great, but I'll take one for the team," Frank said. Elizabeth directed him to a pile and he started looking through.

"What am I looking for?"

"How about any reference to Susan Montgomery. We know she's currently being treated, and Dr Malberg referenced donations when I first contacted him. If she's top of the list I bet there's some money involved," Elizabeth said.

"Right, I'm on it," Frank said. Elizabeth exhausted her stack of patient records and started thumbing through the letters.

They were mostly generic letters, reporting results and getting approval for continued research. However there wasn't anything useful that jumped out at her. She saw a few references to 'CM' but not enough to draw any conclusions about it.

"I keep seeing references to CM, and I know that was a label on Nathan's door. I think it's most likely the codename for the research program Dr Malberg was running."

"Sounds about right. I'll note any references to it in these statements," Frank said. Elizabeth kept flipping through, then stopped and turned back to the letter she had just been looking at. Something had jumped out at her. She read the letter back again.

"This is it," Elizabeth said looking over at Frank with excitement. He looked up and waited to hear more.

"You are hereby granted approval to begin the CANCERMAN program," Elizabeth said, reading out the letter.

"Who authorised it?"

"The head of research."

"Well that's going to come back to bite him."

"It should, it really should. Well we have a name now, and I'm guessing that's what CM stands for," Elizabeth said.

"Has to be. Nice find," Frank said.

"One step closer. But I'm still missing something," Elizabeth said. She went back to reading through the letters, but after a few minutes exhausted her stack.

"I think the really sensitive stuff is not here. But maybe..." she said out loud sweeping through the piles of documents with her hand. She uncovered the USB data stick and held it up.

"You have a computer here?" she asked Frank.

"Yeah, let me show you," Frank said. He led Elizabeth back down the corridor to a separate room set up as a study. There was a monitor and keyboard sitting on a brown desk, with the computer tower sitting on the floor nearby.

"It's an older machine but still works fine. I'll log in for you," Frank said. Once he had done so he let Elizabeth sit down and went to fetch a chair. He plonked one down next to her. Elizabeth inserted the USB stick and waited for the computer to respond. On the drive was a single folder labelled 'CM'.

"This looks like it lets take a look," Elizabeth said. She opened the folder and was prompted for a password.

"You don't think it would be this obvious would you?"

"What are you thinking?" Frank said. Elizabeth typed in 'CANCERMAN' and hit enter. The password prompt disappeared for a few seconds, and then the folder opened, showing a list of documents.

"Bingo. Now we've hit the pay dirt. Great find getting this USB Frank."

"No worries, glad you could crack it open."

"Let's see here," Elizabeth said scanning through the list of documents. She opened up one titled 'Executive Summary'.

"Oh my god," Elizabeth said, once she read the first few paragraphs.

"Does that say what I think it says?" Frank asked, looking at Elizabeth with surprise.

"Yeah. These guys are super literal. When they say Cancer Man, they mean it. Nathan is the man. I can't believe I'm saying this. Nathan is the fucking cure for Cancer," Elizabeth said. Her voice rang out in the room, hanging in the air. It was a preposterous notion, but there it was in the report.

"How is that even possible?" Frank said.

"I don't know enough about this stuff, but it says there's something in his blood. His white blood cells can target and eliminate cancerous cells. That explains all the blood transfusions. And Dr Malberg talking about the problems scaling up his treatment. They were bleeding Nathan to cure other people," Elizabeth said. She leaned back in the chair. It explained so much, but it just seemed so unbelievable.

"This is big. This is really big. How can something like this fly under the radar?"

"Well, you did say Dr Malberg was profiting from it. I'll dig through the financials more. Do you think there was any high powers privy to this?" Frank said.

"You mean the government?"

"Yeah. If they are, this changes everything."

"I'm not sure let me read through more of these documents," Elizabeth said. Frank left the room to go back to the financial statements and documents. As Elizabeth kept reading she discovered that initial trials were done by treating Nathan with the same chemotherapy as used on the patients, to make sure there weren't any strange reactions. However once they noticed the impact on his energy levels, they decided to keep the chemotherapy up at low levels as a safety mechanism to prevent him leaving on his own.

"This is madness. How can they get away with this?" Elizabeth thought. They were not only ignoring their duty of care, they were slowly killing him. And profiting from it.

"Donation method used to subside funding problems," Elizabeth read out loud. It was all there in black and white. Elizabeth just stared at the screen, trying to understand the magnitude of it all. Frank returned carrying some paperwork.

"I've got a theory," he said.

"Sure, throw it at me."

"When did you say the last museum burglary was?"

"Oh it was a few weeks ago."

"Well strangely enough, there was a large donation on behalf of Susan Montgomery about one week later. I think if we look back and corroborate with a source at the museum we might see a pattern."

"So you think Albert was stealing to fund his daughter's treatment?"

"Sounds like the right motive to me. Would also explain why they never publicised the thefts."

"Yeah, it makes sense. That explains the weird connection between the museum story and Nathan's story," Elizabeth said.

"I don't know how you ended up picking those two stories."

"Yeah, pretty strange. Something to mull over, when I'm bored," Elizabeth said. She went back to looking through the files on the computer. Then she stopped and turned to Frank.

"What do we do about this?"

"We sleep on it. We can talk about it with Nathan tomorrow."

"Good idea, I'm going to go crash on that couch I saw," Elizabeth said.

When she awoke, it was early in the morning. She sat up, stretched and then walked off to the kitchen. She saw Nathan up and sitting at the kitchen table.

"Good morning, how are you feeling?"

"I've been worse. Are you impressed?"

"Very. Pretty good mobility for a man who was a vegetable!"

"Ha-ha yeah that's a fair statement. Although getting here myself might be my achievement of the day. I've looked through some of the documents here, wow it seems full on. But I bet you've got something better to tell me."

"Actually yes, with the information that Frank gathered we made a breakthrough last night. Have you seen Frank?"

"He had to go out, said you would fill me in."

"Ok, that's fine. Well there's no easy way to put this. As much as they are despicable people abusing their power of you, they had a legitimate reason to keep you there."

"Oh really? This will be good."

"Nathan, you're the cure to cancer."

"What? Hang on, you're not laughing. Are you serious?"

"Yes, all the information is on the USB stick we retrieved. They were using your blood to cure cancer patients. And they were filling you with chemo and other drugs to keep you weak and compliant."

"Those bastards. I can't believe it. They must have found something back when I went for that first blood test. So when I came back in, they were ready for me. The whole thing is so cold and premeditated. I just can't believe it," Nathan said. He looked like he wanted to stand up and start pacing, but he was stuck in his seat.

"I know, I still can't believe it. But everything adds up. I don't think the government was involved, I think it was restricted to the hospital. We don't know how widespread the information was, probably only a few key doctors really knew."

"What about the nurses? Robin?"

"Not sure, apart from asking them. It's possible that they knew, but unlikely. They were probably told very little."

"Wow, so what is it about me?"

"Something in your blood. Your white blood cells can identify and neutralise cancerous cells without the need for any other treatments."

"So that's why they were always after my blood, and even took more when I destroyed the samples."

"Yeah, they're treating someone at the moment. We would need a doctor we can trust to go through the information in more detail, to determine exactly what they were doing, and what their end goal was."

"I see."

"Yeah, it's a lot to process. But I think you are alright health wise. We should get you checked out, but it's safe to say they kept you in hospital for their own purposes, not your wellbeing."

"So what happens now? This is a huge story. Is my life over? Are you going to out me?" Nathan said quietly. The responsibility of his situation was starting to dawn on him. Yes he had been held against his will, by people without honour. But he had been saving lives while he was there. By running away, he was preventing people from receiving lifesaving treatment. He looked at Elizabeth, not sure how she was going to respond.

"I understand what you are thinking right now. But I want to make something clear. This started out as a story that I wanted to break, for various reasons. None of which are important now. And you know what, it's satisfying as hell to have gotten you out and busted this story open. But now that we are here, it's your story. It's your life," Elizabeth said. Nathan nodded and thought it over. He had a few big decisions to make.

"But I do have one request, for a friend of mine," Elizabeth said, a smile creeping onto her face.

EPILOGUE

Elizabeth was nervous, as she closed the car door and started walking. She checked the address again, and it was definitely the right place. It was an old red brick set of apartments, that looked around forty to fifty years old. She walked down the driveway and opened the glass doors into the main entrance. The smell of mothballs greeted her, and she carefully ascended the staircase, marvelling at the faded blue carpet. After one flight of stairs she stopped and looked at the apartments. There it was, number seven. She paused, and then knocked twice.

"Coming," a voice said and within moments she could hear the door opening. She didn't know what to expect, and found herself holding her breath.

"Elizabeth! So good to see you, please come in," Dean said.

"You too Dean, it's been too long," Elizabeth said and stepped inside. The apartment was small, the kitchen, dining and lounge area were in front of her, with a door off to the right that she assumed led to the bedroom and bathroom.

"Cute place," she said.

"Thanks, yeah it's enough for me. Lucky I have it, you know," Dean said.

"You look good. In fact you look better than I have ever seen you."

"Not bad for an old bloke eh?" Dean said and made a face at her. Elizabeth couldn't help but laugh.

"Can I get you anything to drink?"

"No, I'm fine for now," Elizabeth said. She followed Dean and sat down on the couch next to him.

"Sorry I haven't been in touch, we thought it best if we laid low for a while," she said.

"Oh that's fine. I got your message, and everything happened so quickly. I was so surprised, that I almost argued when they came to move me to another hospital. But I figured you were up to something so I played it cool."

"Just as well!"

"Yeah, trust me to almost ruin things. I know I don't need to say this, but thank you. You saved my life."

"Don't thank me, thank Nathan."

"That's an incredible story, one that I'll take to my grave don't you worry. How's he taking it?"

"Well, given the circumstances, I'm not pushing him for any answers, but I think he's had enough time to make his decision."

"Well, he's done so much for me already. I feel like a new man. It's a strange thing, death. It changes you. You have to change your thinking, start to accept the things that you never could. But here I am, I feel like I cheated. Every day I wake up and just breathe in the life around me and I feel like dancing," Dean said. Elizabeth couldn't help but smile.

"I can totally see that."

"Ha-ha, I know huh? So what else is happening, fill me in."

"Well Dr Malberg and Dr Sterling, the head of research, quietly resigned. I think they wanted to get ahead of any potential scandals. Frank had a word with Albert, the head of Egyptian Antiquities. The evidence we got was unlawfully obtained so he can't be prosecuted, but I think Frank scared the hell out of him. But truth the told, I think the guy is just happy that his daughter is alright."

"What about those goons that were following you around?"

"Turns out they were hired by Albert to protect his investment. I'm kind of glad they weren't affiliated with the government, although Frank reckons Don is a former operative of some kind."

"He's probably right. But what about you?"

"I'm alright, but I don't know what's next. Even after the dust settled I couldn't go back to the newspaper. And that's pretty much all I've done, so I'm at a loss as to what to do with myself."

"You've got the whole world at your feet, take your time."

"I already have, but you're right. No need to rush things just yet. I'll figure it out."

"Of course you will, you're a smart one. You cracked this case, just like I knew you would."

"Hey thanks for pulling me back in. I was in a bad place, and ready to give it all away. But you stopped me in my tracks."

"I don't know why you're thanking me, I just told you what you needed to hear. And after all you have done for me, I don't think you'll never need to thank me for anything!"

"Well, I'll keep that in mind. What are you doing with your newfound time?"

"Enjoying it, not putting labels on things. Like you I have the world at my feet."

"I'm happy to hear that. Hey, did you still want me to write your story?"

"Nah that was going to be a swan song. I'll make a story worth writing about, and may even tell it myself," Dean said. He had a determined look in his eye.

"I can't argue with that," Elizabeth said, then looked at her watch.

"Hey can you pass me the remote?" she asked. Dean handed it over. Elizabeth turned on the television and changed the channel.

"Don't want to miss your favourite show?"

"Trust me, you don't want to miss this," Elizabeth said. A reporter in a red dress and long brown hair sat behind a standard news desk, and started talking into the camera.

"We have with us today a man who has been through an extraordinary ordeal. One so extreme, that we can't show his face or broadcast his voice. He was confined to a hospital bed for months against his will, never told why he was being held and was isolated from other patients. His own family didn't even know where he was and thought him dead. He is here today to share his incredible story, one that even I have not fully heard. We are referring to him as Patient CM. So, Patient CM in your own words can you please tell us why they held you captive in a hospital bed," the reporter said, before pausing. The camera cut to a darkened room, with the silhouette of a man sitting in a chair. He seemed to be looking directly into the camera. Finally he spoke.

"I am the cure for cancer."

ALSO BY VAUGHAN W. SMITH

Have you read these other books by Vaughan W. Smith?

Amy's past is hidden by trauma and fears. A psychiatrist provides an experimental drug that helps her open her mind with wild and vivid dreams. What she sees terrifies her, but she must know more.

A man wakes with no memory, just a fake ID and instructions. He follows along and sets off a chain of events that spiral out of control. After he performs an assassination he has a choice to make: take the money and run or dig deeper and try to understand who he is and what is going on.

ABOUT THE AUTHOR

Vaughan W. Smith is a fiction writer from Sydney,
Australia, who explores big life questions through story.
His favourite genres are Thrillers, Mystery, Science
Fiction and Fantasy.

To connect with Vaughan check out his website:
http://www.vaughanwsmith.com

Made in the USA
San Bernardino, CA
04 March 2020

65275681R00219